PRAISE FOR

The
MISCONCEIVED
CONCEPTION
of a Baby Named
JESUS

"A fun, pithy sendup of one of the best-known origin stories."
—*Kirkus Reviews*

"Bill Burkland has written a sharp, shrewd, witty, and occasionally wacky alternate-universe Bible—though who's to say whether his version might be closer to the truth?"
—Greg Thompson, writer-producer, *Bob's Burgers*

"I swear to God, if Bible class had been as fun as Bill Burkland's *The Misconceived Conception of a Baby Named Jesus,* I would still be enrolled. Fun, funny, and wise, *Misconceived Conception* is the Gospel as written by Matthew, Mark, Abbott and Costello. To say I loved Burkland's humor, wit, and cleverness within this book would serve as an understatement. In Burkland's brilliant hands, cats talk and think, shepherds are high, wise men stoop low, and Mary, Joseph, and the Baby Jesus are lovingly human characters. This book merits book-club discussion and argument. Don't forget the wineskins."

—Glenn R. Miller, author of *Doorman Wanted*

"Take one part of *The Chosen* and two parts of *The Life of Brian* and you end up with a whimsical look at the birth of Jesus in Bethlehem. Bill Burkland's novel is a wild satirical look at the events narrated by the Gospel written by Luke. From overbearing parents to clueless wise men to confused shepherds, *The Misconceived Conception of a Baby Named Jesus* is a funny and creative retelling of the birth story of Jesus."

—Rick Spees, author of *Capitol Gains*

"History depends on the quality of research and perspective of the historian. In *The Misconceived Conception of a Baby Named Jesus*, author Bill Burkland's version of 'the Greatest Story Ever Told' will blow your mind and might even raise a chuckle or two. It's satire that could earn you a ticket to down under, and I don't mean Australia. Take care. If you read it, you just might burst into flames."

—John J. Jessop, author of *Pleasuria: Take as Directed*, *Murder by Road Trip*, *The Realtor's Curse*, *A Fishy Tale*, *The Guardian Angel Series*

The Misconceived Conception of a Baby Named Jesus
by Bill Burkland

979-8-88824-539-2

This is a work of fiction. All the characters in this book are fictitious, and any resemblance to actual persons, living or dead, is purely coincidental. The names, incidents, dialogue, and opinions expressed are products of the author's imagination and are not to be construed as real.

Published by

köehlerbooks™

3705 Shore Drive
Virginia Beach, VA 23455
800-435-4811
www.koehlerbooks.com

The
MISCONCEIVED
CONCEPTION
of a Baby Named
JESUS

BILL BURKLAND

VIRGINIA BEACH
CAPE CHARLES

TABLE OF CONTENTS

For my wife, Shawn, who encouraged, cajoled, and supported me from the uncertain beginning of this novel until the very last word was written—and rewritten and then rewritten again. She has the strength of Mary, the generosity of the Keeper, the kindness of Jude Aya, and a love of wine like Paragus. For my daughter Emily and her partner, Mikaila, for their curiosity and support and encouragement. For my daughter Megan and her partner, Daniel, for their exuberance and always helping me see the world through younger eyes.

CHAPTER I

The Prophet Isaiah
693 BC

Therefore, the Lord himself shall give you a sign; Behold, a virgin shall conceive, and bear a son, and shall call his name Immanuel.

THE OLD TESTAMENT, ISAIAH 7:14

"This is the time in the lesson, my boys, when I'll share a secret of prophecy," Isaiah said as he teetered from side to side. An empty wineskin, which he drained hours ago, lay on the floor by his feet, while a half-empty skin hung loosely across his shoulder, swaying in perfect syncopation with its intoxicated master. Isaiah tried, without success, to focus his glazed grey eyes on the small group of students who had gathered to hear him speak in the Temple of Jerusalem.

"It's actually not a secret. It's the first rule of prophecy." Isaiah stroked his gnarled beard, oblivious to the calcified mutton crumbs from last week's supper and the translucent carcasses of a large family of dead lice that tumbled from his beard onto the white limestone floor. "Make your prophecy far enough in the future so that no one who hears it could ever live long enough to know if it actually comes true."

With an unsteady hand, he lifted the wineskin to his mouth, sending a stream of red wine down his throat; but as his hands shook, the stream splashed from his mouth to his eyes and then down the

1

front of his wine-streaked robe and onto the floor of the speakers' platform. Isaiah resumed, unfazed. "Create prophecy that could occur a month from now, a year from now, or a thousand years from now. Make your prophecies fantastic but feasible; filled with vivid detail, yet ambiguous; infinite, not time bound."

The group of twelve students sat with straight backs on smooth limestone benches in the inner sanctum of the Hall of Hewn Stones. Their eyes followed Isaiah as he swayed. The boys, ranging in age from ten to twenty-five and identically clad in long-sleeve, ankle-length white linen tunics and sandals made of fine leather, were on a path to becoming learned Pharisees in the largest and most important temple in Jerusalem. The Temple Elders and the High Priest had invited the students to hear Isaiah speak. They considered him to be the greatest living prophet and were eager to expose their best, brightest, and most promising students to his divine wisdom. The Elders were not alone in their admiration for Isaiah, for all the citizens of Jerusalem agreed that Isaiah, among all prophets, was closest to God and the most esteemed and prolific prophet since Moses.

One student, a young teen with more pimples on his cheeks than hair on his chin, slowly raised his hand, catching Isaiah's wandering eyes.

"What is it, boy?"

"Your description of prophecy . . . " The student paused, then continued cautiously, "It sounds as though you create the prophecy yourself rather than receive the word directly from God."

"You, boy, are a withering, tapered tip of a long, contemptible turd. What do you take me for, some kind of charlatan, a fake?"

"No, my Prophet, of course not." The student bowed his head.

"The Word of God shapes each of my prophecies. I am a vessel for Him to communicate to his earthly subjects." Isaiah took a long draw from the wineskin.

"Is drinking wine allowed in the Temple, my Prophet?" another student asked.

"Of course not," Isaiah said. He raised the wineskin over his head and, with a drunkard's unsteady aim, missed his gaping mouth, splashing red wine onto his grey beard. He threw the wineskin to the floor, gathered his beard with both hands, lifted it to his mouth, and licked the wine clean until only a few red drops clung to its greying, tapered tip.

"Most commonly, I hear God's voice after consuming a great deal of wine, preferably a Bittuni from the fertile hills just outside of Nazareth." Isaiah snatched the wineskin from the floor and held it high in the air as if giving a toast. "The second rule of prophecy, my boys, is to drink wine and drink plentifully, and as you drunkenly flow into a state of incoherence, God is most likely to appear."

A young doughy boy stood, the distressed threads of his tunic desperately clinging to one another in a futile attempt to keep from splitting. "My Prophet, is God present now?"

"Why do you ask, boy?"

"You are . . . " The student looked at his peers for support. They did not return his glance. He swallowed hard. "You are, well, slightly incoherent, and decidedly drunk."

"Indeed, and quite pleasantly so," Isaiah said as the last remnants of the wine dripped from his beard onto his robe, which was now more red than white. "God, you see, created grapes. God is in each grape. And being a clever God, He endowed man with the strength to squeeze the juice from the grape and the wisdom to ferment the juice into a divine nectar. Drinking wine is like having God sloshing around in one's belly, coursing through one's veins."

"Is He amongst us now?" the doughy student asked, crossing his arms, locking his clammy hands under his sweat-drenched armpits.

"Is who amongst us?" Isaiah slurred as he stared blankly at the boy's cherubic face.

"God."

Isaiah fell silent, his shoulders slumped, his head bent down, eyes fixed on the floor. He knelt, picked up a dried mutton crumb, placed it on his tongue, and chewed it slowly between his front teeth. In the silence, he reflected upon the fact that his prolific stream of prophecies had run dry. God stopped talking to him. Isaiah hadn't heard a word from God, not even a whisper, for nearly three cycles of the moon.

"Do you hear that?" Isaiah asked no one in particular.

"Hear what?"

"That voice?" Isaiah cast his eyes up toward the domed Temple ceiling.

The students shook their heads. "No, my Prophet, we do not. What voice?"

"God's voice. You can't hear it?"

"No, my Prophet, we can't."

Isaiah's head drooped; a trickle of wine-filled saliva fell to the floor. "Neither can I."

"My Prophet," another of the students said, "perhaps you could tell us of another?"

"Another what?"

"Rule."

"Rule for what?"

"For creating prophecy."

"I suppose." Isaiah straightened, cracked his back, and took a long drink from the wineskin. "The third rule . . . " Isaiah paused. "It actually may be the fourth. I don't remember. Either the third or fourth rule. Certainly not the fifth. For simplicity, let's just call it the third rule. A rule that God Himself and the Temple Elders are obsessed with is the desire to hear prophecies of pestilence and plagues, festering boils, and rivers of blood flowing in the cobbled streets from the torn carcasses of sworn enemies. Temple Elders pay generously for death and destruction."

"I heard a prophecy about the destruction of Jerusalem from Micah of Moresheth," a young student eagerly said.

"Micah?" Isaiah shook his head. "He is a second-rate prophet preaching in a third-rate backwater where no respectable prophet would care to go. Micah of Moresheth? More like Micah of more shit."

"You don't believe in his prophecies?"

"Ignore Micah and his stories of the demise of Jerusalem." Isaiah spit on the Temple floor.

"My father says he preaches more to cats than he does to people."

"That's true," Isaiah confirmed. "Don't waste your time with the prophecies of the mentally infirm."

Isaiah drank from the wineskin, wiping his lips and nose with his sleeve. "Rather than reciting more rules, should we instead practice listening for God's words and creating a prophecy among us?"

"Yes, my Prophet," came the students' unanimous refrain.

"Let's begin." Isaiah handed the wineskin to a student in the front row. "Each of you take a long drink, maybe two, of the divine wine and pass it to the next."

As the wineskin wound its way among the students and back to Isaiah, he instructed them to close their eyes and think of God. Isaiah closed his eyes and held his unsteady hands up to his ears. "Listen, boys, let the wine lubricate your mind. Let God speak to you," Isaiah whispered. "Sometimes you hear God's voice with your ears, but more often, His voice is silent. Heard only in the mind. Felt only in the soul."

Isaiah stepped down from the speaker's platform and walked and wobbled among the students. "Now reach into your mind and your soul and if I tap on your shoulder, you are to utter a word, a single divine word, that God Himself placed in your mind, in your mouth, and on your tongue, for me to interpret."

Isaiah stopped in front of a wispy, pale-skinned, sullen boy and tapped his shoulder.

The boy looked down, avoiding Isaiah's drunken stare.

"Go on, boy."

"My word is," the student said and fidgeted with his tunic, "*fig*. No, wait. *Salad*. No. Maybe *cheese*?"

"God put that in your head? I don't think so, boy. Try again."

Dispirited, the student sighed. "Oh Lord—"

"That will do. *Lord*. It's enduring and versatile. Never goes out of fashion. Give me another one," Isaiah barked at the boy, who wet his tunic in fear.

"Another what?"

"Word, you imbecile. Give me another word."

"But I thought you said we were to give only one word."

"Don't repeat back to me what I may or may not have said earlier. Listen to what I'm saying now." Isaiah repeatedly tapped his crooked finger on the boy's forehead.

"Son," the boy whispered, urine trickling down his leg and onto the floor.

"What?" Isaiah said disapprovingly.

"Son."

"Son?"

"Yes, son."

"I find your answer confusing, pee-piddler. Do you mean son as in father and son or sun as in the bright orb that rotates around Earth?"

"I don't know; I didn't think about it. You choose, my Prophet."

"Oh, you didn't think about it. Half-wit." Isaiah shook his head. "Son. Unimaginative and disappointing; I was told you were all among the best and brightest. Instead, I find myself surrounded by dull mediocrity. We have *Lord* and *son* as in father and son. I need one more word."

The eldest student, a tall young man with a full beard and an Adam's apple that rose from the middle of his neck like a horizontal Mount Horeb, raised his hand.

"Go ahead, boy. What's your word?"

"Virgin."

"Ah, you are a clever one." Isaiah approvingly slapped the student on his chest. "The only thing the Temple Elders like to hear about more than festering boils and torn carcasses are lascivious prophecies involving virgins." Isaiah returned to the small platform at the front of the inner sanctum in the Hall of Hewn Stones. "Never forget that, boys."

"Now what?" asked the eldest.

"We work through this. God has spoken through you, and now we must knit together the meaning of these words."

"I am the eldest here. Perhaps I can try," said the bearded boy.

"Go ahead."

The student joined Isaiah on the platform. "What about a prophecy of the Lord's Son coming down from Heaven to marry a beautiful virgin?"

"The Lord doesn't have a son. That doesn't work," Isaiah said. "But you're on to something here. God is working through you, through us." Isaiah repeated the words slowly, "*Lord, son, virgin.* Any other tries?"

"But what if God were to have a son?" The eldest student tugged at Isaiah's sleeve.

"Why would God have a son?" Isaiah shook his head. "It makes no sense. What purpose would that serve?"

"What purpose do cankerous boils and rivers of blood serve?" the pimply boy in the back row asked.

"What if," another student joined in, "a virgin gave birth to a baby—"

"And," the eldest student interrupted as he raised his voice and his eyes toward the heavens, "the virgin's baby turned out to be the son of our Lord! *Lord, son, virgin.* It covers all three."

"Now you're just being absurd. I've never had the misfortune of instructing such an ignorant group of dolts and dullards. A virgin having a baby?" Isaiah shook his head and laughed. "You boys may be too young to understand, but that's impossible, given the definition of a virgin."

"It would have to be a miracle," said the doughy boy.

"Exactly!" said the eldest, embracing Isaiah.

"Ah, ah. Hmm. I see what you've done here. Good. Very good. The Elders will pay dearly for this. You are indeed the best and brightest. There was never a doubt in my mind."

"But what exactly is the prophecy, my Prophet?"

Isaiah thought for a moment, cleared his throat, and began.

"*And . . .* " Isaiah paused, closed his eyes, and put his hand to his chin.

"Wait. Should I begin the prophecy with *and* or *therefore*? I can never decide on such things."

"What would God say?" the pimply student pondered.

"God? Forget God. This is between us now."

"Begin with *therefore*," said the bearded student.

"That's good advice. It's more authoritative." Isaiah raised his hands to the Temple ceiling and said, "*Therefore the Lord himself shall give you a sign; Behold, a virgin shall conceive, and bear a son, and shall call his name Immanuel.*"

"Immanuel? Where did that come from?" a student asked.

"This sort of specific reference gives prophecies additional credibility, boys. Immanuel means *God with us*. A fifth, or maybe sixth, rule of prophecy is to imbue it with memorable detail. It's what separates a first-rate prophet like me from a hack like Micah."

CHAPTER 2

The Prophet Micah
692 BC

But thou, Bethlehem Ephratah, though thou be little among
the thousands of Judah, yet out of thee shall he come forth
unto me that is to be ruler in Israel; whose goings forth have
been from of old, from everlasting.

THE OLD TESTAMENT, MICAH 5:2

The prophet Micah sat in his accustomed spot under the shade of a centuries-old acacia tree, slowly chewing bits of its bark and speaking, as he did every day, to a group of feral cats who had gathered to escape the unbearable Galilean sun. Barefoot and dressed in rags, Micah wiped the sweat from his brow with his sleeve. He pushed back the tangle of greasy grey hair from his eyes and turned his attention to a dusty, rust-colored cat with matted fur and ribs that stuck out like fence posts. Micah loved his entire congregation of decrepit cats, but he had a special affinity for this particular one; not only was he the smartest of the bunch, but in many ways, he was a reflection of Micah himself.

Like Micah, the cat had been full of promise and pride and revered among his feral peers in his youth. The cat roamed the streets of the small hamlet of Moresheth, successfully fighting for scraps of food the villagers had dropped or discarded. Like Micah, the cat had been a fighter in his youth. A bigger cat scratched out the cat's left eye in a bitter fight, and a mean Moresheth mutt bit off the tip of his right ear. Also like Micah, the cat was now old, indolent, and indifferent.

"I'd be interested to hear what you would do if you were in my situation," Micah said as he bit off a fresh piece of the soft acacia bark with his few remaining teeth.

"Remind me, Micah of Moresheth," the cat replied with only the slightest hint of interest, "what situation do you find yourself in?"

"Always answering my questions with questions of your own; an annoying habit of yours. I'll remind you that like you, I've spent my entire life fighting. While you've been fighting for scraps of food and a cool place to sleep in the hot summers and a warm place in the cold winters, I've been fighting for the poor and the underserved—the people of Moresheth, and the people of the small, neglected, shit-upon villages that dot the Galilean landscape."

"Shit upon by whom?" the cat asked as he lazily licked his paw.

"Ah, yet another question. Always full of questions when I seek answers. You know very well by whom—the Pharisees and elites of Jerusalem, the corrupt government officials and morally vacant citizenry who built their wealth on the backs of prostitutes, cheats, and liars."

"And?" The cat had an uncanny knack for knowing when Micah had not quite finished a thought.

"And that arrogant, self-aggrandizing prophet of Jerusalem, Isaiah."

The cat enjoyed steering their daily discussions to the two things that Micah most despised: the morally corrupt city of Jerusalem and Isaiah, the city's most revered prophet and Micah's chief prophetic rival.

As young prophets, many considered Micah to be Isaiah's equal. But over the years, through the much larger population in Jerusalem, Isaiah's reputation grew, far exceeding that of Micah's. In discussions and debates that took place in temples and town squares, people mentioned Isaiah's name amongst the great prophets, like Moses and Solomon and David. They seldom mentioned Micah. There were even whispers in the homes and temples and palaces of Jerusalem, possibly fueled by Isaiah himself, that Micah attracted more cats than people when he spoke.

In his fiery youth, Micah lashed out at Jerusalem, prophesying, *"Therefore because of you, Zion will be plowed like a field, Jerusalem will become a heap of rubble, the temple hill a mound overgrown with thickets."* Micah's prophecy offended and angered the people of Jerusalem, especially the Temple Elders. The Elders, in turn, encouraged Isaiah to sully and discredit Micah's reputation at every opportunity. The two prophets agreed on only one thing: their disdain for one another.

Over the years, Micah retreated farther and farther into the Galilean wilderness, carving out and honing his reputation as the defender of the downtrodden people of Moresheth and of the scorned who lived in the scattered villages described by the Jerusalem elites as "shitholes" or "backwaters" or "backwater shitholes." It was places like Moresheth, Jericho, and Bethlehem that the powerful men of Jerusalem held in contempt. With guidance from God and a few good cats, Micah's mission was to humble and humiliate the people of Jerusalem, then call for the city's merciless destruction.

"I have heard these complaints, these grievances, from you before," the cat said, slowly getting up and walking with a decided limp toward Micah, finally settling comfortably in his lap. "What is new today, Micah of Moresheth?"

Micah gently combed the cat's matted hair, picking out a flea and squeezing it between his fingers until it burst. He looked at the squashed flea, put his fingers to his nose, and inhaled deeply to understand what a flea smelled like from the inside. He wiped his fingers on his sleeve, adding to the colorful mosaic that decorated his entire threadbare ragged cloak that had, as far as Micah could remember, never been washed.

"I have heard—" Micah said.

"From other cats?"

"Not from other cats, but from one of my ... wait ... you sound almost jealous."

"Me? No. You're misconstruing my curiosity for jealousy. I am simply curious, like any good cat. Continue."

"I received news from an ardent follower that Isaiah prophesied the birth of Immanuel, the Son of God. And, the most sensational part of the prophecy, the one that is causing it to spread like wildfire through Judea and Galilee, is—"

"That it will be a virgin birth." The cat yawned.

"How did you know that?"

"Virgin births in prophecy and in myths are not new, my friend. They are quite common. I think this Isaiah fellow is getting lazy in his old age. Why is this sort of well-trodden prophecy troubling you?" The cat resumed his expected role as inquisitor.

"I'm disappointed you don't understand." Micah picked and squeezed the life out of another flea. "From his pretentious pulpit in Jerusalem, Isaiah has certainly implied that the birth will take place in Jerusalem, the least holy city in all of Judea."

"You said *implied*, does that mean Jerusalem was not explicitly part of the prophecy?"

"It was not."

"Perhaps there is an opening," the cat said.

"What do you mean?"

"Well, you still have followers? Human, not feline, correct?"

"A few. Yes."

"And you are still recognized as a prophet, though a lesser one, correct?"

"Thank you for the reminder. But yes, I'm still looked upon by some as a prophet."

"Then it seems reasonable, and certainly well timed, for you to have a prophecy about *where* the birth of the Son of God shall take place."

"So," Micah said, inspired by the cat's thinking, "let Isaiah claim victory for prophesying the birth while I snatch the victory away from him by prophesying where the birth will take place?"

"Exactly," the cat confirmed. "And that place shall not be Jerusalem."

"But God has not spoken to me about this," Micah said.

"But I have," said the cat, somewhat offended. "And have you considered that I'm channeling the voice of God?"

"No, my friend. I haven't. Are you?" Micah rubbed the cat's head, sending the cat's half ear into a spasm.

"It's plausible now, isn't it?" the cat said. "If God spoke to Moses through a burning bush, then why is it such a stretch to think God would speak to you through an old feral cat?"

Micah thought for a moment, unable to challenge the cat's sound logic.

"So," the cat said, "let's get to the business of choosing a place where the virgin birth of the Son of God will take place."

"It must be a place that will humiliate and infuriate the Jerusalem elite, and Isaiah particularly," said Micah.

"A place that is everything that Jerusalem is not," suggested the cat.

"A small village. An insignificant backwater."

"Looked down upon. Scorned and disparaged by the people of Jerusalem," the cat said.

"Poor."

"Beyond poor—downright downtrodden!"

"A small, poor, downtrodden village," Micah said as he continued to rub between the cat's ears, "that is scorned by the people of Jerusalem."

The briefest of moments passed in silence until their eyes met and, in unison, they declared, "Bethlehem!"

"Perfect," said another cat who had been listening intently to the entire conversation.

"Thank you," Micah said, not surprised by the second cat's response.

"What exactly is the prophecy, Micah?" The first cat took control of the conversation, again asking the questions.

Micah pondered the question as he slowly chewed the last bit of bark. He cleared his throat. *"But thou, Bethlehem Ephratah,"* Micah said, emphasizing the word *Bethlehem. "Though thou be little among the thousands of Judah, yet out of thee shall he come forth unto me that is to be ruler in Israel; whose goings forth have been from of old, from everlasting."*

"That does quite nicely," the second cat confirmed.

"Thanks be to me," the first cat said as Micah squished another flea that had been cheerfully exploring the fertile fur between the cat's ears.

"I need to write that down," Micah said, satisfied with his work.

"No need. I've got it all up here," the first cat responded, pointing his aged paw to his flea-free head.

CHAPTER 3

Joseph Comes

MARCH 25, 9 MONTHS BC

Mary sat alone, in the dark, under a blanket of stars that filled the Nazarene sky, wondering if Joseph would come. The blue linen sadhin draped across Mary's body, clinging to the curves that, coupled with her intellect, made her one of the most desired among all the young women in Judea and Galilee. It was her finest sadhin, and unlike her winter clothes, it exposed the base of her delicate neck, her slim arms, and, daringly, even her ankles. Mary's mother, Elisheba, who was far away in Bethlehem, would have found the sadhin scandalous, which is precisely why Mary had worn it to meet Joseph on this night in the secluded privacy of a quiet garden in a remote neighborhood in the Galilean village of Nazareth.

At fourteen, Mary's mother and father sent her from their home in Bethlehem to live with her aunt Deborah in Nazareth. It was a misguided attempt to remove their increasingly independent and strong-willed youngest daughter from the influence of her best friend, Vashti. Mary and Vashti had been inseparable ever since Vashti and

15

her parents moved from the small fishing village of Magdala and into the home next to Mary's parents.

Mary and Vashti became friends from the first time they met. As toddlers, Vashti taught Mary how to weave simple baskets using palm fronds—an activity that Mary's parents saw as beneath Mary, the sort of craft suitable only for peasants. By the age of ten, much to Mary's delight and her parents' disapproval, Vashti taught Mary how to gamble with dice and knucklebones. With each passing year, as the bond between Vashti and Mary grew stronger, and the influence of Mary's parents withered, Mary's parents' resentment of Vashti deepened and hardened.

The final straw, the straw that led to Mary's banishment to Nazareth, was Vashti introducing Mary to the teachings of Greek philosophers and Roman writers. This diverted Mary's attention away from the Holy Scriptures that Mary's pious mother and the High Priest of Bethlehem had prescribed.

Mary arrived in Nazareth in January, and by March she had already explored every path, every garden, and every corner of the village. She spent her mornings helping her impoverished aunt bake the barley bread they ate at every meal. Afternoons were spent cleaning or weaving reed mats that covered the dirt floor of Deborah's simple single-room mud-walled home. Mary picked flowers from the gardens that dotted the village, and she made regular trips to the Nazarene well to fetch water. In early March, while getting water, Mary first glimpsed Joseph.

Mary had arrived late in the morning, just before the sun had reached its midday peak. On her regular visits to the well, she would methodically raise and lower the bucket and pour the water into two clay water pots she would carry back to Deborah. But one morning, as she raised and lowered the bucket, Mary heard the steady, rhythmic pounding of a wooden mallet, the sound amplifying and echoing off the stone walls of the well. She looked up from the well and saw a carpenter building a thick wooden bench in the garden of a

wealthy silk merchant. The carpenter was shirtless, wearing only a
tattered leather work apron on top of his hagor, an undergarment
that resembled a loose loincloth. Mary froze, watching the muscles in
his arms and shoulders and chest ripple as he heaved a heavy slab of
Jerusalem pine onto two sets of equally heavy pine legs. He was a man
among the boys that she had previously met in the village.

Mary fixed her gaze on the carpenter as the water bucket floated
motionless at the bottom of the well. An elderly woman waiting to fill
her own water pots clucked "tsk, tsk, tsk." But Mary did not hear. Her
complete attention was on the carpenter and as she turned to leave,
she tripped over one of her pots and fell to the ground, shattering one
of the pots and sending a stream of water across the honey-colored
stones of the well's foundation.

As Mary struggled to her feet, the carpenter left his work and
walked, in what seemed like giant steps, toward her. Without a word,
he extended one hand to Mary and with his other hand picked up the
remaining filled water pot as if it were an empty teacup. The two walked
through the narrow, crooked lanes of Nazareth back to Deborah's in
a wonderfully intimate but awkward silence. Occasionally, Mary's
hand brushed against the carpenter's hand. So enjoyable did Mary
find walking beside him that she deliberately took the longest route
back to her aunt's house, and as they walked, Mary swung her hand
slightly wider, increasing the frequency and intensity of the brushes
between her smooth, delicate hand and the carpenter's powerful, virile
hand. Upon arriving at Deborah's home, the quiet carpenter set the
pot down, bowed his head to Mary, introduced himself as Joseph of
Nazareth, and left as quickly as he had arrived.

Now, on this night, the night of March 25, just two weeks after
her first encounter with Joseph at the water well, Mary sat alone on
the secluded bench in the quiet garden—waiting for him. Thirty-foot-
tall cypress trees planted tightly together lined the garden, providing a
protective screen. To each side of Mary stood rows of oleanders, their
delicate pink flowers just beginning to bloom. Behind her, a thick vine

of jasmine draped over a wooden arch, its sweet scent filled the air. As she waited, Mary closed her eyes and slowly ran her fingers across the smooth granite bench, feeling the faint residual warmth from the Galilean sun, which had set long ago. She imagined the warm, smooth granite to be Joseph's skin. She pulled her sadhin slightly higher so nearly half her calf was showing.

Joseph, hidden behind a thicket of oleanders, had been observing Mary. He quietly crept from the path behind the bench and put his hands on Mary's shoulders. Mary shuddered. Joseph's hands betrayed his profession. They were strong and calloused, cut and bruised. But they were also gentle.

"Hello, my lamb," Joseph whispered in her ear.

Mary smiled as Joseph sat beside her, their legs, arms, and shoulders slightly touching.

"I am glad you're here," Mary said as she stretched and kissed Joseph's neck, an impulse that surprised even her. "I'm sorry, I—"

Joseph put a finger across Mary's lips. "Don't be sorry. I'm the fortunate one to be kissed by these lips."

Mary traced her fingers along the edges of a birthmark just below Joseph's left ear. "It's shaped like—"

"The Sea of Galilee. I know."

"Exactly. It's distinctive, beautiful." Mary kissed his neck again.

Joseph placed his hand on hers. "You're too kind. I see the same birthmark on my father and my father's father. I know it's not beautiful and certainly undeserving of your attention, let alone your kiss."

"You're wrong. It's beautiful. You are beautiful."

Mary moved her hand from the birthmark to Joseph's bare leg, imperceptibly caressing his knee. She smiled.

"How do I, a poor and simple carpenter, among all men, deserve your favor?"

"You forgot *old*. You are poor, simple, and old." Mary winked at Joseph.

"And you, Mary—beautiful and sharp-witted."

"And," Mary whispered into Joseph's ear, "feeling salacious."

"That's a word this simple carpenter is not familiar with."

"Let me show you," Mary said as she, in a single smooth motion, swung one leg across Joseph. Straddling him, with her chest resting just inches from Joseph's lips, Mary guided his hands to her body.

A cool desert breeze lightly blew; the shrill sounds of cicadas and the croaking of shy tree frogs filled the night air. The row of cypresses slowly swayed, and the breeze heightened the scent of the jasmine and pink oleanders. But Mary and Joseph were not aware of these things. They were aware only of each other. In this moment, on this night, on the bench that was still faintly warm from the day's sun, Joseph filled Mary with joy. It was her first time experiencing this kind of joy. An intense joy, one that grew and swelled and filled her completely and utterly. A joy that brought slight quivers and sublime convulsions. A joy that burst inside of her. A joy that left her exhausted, but energized; numb but tingling. And even as the great joy slowly, achingly left her body, the residual warmth and goodness of that joy remained deep inside.

Sitting beside Joseph, Mary's senses were now filled by the coolness of the night breeze, the fragrance of the jasmine and oleander, and the music of the clicking cicadas and croaking frogs. She rested her head on Joseph's shoulder. "My love."

"Yes," Joseph replied, kissing Mary's forehead.

"Tonight, I wasn't certain that you would come."

"Oh, my Mary, there isn't anything that could have stopped me."

CHAPTER 4

Joseph and the Corinthians
JULY 25, 5 MONTHS BC

Just outside the modest walls of Nazareth and with an easterly view of Mount Tabor sat a sprawling compound built for breeding, training, and housing the finest Arabian horses in all of Galilee, Samaria, and Judea. The compound was owned by the Corinthian family, whose name reflected the city from which they came. Generations before, the family lost every bit of their considerable wealth as they fled Corinth when the ruthless Roman army lay siege to their beloved city. They landed in Galilee with nothing more than what they could carry in their arms and on their backs and with a determination to rebuild their equine empire, which had been their passion and source of wealth and prestige for centuries.

The first generation of the Corinthian family that settled on the fertile Galilean plain immediately took on any kind of work, even the most menial tasks, that allowed them to accumulate enough money to buy their first Arabian. Horse by horse, year after year, they built their reputation as the finest breeders and trainers in Galilee. Soon, their reputation spread to neighboring Samaria and even farther south to Judea and to Perea to the east. The current generation of the Corinthian family, led by the brothers Caleb and Aaron, had developed such a strong following that they could charge prices only the richest kings, wealthiest Wise Men, and largest city-states could afford. Corinthian Arabians, branded with an ornamental *CA*, became a symbol of wealth and prestige.

Joseph stood on the outskirts of the compound, gazing across a tract of land cleared of all vegetation, where dozens of temporary posts stood outlining the perimeter of a new building project. Aaron Corinthian had sent for him for reasons that were not yet clear to Joseph. Over the years, Joseph had performed odd jobs for the family; he built Grandpa Corinthian a sturdy chair on which he sat, in the garden next to the stable, to watch his sons and grandsons train and exercise the untamed foals. Joseph also built a chicken coop and a watering trough for the pigs. His last project for the Corinthians, finished just months before, was a table and a set of shelves where the brothers kept their branding irons and tools to make leather saddles for their horses.

Joseph stood waiting in the compound, looking with wonder at Mount Tabor, admiring its symmetry and the way it majestically rose and towered above the otherwise perfectly flat Jezreel plain.

"Hello, my friend," Aaron said as he affectionally slapped Joseph on the shoulder. "I hope I haven't disturbed you. You looked like you were in a trance." Aaron embraced Joseph as if they were brothers. For all the wealth and power that the Corinthian family wielded, Aaron and his brother, Caleb, were modest and amiable, treating their most humble servants the same way they would treat the most revered king.

"No, of course you haven't disturbed me. I'm here at your service."

"Thanks for making the trek from Nazareth, my friend. I know it's a bother, particularly on that poor beast." Aaron nodded at Joseph's aging, sagging donkey.

"It's no trouble. In fact, it's an honor."

"Joseph," Aaron said as he gripped Joseph's arm and looked earnestly into his eyes, "you know the family is pleased, very pleased, with the work you've performed for us."

"I'm happy to hear that."

"But, have you ever considered more ambitious work, a larger project, something more remarkable than a chair or more challenging than a table?"

"Honestly, I haven't. I'm a simple carpenter with simple tools, quite content with the work you've commissioned me to perform, and I'm proud of what I've delivered. I leave the complex carpentry to the more highly skilled," Joseph said without a hint of shame or false modesty.

"Caleb and I believe you're capable of more. You're too modest about your talents."

"I appreciate your confidence."

"We think you're ready for something bigger, Joseph—a project that, when completed, will be the cornerstone of the Corinthian enterprise." Aaron put an arm around Joseph and then, with his free hand, pointed at the land that stretched before them. "A project that will catapult you to the top of the list of the finest carpenters in all of Galilee."

"You flatter me, my friend."

"A stable, but not just any stable—a stable that will house the entire herd of Corinthian Arabians. A stable that, when completed, will hold more wealth within its fences than all the stables in Galilee, Perea, and Judea combined."

"I've built nothing close to that scale, Aaron."

"We think it's time you did."

"You're offering this work to me?"

"Yes."

Joseph thought of Mary and the approaching need to provide for not only her but also their child. Mary never complained and never asked for anything, but Joseph felt she deserved far more than what he could give. He dreamed of moving from his one-room hovel into a two-room stone house with a courtyard and small garden where their child could play. This job would provide the means to enable Joseph to fully provide for his growing family.

"I humbly accept."

"Have you told him?" Caleb, the brusque older brother, joined Aaron and Joseph.

"I have," Aaron said.

"And did you accept?"

"I have." Joseph nodded.

"Excellent." Caleb grabbed Joseph's shoulders and looked him in the eye. "You have our confidence, of course, but the stakes are higher with this project. You understand that, right?"

"I think so."

"You *think* so?" As Caleb spoke, his hands tightened around Joseph's shoulders and he drew him closer. Caleb's eyes narrowed; his gaze grew more intense. "Let me make it perfectly clear. If Grandpa sat in the chair you built and it collapsed under him, sending his old body tumbling to the ground, but not before a sharp, knifelike splinter of the broken chair leg pierced his skin and punctured his heart, that would certainly be sad, and don't get me wrong, we love old Grandpa, and we'd hate to see anything bad happen to him, but if he died because you built a flimsy chair, life still goes on. Not for him, of course, but for us. And if the chicken coop you built collapsed and crushed the chickens, well, that would also be sad, but we would just eat more chicken and a lot fewer eggs. But these horses, Joseph, these horses are our livelihood. They are the very foundation of our family's wealth. One of our Arabians is as valuable as a handful of gold. To lose just one horse because of some flaw in the fence's design or the quality of the workmanship would be devastating. Now, do you understand how high the stakes are?"

"You've made that clear."

"And you're confident you can build this enclosure, this stable?"

Joseph was unsure he possessed the skill and experience to meet their standards, but his thoughts again returned to Mary and their child growing in her belly. His desire to provide for them outweighed the doubts of his abilities. "I'm confident."

"Good. It's done, Joseph the Carpenter. The job is yours."

As Caleb and Aaron walked around the property with Joseph discussing fence lines, materials, and timing, a compact figure with arms and legs going in all directions and clouded in dust ran toward the three men.

"Hello, Junia," Aaron said as he knelt in the dirt to hug his young daughter.

"Hello, Father. Hello, Uncle Caleb," Junia said, greeting the pair as if she were their peer. "Who are you?" she asked Joseph, studying his face carefully.

Junia, at seven years old, was the youngest of the Corinthian children. The cloud of dust that followed her across the field continued to hover around her as she stood toe to toe with the three men. A towering shock of thick black hair pointed out in all directions from her head as if she had grabbed a lightning bolt and never let go. A thick strand of mucus flowed from her nose to her thin upper lip, where it stayed until she licked the salty goodness away with her tongue. Both knees were scraped and scabbed, and her right knee oozed a thin stream of semi-congealed blood. Junia's demeanor was serious and businesslike, without an ounce of playfulness that you might expect from a seven-year-old. Joseph looked at the girl and smiled—the awkward smile of one who is not accustomed to being around children.

"My name is Joseph."

"Why are you here?" Junia looked Joseph in the eye.

"Junia, mind yourself. This is the man who is going to build our stable. He's a friend of Uncle Caleb's and mine, and he's a friend of yours."

"You ever build a stable?"

"No, miss, I have not."

"What makes you think you can build ours?"

Aaron and Caleb looked at one another with uneasy smiles.

"Well, I've built your grandpa's chair and that feeding trough." Joseph pointed to a wooden manger across the property. "And I've built a few small fences for the villagers in Nazareth, and," Joseph said, placing a hand on Junia's head, "if you work beside me and help with the carpentry, I think we could build this together."

"Do you mean it?" Junia raised her eyebrows and smiled at Joseph.

"I do."

"When can we start?"

Joseph looked at Aaron and Caleb for guidance.

"As soon as you can," Caleb said as Aaron nodded in agreement.

"We're starting tomorrow, Junia," Joseph said.

"I'll be here." Junia hugged her father and raced back across the field with a strand of elastic mucus flying from her nose and an ever-present cloud of dust following closely behind.

Aaron put his hand on Joseph's shoulder. "You have no idea what you just got yourself into, Joseph. She's only seven, but she's a handful and a half."

"She's the least of my worries." Joseph looked out again, raising a hand to shade the late morning sun from his eyes. "How many horses does this enclosure need to hold?"

"We've got twenty-five Arabians now, but we're sending four of our fastest colts to Perea next week. They're going to a wealthy Wise Man who has more riches than he has sense; he paid twice the price that we would normally ask. What's his name, Caleb?"

"Paragus. Paragus of Perea."

"That's him. We'll deliver the colts to Paragus next week, so we'll be down to twenty-one horses, but let's build for twenty-five."

"It shall be done," Joseph assured the two brothers as he walked across the compound back to his donkey, eager to return to Nazareth and relay the good news to Mary.

"And Joseph," Caleb yelled from across the field, "we need to move all the horses into the enclosure before the end of the year. No later than December twenty-fifth. No exceptions."

"Again, my friends," Joseph yelled back to the brothers as he left the compound, "it shall be done."

CHAPTER 5

A Most Unpleasant Couple
DECEMBER 11, 2 WEEKS BC

Mary's parents were, by all accounts, a most unpleasant couple. Jerome, a ruthless, highly successful spice trader, was among the wealthiest of Bethlehem's merchant class. He had built his father's modest spice stall in Bethlehem's central market into a large trading syndicate controlling spice routes by whatever means necessary. Jerome's business empire stretched from Bethlehem to India in the east and Persia to the south. His wife, Elisheba, knew nothing of commerce but was a fervent believer in God. She was an intelligent woman; one of the few women in Judea who knew how to read and write. By her thirties, she had committed all the ancient Scriptures to memory, from the stories of Solomon and David to the laws of Moses and the prophetic words of Isaiah and Micah.

Husband and wife were each unrelenting and uncompromising in their own beliefs, which made them unpleasant individuals. What made them even more unpleasant as a couple was that neither one believed in the other's dogma. Elisheba rejected Jerome's singular focus on acquiring material wealth, and Jerome rejected Elisheba's deep devotion to religious doctrine. But none of this stopped either from using the other at every opportunity to advance their respective causes. Together, they were a force to be reckoned with in the village of Bethlehem—Jerome because of the long reach of his business empire and Elisheba because she used their wealth to influence the Temple Elders and the High Priest of Bethlehem. After eighteen years of marriage, neither could remember why they had married the other.

Physically, the couple couldn't have been more different. Elisheba was a gracefully aging beauty with thick black hair softened by streaks of grey. Her olive skin radiated a warmth that masked an inner coldness. When she smiled, which was not often, delicate lines radiated from her lips and her green eyes. All of this enhanced her aura of commanding authority. Jerome, on the other hand, while powerful in his business dealings, was physically unimpressive; a noodle of a man with delicate features—a dainty, upturned nose and small eyes deeply sunken into darkened, half-moon bags—and rapidly receding hair that looked as though a handful of thin, lethargic worms had been indiscriminately dumped on top of his tiny head.

Elisheba, having completed her morning devotional, sat on a silk-covered sofa stuffed with goose feathers as she read a letter from her sister, Deborah. A servant brought her a cup of Ceylon tea, an exotic drink that Jerome sourced from a large island off the tip of the Indian peninsula and sold for an exorbitant amount to the wealthiest families in Judea. Elisheba slowly shook her head from side to side as she sipped the beverage through her downturned lips. Jerome sat opposite her, drinking sweet Marawi wine and picking at a plate of goat cheese that a second servant had brought at his request.

"What is it?" Jerome asked Elisheba. "Who is it from?"

"Deborah. She says that Mary is returning and that she is traveling with some carpenter who is coming to Bethlehem to register for the Quirinius census."

"Mary's coming back!" Rachel, Mary's older sister, walked into the room, smiling and kindly nodding to each of the servants. Rachel's thick black hair, olive skin, and green eyes mirrored that of Elisheba's in her youth. While her younger sister, Mary, was the rebel in the family, Rachel was a rule follower. Rachel admired Mary for her free spirit, and Mary admired Rachel for her discipline. The two sisters were devoted to one another, and they each missed the other dearly. "That's wonderful news."

Jerome and Elisheba looked less enthused.

"When?" Jerome asked with little interest as another servant refilled his wineglass.

"Can she stay for good? Please let her stay," Rachel said.

"You know how muddleheaded Deborah can be," Elisheba said to Jerome, ignoring Rachel. "It isn't clear when she's coming. Deborah's vague. It sounds like it could be in the next week or so. It's difficult to tell."

"So, can she stay?" Rachel sat next to her father, taking a sip from his wineglass.

"We'll see. We'll see if she has grown out of her insolence and rebelliousness," Elisheba said.

"It's her free spirit, Mother. It's not rebelliousness."

"You can call it whatever you'd like," Elisheba argued. "She is still a bother, an embarrassment at times—both she and that Magdalene girl."

"Vashti?" Rachel said. "Another free spirit. I bet you were just like them when you were their age."

"I most certainly wasn't," Elisheba said.

"Well, perhaps you should have been."

"Any other details or news from the Nazarene north?" Jerome interrupted the female banter, which he felt was beneath his dignity.

"Deborah says Mary carries with her an unwelcome surprise."

"A what? Could she be any less clear? What does that even mean, *unwelcome surprise?*"

"I'm not sure," Elisheba said. "Deborah is cryptic. She doesn't say."

"Typical Deborah."

"Perhaps she's shaved her head or pierced a private body part, or maybe she's joined the Sadducees," Rachel said with the sole purpose of irritating her parents.

"Perhaps it's a reference to the carpenter," Jerome said.

Elisheba rolled her eyes. "Knowing Mary, we should be prepared for anything."

CHAPTER 6

The Conception Story Conceived

DECEMBER 22, 3 DAYS BC

The Roman occupiers had summoned Joseph to appear in Bethlehem, his birthplace, to register for the Census of Quirinius. They used the census to count citizenry, collect taxes, and keep close tabs on every man in the Roman territory that stretched from northern Galilee to southern Judea. The census was compulsory, and the penalty for resisting the Roman authority was imprisonment in some wretched jail where prisoners were often forgotten and left to rot.

Mary, though racked with chronic discomfort and ready to give birth, was eager to accompany Joseph so she could spend time with Vashti and Rachel. The joy in seeing her closest friend and her dear sister outweighed the repugnant prospect of having to spend a night or two in her parents' home. At least that is what Mary thought as they began their journey from Nazareth to Bethlehem. Her love and affection for Vashti and Rachel were as strong and palpable as the day she left Bethlehem those many month ago, while her memory of the maliciousness of her parents had somewhat faded.

31

Their travels began with a steady descent from the rolling hills of Nazareth to the flat and fertile Jezreel Valley, where Joseph gathered oranges and sweet lemons to supplement the dried dates and flatbread that he packed. From the Jezreel Valley, they continued southeast to the Jordan River, where they refilled their goatskins with fresh water to prepare for the last leg of the trip through the Judean Desert. Each day, as Mary rode atop Joseph's donkey, she felt as though her baby, their baby, moved lower and lower in her belly as each plodding step of the steadfast steed reverberated through her body. As they traveled, Mary wrapped an arm around the lower part of her belly to cushion the baby from the jarring ride. In a soothing, lilting voice, she softly sang an ancient Mesopotamian lullaby to comfort both herself and her child. Vashti had clandestinely taught Mary the song many years ago, against the strong wishes of Elisheba, who allowed only hymns of heavenly praise to be sung in their home.

On the morning of the final day of their journey to Bethlehem, Mary called Joseph to the blanket where she had set out breakfast. As Mary took the tea water from the fire, she watched Joseph secure the last of the large worn tent sheets on the back of the donkey. Mary's love for Joseph had grown over the months since they had first met at the water well. Initially, she was attracted to Joseph for the reason women have been attracted to men since the beginning of time: He was strong and virile and what lay under his modest clothing had been a delicious mystery.

A carnal desire had brought Mary to the Nazarene garden that night nine months ago; the promise of exploring Joseph's body entirely; the scent of his sweat and the touch and taste of his body. The idea of a long-term commitment or betrothal felt as distant as the moon that night. But, to her own surprise, on this morning in late December, on the edge of the Judean Desert, as she watched Joseph walk toward her in the morning sun, she realized how deeply her love for him had grown. She loved his grace, his humble nature, and the caring and tender way he attended to her every need. She admired him for knowing who he was and what he desired. And she was grateful that one of his desires was her.

After breakfast, just eight miles outside of Bethlehem, Joseph walked beside the donkey, holding with his left hand the coarsely woven sisal rope that he had fashioned into reins. A bloody ring formed around Joseph's palm and across his knuckles as the rope cut and chafed his hand during the long journey. As Mary rode atop the aging donkey, Joseph caressed Mary's knee. The donkey, with grey whiskers and a badly slumped back, was well past its life expectancy, but he was Joseph's most valuable possession. Although old, the donkey's gait was steady, and on the final day of their trek, he was as strong as the first day. With every rhythmic step of the donkey, Mary's round belly, full with child, moved in unison.

"What do you think of Abigaia?" Mary said as she placed her hand on Joseph's.

"What do I think of what?"

"Abigaia."

"I'm not sure what that is."

"It's a girl's name—for the baby. It means *joy*. I've thought about that—or Rachel or Vashti. But I like Abigaia."

"All beautiful names. I like them all. Have you considered Elisheba?"

"After my mother? Absolutely not. No."

"Abigaia," Joseph said slowly, letting each syllable roll off his tongue. "It's lovely, just as you are and she will be. And she'll bring us joy. It's perfect."

"So, it shall be."

"What about a boy's name?"

"I haven't thought about it." Mary patted the matted hair on the donkey's neck.

"Why not?"

"Do you know Joachim the Healer?" Mary didn't wait for an answer. "He took one look at how small my belly is and how low the baby is positioned and declared that I shall have a girl. He said there was no question. And before we left, I ran into Grandma Hannah, Caleb and Aaron's mother, in the market square. When she saw me, she rushed over—as fast as a ninety-year-old woman can rush—and she closed her eyes, then put her hands on my belly and slowly moved them up and down and side to side. It was strange, a little uncomfortable, but she was also sure that I'm carrying a little girl."

Joseph stopped, raised his eyes to the sky, and shook his head.

"What is it?" Mary asked.

"The Corinthian family. In the rush to leave Nazareth, I didn't tell them I'd be away. That I'd been summoned to Bethlehem for the census two weeks earlier than I had planned."

"You finished the enclosure, though, right?"

"Not entirely. I didn't have a chance. There's a sizable gap in the eastern section of the enclosure, the part that faces Mount Tabor."

Joseph had been tirelessly working to meet the Corinthians' December deadline and was slightly ahead of schedule, but that was before an unsympathetic Roman bureaucrat stationed in Nazareth, and who was backed by a group of brutish Roman centurions, ordered Joseph to leave immediately for Bethlehem to register for the census.

"And you didn't let them know you were leaving?"

"That's the problem. No one was in the compound when I left. I looked for Aaron and Caleb, and I looked for the grandparents. I even looked for little Junia. No one was in or around the compound. I didn't have a chance to tell them. I just leaned some loose boards to fill the gap in the fence."

"Will that hold?"

"I expect it will." Joseph sighed, and his shoulders slumped. "It might. It's possible. I'm not certain. Actually, no, probably not for long."

He walked in silence, stroking his closely shaven beard, shaking his head, his eyes fixed on the dull brown pebbles and sand-colored stones that formed the road to Bethlehem.

Mary attempted to distract him. "What if we had a boy? What if Joachim and Hannah were wrong? What shall we name him?"

"I'm not sure. What are your thoughts?" Joseph said absently.

"Joseph—to honor his father. What do you think?"

"I think I hope it's a girl." Joseph patted Mary on the knee.

Mary smiled, but as the distant silhouette of the low-slung walls of Bethlehem revealed themselves, her mind turned from the pleasant thoughts of the baby to the unpleasant prospect of seeing her parents. "We've talked about what to tell my parents, but we've not settled on anything."

"In her letter, did Deborah tell them you were pregnant?"

"No. She said she told them I was returning but didn't tell them about the baby. She also mentioned you in the letter, but only as my traveling companion. They don't know that I'm pregnant, and they don't know that you and I are to be married. Both things will meet with their vehement disapproval."

"How do you know?"

"My mother is pious, very righteous. No, that's not strong enough. She's a religious zealot." Mary shook her head, frowning. "She surrounds herself with the most extreme Temple Elders and the words of the sanctimonious High Priest nourish her. She believes in the infallibility of the prophets, that their words are God's words."

"A true believer," Joseph said, "unlike us. But I find something admirable in it."

"No, no. That's only half of the story of my mother's faith. You're giving her too much credit. True believers live to serve God. My mother lives to have God serve her. She seeks advantage and privilege, using religion to suit her needs. Growing up, she would have me and Rachel on our knees while we listened to the High Priest read from ancient Scriptures about dark prophecies and plagues and destruction."

"That isn't uncommon," Joseph said.

"And, to ensure that Rachel and I stayed away from boys, she forced us to recite, every morning before breakfast and evening before bed, a passage from some prophet that is now etched in my mind: *'Marriage is honourable in all, and the bed undefiled: but whoremongers and adulterers God will judge.'* We had to read this from the time Rachel was seven and I was only four! When we arrive at her doorstep, she will not wait for God to judge. She will judge. She will deem me a whore and you a whoremonger and rapist."

"Then let's not see them, Mary. Let's register for the census and return to Nazareth. We don't have to stay."

"We can't undo what my aunt Deborah has done. She has sent the message. Bethlehem is small, and my parents exert influence well beyond the walls of Bethlehem. They will know the moment we arrive. They will probably know *before* we arrive. Between my mother's ties to the Temple and my father's ties to the merchant community and political leaders, they will find us. There's no keeping away from them."

"What about your father? Is he more sympathetic?"

"My father? Does he share in my mother's zealous belief in God? No. Well, he does when it suits him. My mother worships God, and my father worships gold. If believing in God helps in accumulating gold, then yes, he is an enthusiastic believer. But if it doesn't serve that end, he couldn't care less about God. His religion is wealth, and his god is power. Neither my mother nor father let truth, reason, love, or compassion stand in the way of their pursuits."

"Do you think you're being a little harsh, a little unfair?"

"I wish I were, but you'll see for yourself."

"So where does this leave us and our Abigaia?"

"If we tell them the truth, that I seduced you in a Nazarene garden, they will accuse you of rape and have you arrested and imprisoned and possibly stoned to death. They'll do this because my mother believes that is what the Scriptures call for and what God would want, and my father would consider me to be damaged goods, unable to marry me into wealth. They would each create their separate truths, but the result would be the same; a High Priest whose lifestyle and status depend wholly on the wealth of my parents would condemn you to prison or death. My mother and father would shun me, banish me from Bethlehem or any other town in Judea where they exert their influence. I would be an outcast, or worse, trapped within the walls of my parents' home."

"What if we say you were my betrothed? That is the truth as well."

"Nine months ago, it wasn't true. For my mother and father, a betrothal is only a betrothal if they consent to it. They never consented, and they never will. You will still be accused of rape. They will still find some way to legitimize your death by public stoning."

"Do the men of Bethlehem have powerful arms and good aim?" Joseph said, attempting to lighten the mood.

"This is serious. I should've never come. I wasn't thinking clearly when we left Nazareth. I wasn't thinking at all."

"Then we'll turn back now." Joseph stopped the donkey and began to turn the beast around to backtrack on the path they had just traveled.

"We can't, Joseph. I'm going to have this baby soon. I don't know when exactly, but it's going to be soon, and I don't want it to be in the middle of the desert or in some underbrush by the side of the Jordan River. We need to continue."

At Mary's urging, Joseph turned the donkey and they resumed their slow march to Bethlehem.

"Damn the Romans!" Joseph said.

"The Romans?"

"If they hadn't come and conquered, there would be no census. No need to return to Bethlehem. I would've completed the Corinthians' stable, and we wouldn't have to explain anything to your parents."

"But that doesn't help us now. This is my mess."

"This is our joy." Joseph placed a hand on Mary's belly.

"I'm a fool. My desire to see Rachel and Vash blinded my judgment, and that is increasingly clear with every step we take toward Bethlehem."

Joseph gave Mary the last of the water and wrapped a threadbare cloth over her shoulders and arms to protect her from the desert sun.

With the walls of Bethlehem close, they would arrive at the home of Mary's parents as the December sun set. The donkey's pace slowed as the hills into Bethlehem grew steeper. As Joseph guided the donkey, the sandal strap on his left foot broke, the leather worn beyond repair. He removed both of his sandals and used pieces of thin tent cloth to wrap each of his chafed and bloodied feet. They continued to climb, but their pace slowed.

"Do you remember," Mary began slowly, considering each of her words carefully, "when we were in Jericho?"

"That was only yesterday. I'm old, but I'm not so old that I can't remember one day ago." Joseph winked at Mary.

"Remember the market in Jericho?"

"The answer is still yes. We bought figs and flatbread."

"Remember the older man, even older than you?" Mary smiled at Joseph. "He was talking with the baker about how his wife had spontaneously burst into flames."

"The lunatic. I remember. What are you getting at?"

"He was so detailed in his description," Mary said with a hint of admiration. "It seemed believable."

"It's a fabrication, a complete lie to shield his guilt," Joseph said. "Tell me you don't believe his story."

"Maybe. But do you remember ten years ago or so, in the village of Husan? A similar story circulated about Zacarias the Tanner. He also spontaneously burst into flames."

"It's well-known lore," Joseph said. "Every child from Nazareth to Bethlehem is told this tale."

"I remember my mother telling me and Rachel several times. She called it spontaneous combustion. She believes the lore surrounding Zacarias the Tanner."

"So, you want to make me burst into flames?"

"No. Well, sometimes, yes." Mary smiled, then grew serious. "But if stories of spontaneous combustion are told and accepted as the truth, particularly by my mother, then why not a story of spontaneous pregnancy?"

"You can't be serious, Mary. No."

"It could work."

"No, that . . . that will not work," Joseph said.

"But she believes the story of Zacarias."

"This is different, very different."

"How?"

"No. Impossible," Joseph said, shaking his head.

"Why?"

"You really think it could work?"

"Maybe."

"What if your mother saw it as a divine sign, like when God took the form of a burning bush to speak to Moses?"

"I don't think she will."

"Can you be sure?"

"I can never be sure with my mother." Mary squeezed Joseph's hand. "But she holds Moses in the highest esteem, next to God. Once, I pointed out that Moses was always alone on Mount Horeb or alone on some other, far away mountain when things like the burning bush spoke or the tablets containing the ten laws appeared. She slapped me for questioning God's word—across both cheeks. Then she summoned the High Priest, who recited passages from the prophet Moses to me. He, with my mother's full permission, then took the scrolls and repeatedly hit my open palms as they lay flat across the table."

Joseph kissed Mary's hands. "I'm sorry. That will never happen again. I'll see to that."

"She didn't react the same way when I questioned her about Zacarias the Tanner. She didn't like that I challenged her word, but she didn't slap me or summon the High Priest or reference Holy Scriptures. She thinks of the Zacarias story as true but not divine. For whatever reason, she has never associated it with an act of God."

"It still seems too farfetched, Mary."

"My mother is smart, but she is also eager to believe in all sorts of stories—some of the divine nature and others not. If she earnestly believes that a man from Husan can spontaneously combust, then it's possible she may believe that my pregnancy was spontaneous. In her eyes, I'd still be a virgin, and you wouldn't be a rapist."

"It's the least terrible of a terrible set of options." Joseph held Mary's hand as they continued up the steep path into Bethlehem. "I know this is selfish, but I want people to know that I'm the father, that this is our baby."

"They will, in time. But for now, and only to my parents, we need to spin the tale of a spontaneous pregnancy. When we're back in Nazareth, far away from my parents, everyone will know you are the father of our beautiful baby girl."

CHAPTER 7

The First Letter from the Corinthians

Dear Joseph the Carpenter,

Hello, friend. We were expecting you today. Where were you? Where are you now? Caleb heard gossip that you were seen leaving Nazareth this morning, heading south with a plump, buxom young woman on your donkey. You rascal! I told him it was impossible; you leaving Nazareth. I said you were fully committed to finishing the job here and that you were probably just giving your buxom friend a ride so you could see her bosoms bounce on your ass. That's what I would have done too, my friend! I'm sending this note to urge you to come back tomorrow to finish the job as we've already moved the entire herd of Arabians into your enclosure despite there being a small section of missing fence. Please don't get me wrong, we understand that these things always take longer than expected, so we're completely agreeable to a later finish. We just hope to have that gap closed as quickly as you can possibly attend to it. Ever since my ancestors moved from the arid village of Corinth to the fertile land of Galilee centuries ago, we have bred and raised our beloved Arabians. They are our past, our present, and our future. Our fortune lies in your trusted and capable hands. We know you won't let us down. We hope to see you (and the buxom young woman!) back on the job tomorrow.

Yours fondly,
Aaron Corinthian

CHAPTER 8

Meeting Mary's Parents
DECEMBER 22, 3 DAYS BC

The late December sun hovered just above the walls and low-lying rooftops of Bethlehem, infusing the evening sky with a mixture of oranges, yellows, and reds. A string of wispy clouds, like the delicate feathers of an angel's wing, added texture and depth to the colors. The long shadows of Joseph and Mary stretched under the arched entrance to the courtyard of Mary's parents' house, arriving a few seconds ahead of their corporeal twins.

The courtyard stood in the middle of a two-story compound, the only marble structure in the modest village of Bethlehem, which was otherwise filled with limestone and mud-brick single-story, single-room homes. A fig tree, laden with small green unripe fruit, grew in the middle of the courtyard. This tree was at the center of many experiences that Mary and Vashti shared as they grew up. It was the central base for childhood games of hide-and-seek, and it also served as a clandestine communication channel when they reached their teen years. With thin twine, the girls would tie notes written on small papyrus parchments around the unripened figs they had picked and hidden in their bedrooms. They would then throw the figs back and forth between their bedroom windows, which were separated by only a narrow footpath. In their notes, they conveyed their deepest thoughts, wildest dreams, and crudest jokes. It was how they communicated with one another when Mary was grounded in her room, which was often.

Joseph had never seen such a fine home. Not even the homes of the most powerful merchants from the wealthiest families in Nazareth could match the size, the quality of materials, and the sheer opulence of this one. The house was magnificent; built with exacting detail, including three perfectly sculpted Doric columns supporting a marbled balcony that jutted out from the second floor above the courtyard. Carved into the west wall of the courtyard were three oval coves, each holding a life-sized marble statue of a prophet. Moses was in the center, while Isaiah was to his right and Micah to his left. The spaces between each of the coves were filled with manicured cypress trees with finely tapered tops pointing to the heavens. At the far end of the courtyard, a small stable housed two sheep and a wooden manger.

The courtyard opened to the ground floor, which contained the servants' quarters and a large kitchen with two enclosed fireplaces, cupboards for grains and dried fruit, and a washing basin made of stone. In the back was a large, cooled room to store wine and olive oil. A curved marbled stairway, also something Joseph had never seen, elegantly connected the courtyard to the second floor, where Elisheba, Jerome, and Rachel lived. Only family members and distinguished guests used the staircase; servants climbed up and down a rickety ladder that rose from the courtyard to the second-floor balcony so they wouldn't sully the marbled steps.

"I don't belong here," Joseph said, gazing at the marbled home, which reflected the soft yellows and reds and oranges of the sunset.

"You belong with me." Mary took Joseph's hand. "They built this home to have that effect—to intimidate. It's a garish monument to their wealth and piety but utterly soulless. And, except for Rachel, it's a home without heart."

One female and two male servants effortlessly descended from the balcony on the ladder, greeting Mary with deep bows, which she returned with a warm hug. Joseph loved this about Mary. She didn't consider herself above anyone; she loved and respected all.

One servant took the reins of Joseph's donkey and led it to the stable in the courtyard. The female servant took Mary's hand and led her to the stairway. When Joseph tried to follow, the remaining male servant, younger and stronger than Joseph, blocked his path. Mary stopped and looked with raised eyebrows at this man.

"Mary, I'm sorry, it's Master's orders. The carpenter is to take the ladder," the servant said, bowing his head to Mary but still blocking Joseph.

"I understand." Mary's voice was kind but firm. "But I desire to have him walk beside me on the stairs. I will deal with my parents later."

The servant held his ground.

"I promise," Mary said, cupping her hand on the servant's cheek, "my parents will not punish you; no harm will come to you."

"As you wish." The servant bowed his head and stepped to the side. "We're all glad to have you back, Mary."

When Joseph reached the top of the stairs, the richness of aromas and colors and textures overcame him. The scent of candles infused with frankincense oil and placed throughout the room filled his nostrils. Large vases stood at the four corners of the room; each contained a different variety of palm. Freshly cut pink desert roses and delicate orange Chinese hibiscus flowers filled small blue ceramic vases on each of the tables. Joseph became acutely aware of the contrast between his bare and bloodied feet and the smooth, darkly stained Jerusalem pine floor. He had never set foot in a home with a finished wood floor covered in tightly woven, beautifully dyed wool carpets. He was also growing more aware of the odor that was wafting from his body after having not bathed for over a week and aware that his clothes were far dirtier, much more worn, and of lower quality than the servants' clothes.

Across the expanse of the grand room, Elisheba and Jerome stood, arms crossed and straight-faced. No loving hugs, no warm welcome, no pleasantries of any sort. They focused their attention not on their daughter, whom they hadn't seen for months, but on her companion.

"You must be the traveling Nazarene carpenter Deborah mentioned," Jerome said. "You certainly look and smell the part. You may leave now. You're no longer needed."

"He'll do no such thing." Mary grabbed Joseph's hand.

"He's not fit to be in this home. He belongs with his donkey in the stable." Jerome waved his hand as if he was shooing a fly.

Despite Mary's warnings, Joseph was unprepared for the vileness of the verbal onslaught, which came without the pretense of a greeting. He thought Mary had exaggerated the unpleasantness of her parents. He was mistaken.

"This is Joseph, to whom I am betrothed."

"To *this* man?" Elisheba crossed the room to get a better look at the pair. "Absolutely not. A betrothal is not possible unless—" Elisheba stopped, turned her attention from Joseph, and looked squarely at Mary's rounded belly. "Are you pregnant or just fat?"

"Were you raped by this peasant, this beast?" Jerome walked with small, quick steps to Joseph, stopping only when he realized Joseph's physical advantage. "I will have you imprisoned."

"Prison?" said Elishba. "I'll see that this rapist is stoned to death, as is God's will."

"Stop this. Stop. Both of you." Mary's tone matched her mother's in sharpness and strength.

Rachel, hearing her sister, ran from her room down a long corridor, crossed the great room, embraced Mary, and then stepped back, placing her hands on Mary's belly. "And you are pregnant! Very pregnant! I had no idea."

"Neither did we," Jerome said.

"You look beautiful." Rachel hugged Mary and then nodded to

Joseph. "And who is this?"

"Joseph, my betroth—"

"According to the Scriptures," said Elisheba, raising her voice over Mary's and locking her eyes with Mary's eyes, "a rapist must be punished. Death by stoning. Praise be to God. And you? You will be seen as a harlot. You may choose to destroy your own reputation, but you will not destroy mine or this family's. Do you remember the words of the prophets?"

"Yes, Mother. You made us recite them to you a thousand times before; '*whoremongers and adulterers God will judge.*' But Joseph did not rape me. The baby that grows inside of me is not of Joseph."

"Who then?" Jerome demanded.

"It was no one." Mary squeezed Joseph's hand tighter. "It's difficult to explain."

"Go ahead," Jerome said.

"Do you remember the story of Zacarias the Tanner from Husan?"

"The man who spontaneously burst into flames?" asked Elisheba.

"Yes, exactly."

"What does your pregnancy possibly have to do with poor Zacarias?" Elisheba asked.

"There are," Mary began slowly, "many such stories. These types of spontaneous, unexplained events."

"But you don't believe in any of these stories, Mary. You told me so yourself. When I told you the story of Zacarias, you expressed nothing but scornful disbelief."

"Mary, what exactly are you saying?" asked Jerome.

"This pregnancy—it occurred spontaneously, not unlike Zacarias the Tanner. Joseph did not do this. No one did this to me. I am," Mary said, "still a virgin."

Rachel's muffled giggle was cut short by a jab to the gut from Mary's sharp elbow.

"Mary," Jerome said, motioning for the servant to bring him wine as he sat on a thronelike leather chair, "do you take us for fools?"

Elisheba, uncharacteristically quiet, paced slowly and deliberately, her eyes transfixed on the floor. Jerome got up from the chair and stood in front of Mary and Joseph.

"Spray the peasant carpenter with cinnamon oil. His stench is sickening me," Jerome commanded a servant, who quickly obliged, spritzing Joseph from his head to his bloody toes.

"Father, Joseph is not a peasant. He's one of the finest carpenters in Nazareth," Mary said, knowing Joseph had many good qualities but being the finest carpenter in Nazareth was not one of them.

"Being the finest carpenter in Nazareth is of no consequence." Jerome daintily sipped the sweet Malawi wine from a gilded chalice. "Where has that gotten him? Our least valued, most pathetic servant," Jerome said, pointing to the young servant who had just filled his chalice moments before, "is, I'm sure, more skilled than this brute, and he certainly smells better."

"Mother, you're unusually quiet. What are you thinking?" Mary asked.

"I'm just thinking."

"About what?" Jerome asked.

"About what Mary said. Leave me alone for a moment."

"Mary . . . " Jerome's thin lips melted into his chin, which melted into his neck, which melted into his concave chest like a cascading flow of congealed candle wax. "I never believed the stories of spontaneous combustion—or spontaneous anything. I know your mother does, but I don't, and I don't believe your story either. You're trying to save this peasant—"

"Joseph. His name is Joseph," Mary said.

"You're trying to save Joseph from a stoning."

"Hush, Jerome," Elisheba said. "There are many stories told over many years of these spontaneous occurrences. Hundreds of witnesses have confirmed the details of these stories. They are to be believed." Elisheba stopped pacing and faced Mary. "The greatest prophet of all, Moses, bore witness to the spontaneous burning of the pistacia bush on Mount Horeb. The flames turned out to be an angel from God. There is no disputing this truth."

"Mother, this has nothing to do with angels, gods, or prophets. You know I don't believe in any of those things. They are myths that old men have passed down to other old men for their own benefit and amusement."

"Watch your tongue." Elisheba pointed her finger at Mary. "You may be a grown woman of fourteen, but you are in my house. Those are blasphemous words, and God hears each one of them."

"All I can tell you and Father is that without consummation, I am pregnant. The only explanation I can offer is that it was spontaneous— not caused by Joseph, not caused by any man, and certainly not caused by some divine intervention."

At this, Elisheba paused, replacing her glare with a softer, more understanding gaze at Mary. She crossed her arms, put her ringed index finger to her mouth, and sighed.

"What is it, Elisheba?" asked Jerome. "When you get that look—"

"Nothing. Quiet. It is late, and Mary and the carpenter—"

"Joseph," Mary said.

"Mary and Joseph have had a long journey; we should let them rest for the night. Mary, you will sleep with Rachel tonight, and the servants will prepare your old room tomorrow. For Joseph, we will set out blankets in the stable where he can sleep close to his donkey."

"No, absolutely not, Mother. Joseph will not—"

"Mary, it's fine." Joseph put his arm around Mary's shoulders. "It will be good for you to spend time with your sister, and I have slept in far worse places." Joseph kissed Mary's forehead and descended the ladder into the moonlit stillness of the courtyard.

Rachel took Mary's hand and led her down the long hallway to the familiar comfort of her room. "We have a lot to catch up on," Rachel said, looking at Mary's belly.

"First," Elisheba shouted from the great room down the hallway, "before Mary climbs into a clean bed in this clean house, see that she bathes in jasmine water. She smells nearly as bad as that carpenter."

CHAPTER 9

The Sisters Confide

DECEMBER 22, 3 DAYS BC

After a long bath in the luxurious comfort of warm water scented with delicate, fresh jasmine petals, Mary sat on Rachel's bed, her sister by her side. Mary had forgotten how soft, comfortable, and pampered life had been in her parents' house. A part of her missed the exquisite things in this home—the sweet fragrance of fresh flowers in each room; the fine leather sofas; the aroma of teas and spices; the smoothness of the wood floor against the soles of her bare feet, which were once soft and supple but were now rough and calloused. This home, compared to her aunt Deborah's one-room mud-floor home, or compared to riding atop a donkey and sleeping on hard ground for the last several nights, felt like Heaven. But Mary would not trade one night sleeping on the ground with Joseph by her side, his caring arms wrapped around her body, for a thousand nights in Heaven.

Mary dangled her feet over the side of the bed as Rachel rubbed her back, pressing firmly with her palms. Growing up, Mary loved these back rubs and the gossipy chats that went along with them; but on this night, the back rub was uncomfortable for the soon-to-be mom.

"I'm sorry, Rachel, but I need to support my back." Mary moved farther onto the bed until her back rested against the cold, smooth marble wall. "I swear this baby is ready for this world. It feels like any moment."

"I'm so excited for you. And for Joseph."

"I'm terrified." Mary's eyes became watery, and she took a deep breath and pursed her lips to prevent even a single tear from falling. She rested a hand on Rachel's knee. Rachel placed her hands on top of Mary's. "I can't imagine this baby coming out of my body. I can't. I'm not sure I'm strong enough. I don't know if I can do this. And, once she's born, I want to be a good mother. I want to be caring and attentive, but what if I'm not? What if—"

"What if what?"

"What if I'm like Mother? Or Father? What if I can't do this?"

"Mary, you can do this. You are stronger than anyone I know. Anyone. You will be a great mother—a mother any daughter or son will be grateful to have. You are caring, and kind, and loving, and generous, and everything that Mother and Father are not."

The two sisters fell silent. Mary smiled an uneasy smile and nodded, thankful for Rachel's reassurance. Rachel patted Mary's hand, tilted her head playfully, and put her hands on Mary's belly. "A spontaneous pregnancy?"

"Is that a statement, a question, or an accusation?"

"What was it like?"

"What was what like?"

"What was *it* like? You know. To be with Joseph?"

"Rachel, I just explained this to Mother and Father. I've not been with Joseph. I've never . . . " As Mary spoke, the baby kicked, first one foot and then the other.

Rachel's mouth fell open as the baby continued to kick against her hands on Mary's belly. "Whoa, did you feel that? I felt that! The baby!"

"Of course I felt it. I think she's going to come out walking. Or kicking."

"Mary." Rachel raised her eyebrows and moved closer to her sister. "What?"

"You can tell Mother and Father whatever you will, but I don't believe it. Father was right—you're protecting Joseph."

Mary closed her eyes and sighed.

"We've never kept secrets from each other. Don't start now," Rachel said as she brushed Mary's hair.

Mary inhaled deeply. "You can't tell a soul. This needs to stay between you and me, at least until Joseph and I are well on our way back to Nazareth."

"Of course. I would never do anything to hurt you, your baby, or Joseph. You know that."

"I know, I'm sorry. It's just that—"

"It's okay. I understand."

Mary closed her eyes again and smiled, remembering the night in the garden in Nazareth. "It was wonderful. At first a bit uncomfortable, a bit strange, but Joseph was so gentle, and loving, and—"

"Large?" Rachel grinned.

"I had forgotten what a foul mind you have."

"And?"

"And there are some things I will not reveal even to you, my dear big sister."

"Did it hurt?"

"Have you not been with a man?"

"No, still not. And I'm already seventeen. I'm getting so old." Rachel moved her hands from Mary's belly and crossed her arms. "Everyone around me—you, Vashti—is either pregnant or already has children. I'm afraid I'm going to grow old without ever having—"

"Stop it. You're young. Not as young as me." Mary attempted to cheer up her sister. "And you're beautiful, but—"

"Not as beautiful as you," Rachel finished Mary's sentence, and the two sisters smiled. "Look at you, my younger sister. You're going to have a baby, and I will be a doting aunt."

"And Mother and Father will be doting grandparents, I'm sure," Mary said, rolling her eyes.

Rachel fell quiet, her smile faded, and concern replaced the playfulness in her eyes.

"What are you thinking?" Mary asked. "You went blank. I lost you for a moment."

"Mother."

"What about her?"

"She was quiet. Eerily quiet." Rachel held Mary's hand. "Unusually calm. I'm surprised she didn't have the servants hold Joseph down while she called for the High Priest to condemn Joseph to a stoning right on the spot. She was too quiet, don't you think?"

"Honestly, I was relieved. I expected the worst. I expected shouting and more accusations."

"I'm not sure it is better. You think she believes your story of spontaneous pregnancy?"

"That's my hope," Mary said with some hesitancy. "And you don't?"

"She took it too well. She's ruminating."

"About what?"

"I don't know. But when she gets like that—quiet, nonconfrontational, somewhat agreeable, almost pleasant—nothing good ever comes from it."

"You're overthinking this," said Mary. "The spontaneous pregnancy is a plausible story."

"Not really. It doesn't seem plausible. If Mother told you a similar story, would you believe her?"

Mary didn't need to answer.

"But worrying about this tonight," Rachel said, "won't do any of us—you, me, or your baby—any good. Let's get some sleep."

Mary lay down on the soft bed, her head resting on a pillow of goose down wrapped in silk. She sighed and closed her eyes, and her entire body relaxed. "God, this bed is comfortable," she mumbled just before falling into a deep and satisfying sleep.

CHAPTER 10

The Conception *Story* Reconceived

DEC 23, 2 DAYS BC

The morning sun had not yet risen as five messengers on horse-back arrived in the courtyard of Elisheba and Jerome. The click-clacking of hooves woke Joseph out of a deep sleep as he lay curled up on a small, thin blanket in the courtyard stable. Dust from the horses rose, stung Joseph's eyes, and triggered a fit of coughing. For a moment, Joseph was uncertain of his whereabouts. He knelt on the blanket that served as his bed and surveyed the scene in the low light of the receding moon. The smell of shit surrounded him. During the night, as he lay asleep, the servants, as Mary's father had directed, had hauled shit-filled pots from outside the courtyard walls and arranged them neatly around the head of Joseph's makeshift bed. Joseph covered his nose with his sleeve to block the rancid fumes and walked in a sleepy daze through the dust toward the horsemen.

"You," a horseman called to Joseph, "take these reins and give the horses food and water and have them ready in a short time. We have long rides ahead."

Joseph rubbed his eyes to get a better look at the men; the dust and sleep made it difficult to see clearly.

A servant quickly descended the ladder from the balcony. "I'll take them, sir. I'll take the reins," he said to the horsemen. "Please go inside. My masters have been waiting for you. I'll feed and water your horses and have them back in the courtyard."

Four of the horsemen briskly brushed past Joseph and effortlessly climbed up the ladder. The fifth horseman, reeking of wine and smoke, stumbled by Joseph and began to climb, his feet slipping on each rung as he made his unsteady way up the ladder to the balcony with the others.

Joseph stood in the courtyard, admiring the horses—strong Arabians, perhaps as fine as the horses that Aaron Corinthian and his family raised. The riders were serious men, expressionless and dressed in the clothes of long-distance messengers, carrying only a small leather satchel strapped across one shoulder.

"What's happening?" Joseph asked the servant. "Who are the riders?"

"They're messengers, called here by Master Jerome at the urging of Madam Elisheba."

"Why?"

"Madam said she wants to spread the good news," the servant said as he led the horses by the reins through the courtyard.

"What good news?" Joseph asked, but the servant was already outside the archway, taking the horses to the larger stable.

As Joseph began to climb the ladder, a barefoot man wearing heavily soiled and tattered clothes wheeled a large cart into the courtyard. A putrid aroma wafted from his cart, making Joseph gag.

"I'm here to pick up the filled shitpots, and replace them with clean pots, sir," the man said deferentially to Joseph, "but I don't see them. They're typically placed outside the archway."

"Please, friend, there is no need to be formal. No need to call me sir. I'm a poor and humble carpenter from Nazareth and a guest of this house. My name is Joseph."

"I'm Jude Aya, the collector of the shitpots in Bethlehem."

The man's unapologetic pride in his low vocation impressed Joseph. He felt an affinity for Jude Aya. "It's nice to meet you. The shitpots aren't in the archway because someone placed them all around my head as I slept." Joseph pointed to the crumpled blankets. "It was a sign of welcome, I'm sure."

Joseph could hear the faint voice of Elisheba on the second floor, apparently addressing the messengers.

"I'll give you a hand." Joseph hoisted a pot on his shoulder and carried it to the cart.

"Thank you, my friend. No one has ever offered to help me before." Jude Aya followed with another of the shitpots. "Understandable— the smells, the mess."

Jude Aya and Joseph worked quickly, loading the filled pots on the cart and replacing them with empty, clean ones.

"This is kind of you," Jude Aya said. "I don't want to seem ungrateful. I'm very grateful. But why do you help me?"

"Because I could. And because you looked as though you could use some help."

Jude Aya thanked Joseph and pulled his cart under the arch of the courtyard into the narrow lane, where he would go on to the next house and the next and the next until his cart could hold no more of the filled pots.

Joseph brushed his hands together to get rid of the dirt and dust and climbed the ladder to the balcony, where he stood at some distance from the gathered crowd. No one noticed him. All eyes in the room focused on Elisheba.

The five messengers stood in a semicircle on one side of an imposing table, a large thick slab of Aleppo pine polished so finely that the top served equally well as a mirror. The messengers stood like obedient soldiers facing their supreme commander Elisheba, who sat on a thronelike red silk chair with gilded armrests. Jerome stood on Elisheba's left, and an older man stood on her right.

The older man dressed impressively in an azure silk ceremonial robe with pomegranates embroidered around the neck and cuffs. A thickly woven decorative belt with long golden tassels adorned his waist. His long, impeccably manicured black and grey beard jutted out from his chin like the tip of an arrow. Atop his full head of silver hair rested a ceremonial azure hat embroidered with pomegranates to match his robe. He wore the unmistakable clothing of a High Priest.

Five elegantly ornamented papyrus scrolls placed perfectly parallel to one another, each ornately fastened with two thinly cut palm reeds, sat upon the finely polished table. A satchel that matched his robe and carried additional scrolls lay at the High Priest's feet. Joseph began to worry.

Elisheba nodded and a young servant girl ceremoniously took the scrolls from the table, gave them to Elisheba, and bowed deeply as she walked backwards out of sight. Jerome surveyed the room, glanced at Joseph, and smiled—a menacing, dismissive smile.

Elisheba turned her attention to the messengers, who awaited her instruction. She held up a scroll with both hands, raising it over her head reverently. "This," she said ceremoniously, "will be the most important message you will ever deliver." She paused and looked each messenger in the eye, one by one. "With each scroll is the name of a princely Wise Man to whom you must deliver the scroll before the sun rises to its peak tomorrow. Distances are long. You must ride swiftly and without stopping. You mustn't fail me."

The High Priest stood impatiently, waiting for his turn to address the messengers. The only thing that exceeded his arrogant piety was his love of hearing his own voice. He quickly began as Elisheba paused, "We have chosen each of you carefully, based upon your reputation as the swiftest messengers in Bethlehem. The scroll you are to deliver will alter the course of the earthly and heavenly worlds. You are to deliver this message on behalf of God Himself and all the people on Earth. You carry the words of the prophets, to whom God Almighty spoke directly. God will reward you for delivering His message on time, and

He will leave you withering in a lake of fire, scratching your own eyes out and gnashing your teeth should you fail."

One by one, each messenger bowed and stepped forward. They solemnly received a scroll in one hand and in the other they received the name and location of a Wise Man. Each messenger tucked the scroll in their satchel and again bowed to Jerome, Elisheba, and the High Priest before climbing down the ladder.

Mary emerged from her room as the last rider descended. She walked to Joseph on the balcony and peered into the courtyard just as the five messengers mounted their horses, whipping them as they sprinted out of the compound and on to their divine journey.

Mary grabbed Joseph's hand, and together they crossed the room to seek answers. The scrolls that had been on the table were replaced with a different set of scrolls, ones the High Priest brought with him. Ones that were far older, relics written centuries ago.

"What is this?" Mary pointed at the documents, looking first at her mother, then her father, ignoring the High Priest.

"Mary, come." Elisheba patted the cushion of an empty chair beside her own.

"I am quite comfortable here," Mary said, planting her feet on the floor.

"Please sit," Jerome said, pointing to the empty chair beside Elisheba, "next to your mother."

"I prefer to stand." Mary gripped Joseph's hand.

"We have wonderful news," Elisheba said in a tender, caring tone—a tone that was completely unfamiliar to Mary.

"Mother, you're wearing the same simlah that you had on yesterday. Did you sleep last night?"

"There was no time for sleep, my dear. The energy of God filled me."

The baby kicked and fussed deep inside of Mary. She rubbed her belly and winced.

"Maybe you should sit," said Joseph, pulling out a chair.

"Thank you, but I will stand," Mary repeated, then turned to her mother. "Who were those men?"

"Messengers. The most experienced, fastest messengers, gratefully loaned to us by the High Priest."

"And why do you need messengers?"

Elisheba looked only at Mary, with complete disregard of Joseph. "Mary, after you described the circumstances of your pregnancy last night, I couldn't rest; my mind raced."

Mary and Joseph exchanged glances.

"Why is he here?" Mary nodded toward the High Priest. "Why would you summon the High Priest and send five messengers on an errand? And why these scrolls?" Mary picked one up and threw it back down on the table.

"Wine!" Jerome shouted at a servant. "I'll need some wine for this."

"Make it two," the High Priest called to the servant, who was already halfway down the ladder on his way to the wine cellar.

"Mary," Elisheba said in a respectful, almost reverential tone, "the circumstances you described are more than just coincidences, they are prophecy fulfilled."

"I'm sorry, but I don't understand," Joseph said.

"Ignorant carpenter. We didn't expect you to," Jerome said as he nibbled, with small ratlike bites, on a dried date.

"Father, if you don't treat Joseph with more respect, he and I will leave this very moment and you will never see us again," Mary said through a clenched jaw and with tightened fists.

Elisheba shushed Jerome and turned to the High Priest. "Please, read from the prophets."

The High Priest, always eager to hear his own voice, picked up a scroll from the table and with much pomp untied the reed, rolling out the scroll in his outstretched arms. The blue sleeves of his robe hung like suspended waves of water propelling the scroll to his manicured fingertips. "This is from the prophet Isaiah, who, after Moses himself, is the most revered of all prophets. His prophecies, like those of Moses, resulted from speaking to our God in Heaven directly. He was a prophet pure in soul, a virtuous man, never corrupted by women nor tempted by wine. God looked upon Isaiah with great favor. As the orator of Jerusalem, he was the most celebrated prophet in six hundred years. His words—"

"Oh, please!" Elisheba said. "Get on with it. Read the prophecy."

The High Priest continued to hold the scroll high in his outstretched arms, glanced at Mary, cleared his throat, and began, "Reading from Isaiah: *Therefore the Lord himself will give you a sign: The virgin will be with child and will give birth to a son, and you will call him Immanuel.*"

"You see?" Elisheba said to Mary.

"No, I don't," said Mary, clearly seeing where her mother was headed.

"*You* are the virgin. Yours is not a spontaneous pregnancy," explained Elisheba.

"It is a divine conception!" The High Priest bowed to Mary.

"You carry the seed of God Himself," Elisheba said and gently grabbed Mary's hand. Mary pulled away.

"No. Mother, no, no." Mary pounded her fist on the table. "I'm not part of some prophecy from hundreds of years ago." Mary shook her head, her lips pursed. "And I am not carrying God's seed."

"Mary, I think you should sit." Joseph moved a chair closer to her.

"No, not among this treacherous triumvirate." Mary spoke through clenched teeth.

"Your mother is right, child," the High Priest said, "you shall deliver God's Son unto this earth."

"We're fairly certain Mary is having a girl." Joseph's input was appreciated by Mary but went unnoticed by the triumvirate.

Mary gave him a nod of gratitude before continuing with the fight. "You're not listening to me." She glared at the three. "I will not be part of your scheme based on the writing of a prophet who lived hundreds of years ago and whose prophesies are questionable."

"Read from Micah!" Elisheba stood, her voice rising as she commanded the High Priest. "Mary needs to hear more."

"I've heard enough." Mary cringed and grabbed her belly. She reached her arm out to Joseph, who eased her into a chair.

The High Priest picked up a second scroll from the table, ceremoniously unfurled it and began, "This, Mary, is from the prophet Micah, who, like Moses and Isaiah, spoke directly to our Almighty God. He bore witness to miracles and preached and served the poor people in small villages that dotted the countryside in northern Galilee. Villages such as Moresheth and—"

"For God's sake, read the scroll. Now." Elisheba hit the High Priest on the shoulder, sounding more like the mother that Mary was accustomed to—prickly, rude, always impatient.

"All right then," the High Priest said with a somewhat bruised ego. "I shall read from Micah: *'But thou, Bethlehem Ephratah, though thou be little among the thousands of Judah, yet out of thee shall he come forth unto me that is to be ruler in Israel; whose goings forth have been from of old, from everlasting.'*"

"Mary, you must see now." Elisheba's voice was again calm and tender. She sat at eye level with Mary. "When you combine the prophecy of Isaiah with the prophecy of Micah, it is indisputable proof that you, a virgin, here in Bethlehem, are carrying in your womb the Son of God. These are not coincidences, Mary. This is God's indisputable truth unfolding."

"I think it is quite disputable," Mary said. "These prophecies are not facts. They are stories, myths. They have nothing to do with me. And Micah? Isaiah? How many of their prophesies have come true?"

"Well," said the High Priest, who had a habit of beginning a sentence with the word "well" when he was uncertain of his answer, "they unfold over the goodness of time, over very long periods."

"So, none."

"Well . . . " The High Priest drank from his cup, set it on the table, running his nervous fingers around its rim. "It's difficult to say. No one can really be sure. There were a great many prophecies. Isaiah was, my dear, a prophet who produced a prodigious amount of work.

I can't be certain, but this could be among the first to come true."

"Did you hear that, Mother?"

Elisheba glanced at the High Priest with clenched teeth and a furrowed brow. The vein in her neck popped out, visibly pulsating.

The High Priest, seeing Elisheba's reprimand, added quickly, "That means the odds are with us! It's not a matter of *if* they are true, it is a matter of *when* they shall be actualized. Just as sure as the Earth is as flat as this table and angels live on weightless clouds in the heavenly skies, you, my dear, are carrying the child of God."

"Read from Psalms." Elisheba handed a scroll to the High Priest.

The High Priest held the scroll high in the air. "This," he began and then followed with his familiar dramatic pause, "is from the book of Psalms. It reads—"

"Is Psalms the name of a prophet?" Joseph asked.

"No, my son, it is the name of a book of important prophesies and parables and poems."

"And who wrote it?" Mary asked.

"Well, it was likely Moses, but it could have been King David, or perhaps King Solomon. There are other holy men and scholars who believe it is a compilation of writing from all three. It is difficult to know for certain."

"When was it written?" asked Joseph as he sat down at the table and stretched to take a date from the plate that was in front of Jerome. At this, with a swift motion of his delicate hand, Jerome summoned a servant to move the bowl away from Joseph and closer to himself.

"Well, that is also hard to know," the High Priest explained. "Most likely over hundreds of years and certainly a long, long time ago. A very long time ago."

"So," Mary said, alternating her glance between the High Priest and her mother, "you're going to reference a prophecy from an unknown prophet who wrote it for unknown reasons, at an unknown time, from an unknown location."

"Exactly! Yes." The High Priest raised his glass as if to toast Mary's understanding.

"And that doesn't bother you?"

"Oh, Mary," Elisheba said. "That is the very essence of faith. Isn't it? It is the willingness to suspend reason and put critical thinking aside. This allows one to fully put their head and their heart and their soul in God's gentle hands. To fully submit to his wisdom, and to fulfill, without question, God's commands, including those spoken through the prophets. I think, my child, you understand."

"No, I do not. I don't understand. It's absurd to refer to these prophecies as truth. It's nonsense."

"Enough blasphemy!" shouted Elisheba, now her turn to pound the table. She turned to the High Priest. "Read!"

The High Priest read, this time without dramatic pause, as he wanted only to finish. "From the book of Psalms, *'May the desert tribes bow before him and his enemies lick the dust. May the Kings of Tarshish and of distant shores bring tribute to him. May the Kings of Sheba and Seba present him gifts.'*"

"The messengers," Joseph said to Mary.

"Yes, the messengers," Mary said, then turned to her father. "You've sent messengers to kings and princes?"

"Actually, to Magi," the High Priest said. "The wisest of Wise Men."

"And I pray the holiest of Wise Men," Elisheba said.

"And I pray the wealthiest of Wise Men," added Jerome.

"And you've told them that the Son of God will be born in Bethlehem? That they are to bring gifts and to bow to the true king?"

"This is not good." Joseph stood behind Mary, rubbing her shoulders.

"This is not by choice," Elisheba said. "It must be so. It's God's will."

Mary rose from her chair with difficulty and walked to the half-empty satchel on the floor resting by her mother's foot. Grunting, she bent, snatched a scroll from the satchel, and walked back to Joseph. She untied and unrolled the document, reading it silently and shaking her head with each word until she finished.

"This is the message you've sent?" Mary asked.

"My child, we have sent the truth," the High Priest answered as Elisheba nodded in agreement.

"What does it say?" Joseph asked.

"It says, *'Let it be known that the Son of God, as foretold by the great prophets Isaiah and Micah, will be born of a virgin, in the town of Bethlehem.'*"

"This is not right." Joseph drew closer to Mary.

"There's more. It goes on to say, *'We invite you to witness the birth of our Savior, at the marble palace of Elisheba and Jerome of Bethlehem.'*"

"We need to stop this," Joseph whispered to Mary.

"There is more still. After that, it says, *'As instructed in the book of Psalms, gifts that are suitable for a King, the Son of God Himself, are welcomed and expected.'*"

"I added the part about the gifts," Jerome said, popping a date in his mouth and chewing with a smug smile.

"I assumed so," said Mary. "Mother, Father, you must call the messengers back. Please, stop this."

"We will do no such thing, Mary. It would be against God's will," Elisheba said.

Mary closed her eyes and took several deep breaths, her belly moving up with each inhale and down as she exhaled. "Joseph and I need a moment. Please. Can we have a moment? Alone."

Elisheba nodded to Jerome and the High Priest. As they left the great room and walked down the corridor, the High Priest commented, "I think this is going quite well."

Joseph took the chair next to Mary and sat, resting his hands on her belly. Mary placed her hands on top of Joseph's. This was the first time Joseph had seen Mary on the verge of tears.

"I'm at a loss," Mary confessed. "I'm a fool."

"We're both fools. This is not your fault, Mary. We must tell them the truth and accept their reaction."

"They will react by ensuring you are arrested and stoned to death. You heard them yesterday. I won't let that happen."

"Mary, we have no choice at this point. If we tell them now, there is still time to stop the messengers. That will be the end of it."

"No, your death will be the end of it." Mary stood and paced, taking small steps to not disturb the baby. "That is not an option."

"Maybe they're bluffing." Joseph, still in his tattered tunic, still with blood crusted on his ruined feet, got up and paced alongside Mary, wrapping one arm around her waist. "It doesn't matter. We need to tell them the truth. Whatever the consequences, I will accept them."

"But Joseph—"

"Stop. Mary, we're out of options. We need to protect our little girl. We need to tell them the truth. Your parents and the High Priest do not have her best interests in mind. You were right—they will use her to suit their own ends."

Elisheba, Jerome, and the High Priest filed back into the room, each taking a seat at the table. Elisheba sipped on a cup of hot hibiscus tea. The High Priest and Jerome refilled their cups of red wine and prepared for the battle to continue.

Mary and Joseph sat directly across from the triumvirate.

"What were you two squabbling about?" Jerome found delight in their discord.

"Mother, Father," Mary began quietly, "we have not been honest with you. I need to make this right."

"*We* need to make this right," Joseph said.

"The first thing I want you to know is that I love Joseph."

Jerome rolled his eyes, and Elisheba made a gagging noise before spitting a small splash of tea back into her cup. The High Priest gulped the rest of his wine and summoned a servant for a refill.

"I love Joseph. It was I who pursued him. It was I who seduced him. My actions led to this." Mary placed her hands on top of her belly. "And I'm not sorry. I'm not ashamed. I should have told you the truth from the beginning."

"Stop!" Jerome limply pounded his soft fist on the table, producing a muffled, squishy thud, knocking over the priest's wine. "I will not hear of this, Mary. A carpenter? A peasant?" Jerome used the High Priest's long blue sleeve to wipe up the spilled wine. "No. Not now. Not ever. Not for my daughter. I will not have a grandson who is the seed of a carpenter."

"This is the truth, Mary," Elisheba said and stood holding the scroll of Isaiah above her head. "You may not accept it, but it's God's truth."

"But it isn't, Mother!"

"This is just the humble, self-effacing sort of thing the mother of the Son of God would say," the High Priest said, taking a self-satisfied slurp from his refilled chalice. "My dear girl, as we explained earlier, God has chosen you to give birth to His Son. You are the Chosen One. You have all the qualities God would want for the mother of His child. It further validates the prophecies."

"But I am not a virgin." Mary rose from her chair and leaned in, her belly resting on the table. She met her mother's steely glare and the High Priest's silly smirk. Her voice was steady and resolute. "I am not carrying the Son of God. I am carrying the daughter of Joseph."

"Mary," Elisheba said with growing impatience, her eyes locked on Mary, "the prophecies speak the truth. At no other time, in no other place, has there been such a prophecy of a virgin birth."

"Well, that isn't exactly true," Joseph said. "There are stories throughout history about virgin births; the tale of Romulus and Remus born of the virgin Rhea, of Attis, born of the virgin Nana, and Jason born of the virgin Persephone. Then there was—"

"You, peasant carpenter, are a blasphemer!" The High Priest stood alongside Elisheba and pointed his crooked index finger at Joseph. "A Nazarene carpenter is certainly not capable of understanding such things. If there are any more venomous words that your forked tongue spews from your foul mouth you will find yourself in front of a mob of angry holy and righteous people with sharp stones in their hands and bloodlust in their hearts, and they will take aim at your evil head and strike you dead for the glory of God. Their stones will be guided from their fingers to your head by the hand of God Himself until your skull cracks, your eyes pop out, and blood streams down your body and into the alleyways of Bethlehem. So, carpenter from Nazareth, we could add blasphemy to the charge of rape." The High Priest sat down heavily and clinked cups with Jerome, who nodded with approval.

"And we could add hateful ignorance to the charge of malpractice, High Priest of Bethlehem," Mary fired back.

"Stop it. Both of you." Elisheba took a deep breath.

An icy, uncomfortable silence settled over the room. Joseph held Mary's arms as she lowered herself back into her seat and slowly rubbed her belly with gentle, circular strokes.

In an eerily calm and menacing voice, Jerome said, "Mary, there are two alternatives. The first is that this foul carpenter viciously raped you and now he has blasphemed God's good name and will face the severe and deadly consequences of his actions and of his words."

"Death by stoning," said the High Priest.

"Praise be to God," Elisheba added.

"The second alternative," Jerome continued, "is that you fulfill the prophecies. You, a virgin chosen by God, will give birth to His Son. Further, a small group of very wealthy Wise Men will praise His birth and bestow riches upon us. Afterward, you, the baby, and the carpenter can go back to Nazareth."

"But neither is true," Mary said.

"You misheard me, Mary. I said nothing about the truth. I said *alternatives*. These are the two *alternatives*. The first alternative has your baby being raised without a father, and you, a disgraced and displaced nomad with nowhere to go and without a husband to help. The second provides the baby with a father—"

"God is the true Father, the Heavenly Father," Elisheba said. "Your father is referring to an earthly father."

"And you and your baby," Jerome continued in the same menacing tone, "can return to Nazareth with the pathetic, inconsequential carpenter."

CHAPTER 11

The Second Letter from the Corinthians

Dear Joseph the Carpenter,

A second day has passed, and we have not seen hide nor hair of you. One of our Arabians escaped. He bolted through the gap in the fence and raced across the valley and up the slopes of Mount Tabor. Grandpa claimed to see the whole thing. He said when the horse reached the top of the mountain, it burst into a radiant light and disappeared. I don't know about Grandpa; he seems a little fuzzy headed lately (at least he wasn't skewered by a splintered leg of a broken chair like Caleb had gruesomely described)! But let's not dwell on the past. Let's look to the future. We sincerely hope to see you back on the job, tomorrow at the very latest as we, of course, would hate to lose any more horses. This absence is very unlike you, Joseph. What has gotten into you? You've been a reliable carpenter and general handyman for the Corinthian family for many years, and we've never known you to suddenly walk off the job. I'm sure there is good reason (perhaps the buxom young woman?), but our Arabians need you! Also, Junia, who absolutely adores you, is asking me about a joke you *told her. Something about a blind carpenter who picked up his hammer and saw. She desperately wants to know the punchline, and you know how she gets when something is stuck in her head; she's simply unbearable. Placating little Junia is one more reason we want you back on the job. Our Arabians and my little Junia need you. Please travel back quickly and safely to finish the job.*

Yours fondly,
Aaron Corinthian

CHAPTER 12

The Messengers and the Magi

DECEMBER 24, I DAY BC

The first messenger sent by Jerome and Elisheba arrived exhausted and dehydrated at the palace of Melchior of Persia. A long marble walkway, shaded by tall palms, curved through lush green gardens and past pools of clear blue water to a grand entrance. The messenger knelt beside a pool and drank the cool water to soothe his dry throat. He then cupped the water in his hand and splashed his face until the sand washed away. The shade from the palms was a welcome relief. He walked to the main door, a portal painted deep red and trimmed with inlaid golden triangles that reached the height of what must have been six Arabian horses. In his childhood, the messenger had heard stories of palaces like this, but he never imagined he would be called to one, finding a respite from the heat in the shade of its palms and relief from thirst in the coolness of its pools.

A high-ranking servant, wrapped elegantly in a long white shawl trimmed in gold, greeted him at the door. The servant explained that Melchior had left his palace over a week ago to celebrate the Roman festival of Saturnalia at the palace of Paragus of Perea.

This scene repeated itself in the palaces of Balthazar of Arabia and Caspar of India. In each case, high-ranking servants greeted the messengers and informed them that the Wise Man had left his respective palace several days before to gather at the palace of Paragus for Saturnalia. The fate of the remaining messenger, the one sent to find the Wise Man of Judea, was less clear.

Saturnalia was an annual festival introduced in Judea and Galilee by the occupying Romans to celebrate the winter solstice. While citizens of the occupied territories despised the ruthless Roman soldiers and the middling Roman bureaucrats, the same citizens enthusiastically embraced the Roman festivals. This was particularly true of Saturnalia with all its excesses, and no one embraced the excesses more enthusiastically than the four wealthy Wise Men: Melchior, Balthazar, Caspar, and Paragus.

Each year, Saturnalia took place for seven nights, starting on December 17. For citizens of the occupied territories, it was a time of cheerful merrymaking, but for the four Wise Men, the merrymaking devolved into a world of hedonistic debauchery fueled by excessive wine consumption and cannabis delivered through long, ornately crafted bronze pipes scattered throughout every corner of Paragus's palace. Singing, gambling, voracious feasting, gift exchanging, and the constant presence of scantily clad dancers, male and female, were the hallmarks of Paragus's Saturnalia celebrations. The festival was also a time of role reversals. Servants played the role of masters, and masters, willingly and often eagerly, played the role of servants. It was a window of opportunity, no matter how briefly opened, for unabashed equality and the freedom to say and act as one liked without consequence. Masters and servants dined and drank and danced and gambled together. Masters gleefully accepted their servants' insults and insinuations.

Paragus lived in Perea, a region directly east of the Dead Sea, on the border of Samaria and Judea, and a short distance from Bethlehem. The messenger sent to deliver Elisheba's message to Paragus, like the other messengers, arrived at the palace drained of all energy and parched. His riding clothes, a thin tan simlah and tightly wrapped turban, were caked with desert sand in the front but remained unsoiled in the back. As the messenger dismounted his horse, his knees buckled from the intense ride, and he fell into a crumpled heap to the ground. Squinting, wiping the sand from his eyes, he slowly stood up, took the scroll from his rucksack, and staggered to the main palace gates. They led to a garden that exposed an enormous compound consisting of three separate palaces. Those in the know widely agreed that no Wise Man was wealthier than Paragus.

A dozen different varieties of palm trees, hundreds of desert roses, flamingo flowers, and multi-colored coleus plants filled the meticulously manicured garden. Small streams of water fed into larger streams, which fed into pools that ran the length of the garden, lined by tall, uniformly shaped cypress trees. The messenger felt like he was in a vast oasis. Legs aching, he struggled to walk through the garden, needing to stop several times to dip his hand in the cool water to splash his face and the back of his neck.

He arrived at the white and grey marbled grand hallway lined on each side with large, sleek, black granite statues of fierce salukis. Ceramic wine vessels lay broken on the floor, their contents splattered, forming small red pools on the white marble. The messenger tried to call for a servant to signal his arrival, but when he opened his mouth, no sound emerged from his parched throat. His bloodied lips ached, swollen from the sun and dozens of imperceptible cuts caused by the swirling desert sand. He sat next to the spilled wine and lapped up a small puddle. He slowly pushed himself up from the floor and walked from the grand hall into an expansive, exquisitely furnished great room.

The stench of dried vomit, urine, and stale cannabis smoke made the messenger gag. He brought his hand to his nose and stopped momentarily to gather himself. Gold-trimmed vases that, when standing, were as tall as the messenger, lay broken, their shards scattered among women's clothes strewn across the floor. The ashes from a sofa that Paragus had transported in a caravan from the Orient smoldered in the middle of the room, the faint essence of burnt silk and gingko being the last vestiges of a grand piece of furniture. Every year, the same level of drunken destruction characterized Paragus's Saturnalia celebrations, and every year Paragus happily replenished the damaged furnishings with even finer ones.

As the messenger surveyed the room for signs of life, he saw four men, as still as stones and soundly sleeping, draped over, or on, or under the sofas and chairs that spread throughout the room. A small monkey, a long-tailed grivet with white whiskers and alert, darting eyes, picked cautiously at a pile of chunky, green vomit, which stained the center of a woolen rug that had taken five artisans three years to weave to exacting standards. Behind a red silk sofa at the farthest end of the room, a second stream of smoke floated.

Stepping over pieces of broken pottery and zigzagging to avoid the pools of urine and spilled wine, the messenger made his way across the room to the red silk sofa. A slender teen, a mischievous servant, sat cross-legged and shirtless, deeply inhaling from a bronze hash pipe decorated with figures of elephants, camels, and tigers. He slowly exhaled a cannabis-infused cloud of bitter smoke. The servant, whose normally wide eyes were now thin slits, looked at the stranger unfazed and offered him a seat on the floor and a turn at the pipe.

"No, thank you. I'm here to deliver a message to Paragus. My clients have instructed me to give it to him personally. Where may I find him?"

"Happy Saturnalia!" the servant said through a cloud of smoke. He squinted to get a better look at the visitor. "You look horrible, all dusty and tired. Are you sure you don't want a puff? It may help."

"Maybe later, but now I need to deliver this," the messenger said and held up the scroll, "to the Wise Man Paragus."

"He is here, somewhere. This is his palace, for sure," said the servant, just before inhaling. "To bad you didn't come a few days ago.

Saturnalia ends soon. You're here for the festival, right?"

"No. I am here to deliver a message, an urgent message, to Paragus."

"Right. Well, this is his palace," the servant said again. He giggled as he exhaled a cloud that floated across the room, hovering over the four sleeping Wise Men. "And I'm one of many servants. My name is Zacharia. It's nice to meet you. You said you're here for the festival?"

"Could you just point me in his direction?" the messenger asked with growing impatience.

The servant wobbled to his feet, squinted, and looked across the room. He smiled. "You see that one?" Zacharia pointed to a large man lying on his back on an overstuffed sofa. "The fat one, the fattest of the four. Red pants, no top, with a woman's red silk scarf wrapped around his head?"

"Yes, I see him."

"Well, that's not Paragus."

The messenger cocked his head and looked as though he would hit the servant.

"Just kidding." The servant giggled. "Just having fun. It's all part of Saturnalia. That's why you're here, right? Are you sure you don't want a puff? Yes, that fat one is him."

With purpose, and not bothering to avoid the shards of ceramics or puddles of piss and wine, the messenger walked straight across the room to where Paragus lay sleeping. He had never been face-to-face with a Wise Man and was disappointed by what he saw. Paragus lay shirtless. His massive belly, shaped like a rounded mountaintop, heaved up and down with each slumbering breath. His long, thick white beard hovered over his belly, a cloud above the mountain, and a tuft of equally white hair sat scruffily atop his big head. And the messenger, having seen all styles and types of tunics, sadhins, and simlahs, had never seen pants.

Pants were indeed luxurious clothing, seldom—if ever—worn in Judea or in the surrounding city-states. Paragus had become enchanted with this fashion years ago on one of his many journeys to the farthest reaches of the Orient, well beyond Caspar's noble land. Every year since then, Paragus sent a servant, one who had a particularly sharp eye for fashion, to bring piles of this rare and expensive clothing not only for himself but for his fellow Magi too. Rather than rare and luxurious, the messenger thought the pants looked more like something a circus performer might wear, not like clothing for a Magi.

The messenger crouched down, clutching the scroll in his left hand, and softly shook Paragus's shoulder with his right. "Magi . . . sir, wake up. I have an important message to deliver." No movement. The faint sound of a shy, lazy morning fart came from across the room; the others were waking. The messenger shook a little harder and spoke a little louder. "Sir! Sir! Please. Wake up, I have . . . "

The large man convulsed out of his sleep, his belly shaking like an undercooked mound of gelatinous custard. The scarf that had covered his face fell to his belly as he struggled to sit up.

Coming out of deep sleep, blinking slowly, Paragus tried unsuccessfully to bring the stranger's face into focus. "Do I know you? Are you here for the festival? You must be one of the dancers."

The monkey made his way from the vomit and climbed atop Paragus's lap. "Why does this monkey," Paragus asked the messenger, "smell like Balthazar's vomit?"

"I am sorry, sir. I don't know. He was picking at a pile of vomit when I arrived."

"Balthazar was picking at vomit? Disgusting. We have lamb, and chicken, and fish, and the finest fruits. There's no need for that."

"No, sir, the monkey was picking at the vomit."

"Ah, that makes more sense." Paragus nodded as he was slowly wakening. "I'm a bit fuzzy headed—hungover. Perhaps still drunk. I'm not sure. It's hard to tell. I need a magic puff to help clear my mind." Paragus craned his head, looking around the great room. "Zacharia! Zacharia!"

The young servant who had guided the messenger to Paragus

peered over the red sofa from across the room and stood. "Yes, sir."

"None of this *sir* stuff," said Paragus. "It's Saturnalia, and during the festival we are all equals. We are all brothers, here to serve one another equally. But you could do me a favor by bringing pipes for me and each of my guests."

"Yes, sir. I mean yes, my friend," replied Zacharia.

"And on your way over, wake up Balthazar, Caspar, and Melchior. I hear them farting, and I don't want them to shit themselves before they've met the new dancer who just arrived." Paragus pointed to the messenger.

"No, sir. I'm not the—" the messenger started.

"Just as I told Zacharia, don't address me as *sir* or *prince* or *Magi* or *Wise Man of Perea,* because this is—"

"Saturnalia," the messenger said, beginning to understand the customs of Paragus's festival.

"That's right! And during Saturnalia, we're all equals. Even dancers."

"But I'm not—"

"Do you know the first rule of Saturnalia?" Paragus interrupted the messenger.

"There are no fucking rules!" said Caspar as he stumbled across the room with a freshly opened flask of wine, taking a seat next to Paragus. Caspar, not yet thirty, was the youngest, least refined, and least welcome of the four Wise Men who had gathered. He was the spoiled son of Azriel, a respected and kindhearted Wise Man of the East and a good friend of Paragus. The title of Magi was bestowed upon Caspar due to the unfortunate and untimely death of his father and the fortunate and timely bribe that Caspar's mother paid to the elders in his region so Caspar could retain his father's title. He punctuated his limited vocabulary with an unlimited set of foul words; he had a particular affinity for the many derivations of the word "fuck." Paragus dutifully invited Caspar to his Saturnalia celebration to honor his deceased dear friend and appease his deceased friend's wife.

"Is this the juggler or the jester?" Balthazar asked in a near whisper, pointing to the messenger as he slunk onto the sofa next to Caspar. Balthazar, the oldest of the four Wise Men, was affable and kind in his youth, but aging did not agree with him. The years transformed this once light and genial Wise Man into a cantankerous old crank. He stopped caring about his appearance years ago, often not bathing or changing his garments for weeks. He smelled of musty, sour goat's milk even though his lips had never touched a drop of milk, preferring only wine and water. Mainly wine. His grey hair looked like a windblown field of silvery wheat stalks, his beard a desert tumbleweed glued on his chin unevenly and without care.

"He's the dancer!" replied Paragus just before inhaling from his pipe.

"He doesn't look like a fucking dancer," observed Caspar. "He is not nearly pretty enough."

"To be clear—" the messenger tried to clarify.

"Why does the dancer carry an ornately decorated scroll?" asked a rich and regal voice. Melchior, the only God-fearing and devout Wise Man among the four, made his way across the room. He differed from the other Magi. He looked and spoke the way the messenger imagined a distinguished Wise Man should look and speak. Unlike the other three, he was fully clothed. And his clothes were not just functional, they were extravagant; tailored with the finest Persian silk, gleaming white pants and tunic decorated with thin yellow stripes, and a purple cape decorated with small, precious jewels, sewn with golden thread. There was not a hair out of place on his sharply groomed, dignified moustache. Melchior picked up a chair midway across the room and placed it next to the sofa, to the left of the messenger. The delicate aroma of rare Persian frankincense enveloped Melchior as he sat.

"Melchior asks a good question," Paragus said. "Why would a dancer possess such a fine scroll?"

"I am not a dancer."

"Then why tell Paragus that you were?" Balthazar drank from a large wine flask, holding it with both hands as if he would never let go.

"So, you're the jester?" asked Caspar. "You don't look like a jester.

You're much too fucking serious to be a jester and too ugly to be a dancer."

"I, well, I'm not sure what . . . listen, kind gentlemen, I am a messenger."

"Hence the scroll," said Paragus, exhaling an enormous plume of cannabis smoke.

"I have been sent," the messenger said, then coughed as the smoke reached his nostrils, "from the village of Bethlehem in the region of Judea—"

"Yes, we're all aware of where that shit-smirched backwater of a village is located," said Caspar.

"Gentlemen, watch your tongues in front of our guest," Melchior said.

"And I've come to deliver a message to Paragus."

"Please," Paragus said, "if you can't dance or juggle flaming sticks or perform tricks of magic, if you are not here to entertain us, then read what you've been sent here to read."

As the messenger read aloud the news of the imminent birth of the Son of God to a virgin, Paragus shook his head and frowned, Caspar cursed, Balthazar took an extended swig from his flask, Melchior raised his devout and hopeful eyes to the heavens in praise of God, and the monkey returned to the neglected pile of vomit to resume his snacking.

Melchior grew up studying the words and acts of all the ancient prophets; among those he most studied were Abraham, Moses, Ezekiel, Micah, and Isaiah. He conducted research at the oldest and most respected temples and libraries in Persia and studied under the tutelage of the holiest of Wise Men. He had waited his entire lifetime for the coming of the Son of God. His spirits rose, his soul lifted.

"How many virgin births does that make this year?" asked Balthazar. "Two, maybe three?"

"Doesn't anybody fuck anymore?" asked Caspar.

"Well, Paragus, it looks like you'll be on your way to Bethlehem." Balthazar raised his flask in an insincere toast.

"Oh," the messenger said, "you were all sent messages. While I was sent to deliver this message to Paragus, they also sent messengers to each of you and a fifth Wise Man in Judea. I don't recall his name."

"Please," Paragus said and pointed to the scroll, "if you don't mind, I'd like to see that." He read silently, stroking his white beard, shaking his head, and grunting. "I'm not going. Not during Saturnalia. We have one more night left to celebrate."

"But it is our duty, Paragus," Melchior said, "especially during Saturnalia. It is an obligation that arises from our position in society and our obligation to God Himself."

"But it's camel shit," said Caspar. "If we were to attend every virgin birth, every occasion where some social climbing, newly rich member of society wanted to enhance their social status by having Magi in their midst, it would be a full-time job."

"It is indeed our obligation, our full-time job, my young friend." Melchior said, like a father addressing a petulant child. "And the circumstances of this virgin birth differ greatly from the others. Did you hear what the invitation said? It is the fulfillment of the prophecies of Isaiah and Micah. To have two prophecies converging, intersecting at this moment of time, is surely God's will. There may have been other reported virgin births, and perhaps you scoff at those, and rightfully so, but this particular virgin birth, which Isaiah foretold, is taking place in Bethlehem, which Micah foretold. This is not a coincidence, my friends. The hand of God is guiding this. We must fulfill our part."

"Spoken like a true believer," scoffed Balthazar.

"And you are not?" Melchior replied.

"Once a year, just one time, we come together from the four corners of the earth to celebrate Saturnalia," said Balthazar. "I am old. I can't be certain how many Saturnalias I have left in me. And you, Melchior, would instead have us trudge across the Judean Desert to bear witness to this?" Balthazar held up the scroll. "I don't agree. This needs some discussion."

"The three of you can talk all you want, but I've decided. I shall leave in the evening's coolness, just after the sun sets, and by morning I'll be in Bethlehem."

Zacharia carefully crept in between the Magi and lay bronze pipes in front of each of the guests, after which he poured Paragus's finest wine into golden chalices. Paragus invited the three other Wise Men and the messenger to sit on the overstuffed cushions, which formed an intimate circle from which they would all smoke their pipes and drink their wine.

"What about the matter of gifts, Melchior?" asked Paragus. "The invitation included an audacious request for a gift."

"I came to the Saturnalia festival with gifts of frankincense for each of you, but I will, please forgive me, instead present it to the Son of God."

Balthazar exhaled a plume of smoke. "If I go, and I'm not saying I will, I'll bring nothing of great value, and I certainly wouldn't use a gift intended for old friends to give to a baby who we'll never see again."

Caspar nodded in agreement. "I brought no valuables. Besides, Melchior, what would the Son of God do with frankincense?"

"You're not seeing this clearly, my friends," said Melchior. "Have you no sense of history? This is an epic event. There will be only one Son of God for all of eternity. For generations after his birth, stories will be told and songs will be sung about the heroic journey of the four Wise Men who traveled through the night, guided by the brightest moon and stars, to bear witness to the birth of the Son of God. Not only will we honor God, but we will also secure our place in history."

"I have a bit of myrrh," said Balthazar. "Rich people love myrrh. I don't know why. At my age, I use it as an ointment to soothe my groin after long camel rides, but to each his own. But I agree with Paragus on this. I'm staying here."

"The virgin," the messenger said, lightheaded from the cannabis, "is quite attractive. I only got a glimpse of her as I received the scroll, but she has long black hair, beautiful eyes that defy any single color, a slender neck, and her bosoms are fully in bloom."

"Maybe I need to reconsider," Balthazar said.

"And I hear her sister—" continued the messenger.

"She has a sister?" asked Caspar.

"Equally beautiful, I hear," replied the messenger.

"Why didn't you mention this before?" Caspar said. "This is getting more interesting."

"And what gift would you bring, Caspar?" asked Melchior.

"Myself. I'm young and virile. My presence alone should be enough."

"But of course it isn't," Melchior said, shaking his head.

"Well, you're bringing frankincense; Balthazar has his myrrh. I'm not sure what I'd bring." Caspar scanned the room, looking for decorations or small furnishings he could present as a gift. "What are those?" Caspar pointed to golden nuggets that had spilled from a broken bowl and lay scattered on the floor.

"Those? They're talus bones and back teeth from a sheep that died from old age months ago. I had Zacharia dry and then coat them with a thick gold paint so we could play knucklebones during the festival. I love a good bit of knucklebones, but there is something repugnant about throwing animal bones as sport, so I had them painted gold. It seemed more dignified," Paragus said. He suppressed a burp that, by his expression, contained a small piece of last night's feast.

Caspar walked over to the gold-painted bones and bent down to examine them. He picked one up and hit it repeatedly on the marble floor, then picked another and hit the two together with as much force as a stoned, hungover man could muster. He then threw, with surprising accuracy, the two bones to Balthazar, who caught them with equally surprising agility.

"Does that resemble a gold ingot or a gold-colored bone?" Caspar asked, settling back to take a puff from his pipe.

Closing his left eye, Balthazar raised a bone to his right eye and turned it slowly. "Can't tell."

"Please do tell. I'm asking for your opinion."

"No. Caspar, I can't distinguish. I can *tell* you my opinion. I just can't distinguish."

"You're not making any sense. Hand the pieces to Melchior. He's the only semisober one here—him and that goddamned monkey."

Melchior took the pieces and examined them, slowly turning them in his hand. He then set them on the sofa and squinted. "If you look closely, they look more like painted animal bones than gold ingots, but from a distance, and in dim light, it's very difficult to distinguish."

"I'll need a gift," Caspar said, "if I'm to see the beautiful virgin and her equally attractive sister."

"That is sacrilege, Caspar. You displease God with your intentions," Melchior said.

Caspar asked the messenger, "What did you say her name was?"

"Who, the virgin?"

"Yes."

"Mary."

"If I am to see the Virgin Mary and her equally attractive sister—" Caspar snapped his finger at the messenger.

"Rachel."

"And her sister, Rachel, then I need to bring a gift."

"Caspar, the gifts are to be bestowed upon the child," Melchior said. "The purpose is to honor the Son of God, not to gain the favor of young women."

"Maybe. I would give a little to the baby, and a little to the virgin, and a bit more to the virgin's more eligible sister," replied Caspar.

"It's Saturnalia," Balthazar said, patting Caspar on the back. "We should be generous and give our large endowments to the fair maidens as well. The kid has a point."

"So, Caspar, you plan to gift my knucklebone pieces?" asked Paragus. "You're expecting the Son of God to be a gambling prodigy?"

Caspar walked back to the scattered golden bones. "He's the Son of God, Paragus. He could be any goddamned thing he wants to be. But no, I don't intend to bring him knucklebone pieces. That would be insulting after having received Melchior's frankincense and Balthazar's myrrh."

Caspar gathered a handful of the bones and set them in the red scarf that once covered Paragus's head. "But, if you place a handful of the knucklebones like so," Caspar said, wrapping the bones in a scarf, "and you place the red scarf filled with golden knucklebones in an expensive box like so," Caspar continued, grabbing an intricately carved silver box from the table, "and the gift is ceremoniously presented by a young, handsome, rich, generous Wise Man like me, then these are not some gold-painted sheep bones. No. They transform into rare ingots of gold mined from a rich vein in the remotest part of the Garhwal Himalayas." Caspar took a bow as he finished.

Paragus and Balthazar clapped their hands approvingly, each alternating between puffs on the pipe and gulps from their golden chalices.

"You will burn in each of the layers of Hell." Melchior shook his head and pointed a finger at Caspar. "You are my friend, but you can't deceive the Son of God."

"*If*," Caspar said, "he is indeed the Son of God. And that is where you and I will have to agree to disagree."

"You'll burn entirely in the first level of Hell," Melchior said, turning away from Caspar. "You won't even make it to the second."

"Let's drink to that, my friend." Caspar put his arm around Melchior and kissed the top of his head. The four Wise Men clinked chalices as the messenger passed out, spilling his wine and bashing his forehead on the sharp edges of a bronze bowl that lay on the hard marble floor.

"Prepare the most rested camels for the long evening's journey to Bethlehem," Paragus barked at a servant.

"We'll never reach Bethlehem by tomorrow morning on camel," Melchior said.

"What about the Arabians?" Zacharia suggested. "They could easily be in Bethlehem by early morning."

"Messengers and merchants ride horses. Wise Men ride camels," Balthazar protested, thinking more about his tender groin than arriving in Bethlehem in time for the birth. "Wise Men elegantly parading in a caravan of well-decorated camels is much more dignified. It's the image commoners think about when they think about Wise Men. It's expected of us. We would disappoint our hosts if we did otherwise."

"But camels will never get us there in time," Melchior persisted.

Paragus waved his servants on. "It's settled. Prepare the Arabians. Fashion them with the finest ornamented riding gear that is fit for this distinguished group of Wise Men."

"And a soft saddle for me," Balthazar grumbled, thinking of his chafed groin as he refilled his chalice to the rim with wine, "with a layer of soft blankets on top."

CHAPTER 13

A Misguided Messenger
DECEMBER 24, 1 DAY BC

The fifth messenger left Jerome and Elisheba's house with good intentions. He set out, as had the other four messengers, on his stallion at a torrid pace through the narrow lanes and crooked back alleys of Bethlehem. He was on his way to deliver the message to the Wise Man of Judea. As he was entering the Nakhleh slum, the poorest neighborhood in all of Bethlehem, he stopped for a beer, just one beer, to wet his throat before continuing his strenuous journey through the southern part of the Judean Desert.

The barkeeper offered the messenger a chair, but the messenger, resolute in his mission, refused, choosing instead to stand so he could gulp a single beer and quickly be on his way. The sun was rising, the air was dry, and the beer felt good on his tongue and sloshing down his parched throat.

"Just one more," he called to the barkeeper, "but this time in a larger cup. And be quick. I have a long, important ride ahead of me."

The barkeeper brought a large beer to the messenger, which he drained in a series of three greedy gulps, finishing with a loud belch that was so violent it made his nostrils shiver and burn.

"Where does your journey take you?" asked the barkeeper. "Surely you have time for another."

"No, no," insisted the messenger. "I must be on my way."

"But the heat rises with each moment. You need to be refreshed for your ride, no?"

"Perhaps, my good man," the messenger said, reconsidering the offer. "One more. No. Make it two. Two large cups. But be quick. I must leave immediately, for I have an important assignment on behalf of God Himself. I don't have time to linger or loaf."

The barkeeper filled two large cups, handed one to the messenger and set the other on a makeshift table of wooden scraps held together by fraying strands of thick manila twine. "Here, sit down. I know you must leave with haste. I know you must deliver an important message on behalf of God, but you'll need fresh, rested legs. Please, my fine sir, rest your legs, but only for a moment and then, in a flash, you will be on your way."

"You're right, my good man." The messenger found comfort in a chair that, like the table, was poorly assembled using wooden scraps and held loosely together by thick twine. "Your reasoning is sound. Your advice is wise. I'll be much more capable of finishing my mission with well-rested legs."

A fifth beer magically appeared on the table, so it seemed to the messenger, who didn't remember ordering it. He gulped it down as easily as the first. The sixth beer came and went in the same fashion. In the cool comfort from the shade of an acacia tree that sat in the middle of the tavern, the messenger laid his head on the table, closed his eyes, and thought, *I must first rest, but only for a short while, to prepare for my journey to deliver God's message.* A thick stream of drool flowed from the corner of his lips, forming a small pool on the table. He slept soundly and dreamed of galloping through the desert on his stallion with the scroll safely tucked away in the leather satchel on his back. And, as he slept, the barkeeper discreetly plucked the pile of coins that had fallen from his torn pocket and placed them in his own.

Several hours later, as the afternoon Saturnalia crowd swelled, the barkeeper shook the messenger out of his deep sleep. His earlier convivial tone was replaced by direct, stern orders. "You need to leave or buy more beer. I have paying festivalgoers who want your chair and table."

Still pleasantly drunk, the messenger stood up, staggered, and explained that he must go immediately, for he had an important message to deliver. "By the way," he slurred, "do you know where I can find a Judea Wise Man?"

"That's who your message is for?" the barkeeper said. "Are you sure?"

"Quite sure." The messenger accentuated his certainty with a wet burp.

"You won't need to get back on your horse to deliver that message."

"What do you mean?"

"He lives there." The barkeeper pointed at a hovel of poorly assembled dwellings, a loose collection of lean-tos and makeshift shabby tents—the poorest part of the Nakhleh slum. "Go through that alleyway, turn left at the first corner, and it's only ten, maybe twenty, paces past that."

The messenger squinted through his beery eyes, and with the scroll in his rucksack, made his way up the narrow alley, occasionally careening into a wall or tripping over his own feet. He stood, blinking in drunken disbelief at the sordid collection of shoddy dwellings.

"Can I help you?" A man appeared from one of the disheveled tents, the smell of filth and shit wafting behind him.

"I don't think so," the messenger said, clutching the scroll. "I've been sent to deliver this to a Wise Man, a Judea Wise Man. But I think I've got the wrong—"

"I'm Jude Aya Weissman. I live here. I am the collector of the shitpots of Bethlehem," Jude Aya said with a sense of pride. "This message is for me?"

The messenger glanced back down the alley, imagining the lively crowd gathered at the tavern, talking and laughing and gulping down large cups of beer and wine. He inhaled the aromatic smoke of the rosemary-encrusted lamb and whole chickens slathered with lemon juice cooking over the tavern's open fire. His stomach growled. He thought about how good it would feel in this heat to drink just one more beer, to have just one bite of the juicy grilled lamb in the shade of the tavern's tattered awnings.

"Yes, my good sir," the messenger said, handing Jude Aya the scroll. "This is indeed intended for you, Judea Wise Man. My work here is done. I am now free to return to the tavern." With that, the messenger patted Jude Aya on the back, turned, and stumbled down the alley, making his uneven way back to the tavern.

Jude Aya marveled at the quality of the papyrus and the scroll's decorative calligraphy. He had never seen a scroll quite so beautiful. But he was an uneducated man, unable to read. Few Nakhleh slum dwellers could read. Juda Aya cradled the scroll and walked two tents down to the dwelling of the Singer family. He was in search of their eldest daughter, Alma, a girl of ten, maybe twelve, who could read and write but whose true passion was playing a small drum that constantly hung around her neck.

Alma and some other children from the slum had formed a small, ragtag minstrel group and performed for their fellow slum-dwellers, often their only form of entertainment. With bare feet and her ever-present drum, Alma greeted Jude Aya, tucked her drumsticks into a large pocket in her ragged clothes, and examined the scroll. She read aloud to Jude Aya with reverence and wonder about the invitation to witness the birth of the Son of God. Jude Aya, a man who did not question God's mysterious ways, felt honored and humbled that he, of all people in Bethlehem, should receive such a divine invitation. He immediately began to think about a gift suitable for the Son of God.

CHAPTER 14

The Magdalenes

DECEMBER 24, 1 DAY BC

"Hello?" came a young woman's voice from Elisheba and Jerome's courtyard.

Jerome curled his thin upper lip and shook his head. "What could she possibly want?"

It was late morning and Jerome, Elisheba, and the High Priest sat comfortably on the large sofa and overstuffed chairs, plotting, planning, and carefully orchestrating the events that would unfold in their home leading up to, during and after, the fulfillment of the prophecy. Mary lay resting in the quiet and comfort of her old bedroom, and Joseph sat in a chair by her side. Servants scurried about, preparing rooms for each of the Wise Men, ensuring there was an ample supply of wine, fruit, nuts, and meat to lavish upon their distinguished guests to gain their favor.

Elisheba could hardly contain her excitement about her daughter being the Chosen One. She found energy and divine purpose in these preparations. Jerome could hardly contain his excitement about the prospect of having five of the wealthiest and most influential Wise Men stay in his Bethlehem home. He was certain there would be plenty of opportunities to extend his trading network by worming his way into the world of the five captive guests. The three conspirators sipped sweet, syrupy Jericho wine in delicately stemmed silver chalices and ate dried figs.

"Hello-o?" Again, it was the voice from the courtyard below.

"Who is it?" the High Priest whispered to Elisheba.

"It's Vashti," Jerome whispered back with disgust, "Mary's friend, and the primary reason we sent her to live with her aunt in Nazareth."

"She and her family are no good," whispered Elisheba to the High Priest. "Vashti, in particular, poisons Mary's mind. She had the audacity to introduce Mary, without our permission, to the wicked philosophical drivel of Epicurus and the vile musings of Lucretius, distracting her from the truths and goodness found in the old Scriptures."

Mary's questioning of her mother's deeply held religious beliefs, her distrust of the Temple Elders, and her rejection of how her father pursued material gain at the expense of all else were all laid at the feet of Vashti.

"Hello?" the voice coming from the courtyard persisted. "Is anyone home?"

"Yes, yes, yes. We give up, Vashti. We are here," Jerome called down.

"May we come up?"

"If you must," Jerome said.

"But use the ladder," added Elisheba.

"But I have my baby with me. The stairs would be safer."

"No dear, the ladder will do," insisted Elisheba. "I'm sure you can manage."

Jerome, Elisheba, and the High Priest saw the delicate but determined hand of Vashti reach the last rung of the ladder. Her head was not yet visible. No one moved a muscle to help the young mother and her baby reach the last step. With a final push from her left leg,

Vashti's head crested over the top of the ladder, and she was soon standing on the fine wooden floor with her baby cradled in the crook of her right arm.

"Is it just you? Not your parents?" Jerome asked, relieved to see only the two of them.

"Just me and my baby."

"Oh," Elisheba said. "I didn't realize you had a baby. I didn't even realize you were pregnant. I commented to Jerome this past summer how obese you had become—fat in the belly and thick in the ankles—but I didn't realize that was the reason."

"Elisheba, you've seen my baby. Several times. You even held her, for just a moment, the week after she was born."

"Oh, dear. I don't recall that," Elisheba said with a perfect recollection of Vashti's pregnancy and holding that repugnant Magdalene child.

"Do you mind if I sit?" Vashti asked. "My legs are a bit wobbly from climbing the ladder."

"Oh, I'm sure that won't be necessary." Jerome combed his thin, wormy strands of hair from one side of his pointed head to the other. "Standing is just fine. I'm sure you won't be long. No need to sit."

"Vash!" Mary's voice carried from down the long hallway, and she walked quickly, holding her stomach with one hand and Joseph's hand in the other. Mary and Vashti shared a long embrace, each holding back tears. Mary kissed Vash's baby on her forehead and introduced Vash to Joseph, giving her another long hug.

"It's so good to see you. And look at your baby!" Mary reached out to hold the baby's hand. "She's beautiful, just like her mother. What's her name?" Mary kissed the baby's forehead and held Vashti's hand.

"My baby's name is Mary," said Vashti. "I named her after my dearest friend, someone I love and admire."

Jerome forced a gagging sound, and Elisheba looked as if she had bitten into a sour lemon.

"I am honored. Mary Magdalene—it's lyrical, poetic. Beautiful.

Just as she is." Mary again kissed the baby's head.

"And you!" Vash said. "Look at you! When are you expecting?"

"Any day now." Mary took Joseph's hand and pulled him closer. "Joseph is the fath—"

As if well-rehearsed, in unison, before Mary could finish, the High Priest coughed loudly, Jerome bellowed something indistinguishable, and Elisheba faked a loud sneeze. The triumvirate then raced out of their chairs and surrounded Vashti, her baby, and Mary and Joseph like Roman centurions surrounding a gang of plotting thieves.

"Joseph has been kind enough," the High Priest said to Vashti, "to bring Mary all the way from Nazareth to be here for the baby's birth."

"He's also the fath—" Mary began.

"He's the farthest," Jerome raised his voice over Mary's, "from his Nazarene home than he's been in years, and he's leaving first thing in the morning."

"He's doing no such thing. This has gone far enough; Joseph and I have agreed to—"

Startled by the loud voices, the baby began to cry. Despite Vashti's best effort to calm her, the wailing continued. "I've come at a bad time. I'm sorry. I should get the baby home."

"A splendid idea," the High Priest said.

"No, Vash, don't mind them. Please stay."

Elisheba clapped her hands by the baby's ear, and the cries grew louder.

"Why did you do that, Mother?" Mary asked, but Elisheba ignored her, instead taking a long sip of her wine, her lips firmly glued to the chalice.

"I really should go. I need to settle the baby."

"Vash," Mary said and cupped her hand on top of the baby's head, "your precious Mary and my daughter—"

"You mean your son," Elisheba said.

"Your daughter and my child," Mary said, "are going to be best friends, just like the two of us. Inseparable."

"Not if I have anything to do with it," Jerome whispered to the High Priest and Elisheba.

"Over my dead body," Elisheba added.

CHAPTER 15

The Keeper

DECEMBER 24, 1 DAY BC

Everyone simply knew him as "the Keeper." He had been a fixture in the village of Bethlehem for decades, some thought for centuries. He was, most believed, the oldest living person in Bethlehem. No one knew his name. Even the Keeper himself, just having turned one hundred and three, failed to remember his own name on most days. Having outlived his friends, his beloved wife, and even his two sons, each of whom had lived long, good lives, he had no reason to remember his name. There was no one to talk to, and even if there were, he was nearly deaf and likely wouldn't be able to understand. All the Keeper had left in his life was the inn.

The Keeper often let his mind wander to the quiet, intimate times he had spent with his wife. He missed the way she brushed his thin, white hair through her delicate fingers and yearned for her demure smile and her quick wit, which brought laughter to his life. The Keeper also frequently dreamed about his two boys and the long discussions and spirited debates they would have as they worked alongside one another, repairing their modest inn. He missed his family dearly.

Over the years, as his deafness grew, he taught himself to lip read. But now his failing eyesight was as bad as his hearing, which made lip reading a challenge, even in the closest quarters under the brightest light. Neither deafness nor failing eyesight bothered him, but the constant loneliness and longing for his wife and children did.

He was as gentle and kind as he was old and deaf; he was slender, almost wraithlike, and his once tall frame was now hunched from decades of laboring, performing every menial task and backbreaking chore needed to keep his inn operating. The three-room inn was in a constant state of disrepair, and the Keeper didn't have the energy or the money for repairs. Each of the rooms were identical, with crumbling mud-caked walls, crooked doors, broken window shutters, and dirt floors strewn with straw. There were no beds, only thick woolen blankets to sleep upon and a single unbalanced three-legged stool.

A large, dusty, pebble-strewn courtyard with an olive tree sat outside of the rooms. The Keeper had planted the tree when he was five, when his father ran the inn. At that age, the inn, with its three rooms, large courtyard, and adjoining stable, felt like a kingdom, and he, its prince. But that was nearly a hundred years ago, and the olive tree, whose life paralleled that of the Keeper, hunched badly to one side, its bark rough, tired, and gnarled and its leaves more grey than green.

Mainly poor shepherds coming from the grassy hills to the west of Bethlehem stayed in the inn, one of the few places they could afford. They typically rested there a few nights to reinvigorate themselves from the weeks and months spent in the grasslands tending their flocks. The inn's cheap rates attracted them initially, but it was its location next to a tavern known for its cheap wine and even cheaper women that kept them coming back. Rarely were each of the three rooms occupied on any given night, except for the Roman festivals of Vestalia in the summer and Saturnalia in the winter.

On this night, the Keeper slowly led six ragged, rugged shepherds through the stable and then the courtyard until they stood outside of the three rooms. The shepherds, hoping to celebrate the last days of Saturnalia, had left their flocks in the hands of their young sons.

"Does the tavern stay open past the setting of the sun during Saturnalia?" one of the six indistinguishable shepherds said.

"You sat on a nail?" the Keeper replied. "You'll want to wash that out. I can fetch some water from the well."

"No, no. I'm fine," the shepherd said.

"Find? What do you need to find? The well? It is just over there." The Keeper pointed past the courtyard to the middle of the adjoining stable.

"But when does the tavern close?" another shepherd said in a loud voice.

"Your clothes?" said the Keeper, showing the shepherd the back of the uneven, decaying wooden door. "You can hang your clothes on this knob."

The shepherds nodded, finally understanding the extent of their host's deafness. They thanked the Keeper, dropped their long wooden crooks and short heavy rods in the three rooms, and walked with great anticipation and greater thirst to the adjacent tavern.

The Keeper bade them farewell and hobbled out of the last room and into the stable. While large, the stable was in worse shape than the inn. Long strands of well-worn rope tethered the Keeper's ox and ass to a tilting wall. The stable, the ox, and ass were all past their useful lifespan. A small stall, a hodgepodge of uneven vertical slats of wood, contained two lambs the shepherds had brought down from the hills to exchange for money that they would use for food, wine, and women—not necessarily in that order.

If any of the animals, even the smallest of lambs, ever took the initiative to free themselves from their ropes or knock down their jaillike stall, they could easily tug, pull, and push their way free and, in doing so, bring down the entire three-sided structure. But, like the Keeper, the animals were old and resigned to their station in life, content to think of this stable as home and the only place they cared to be.

As the Keeper walked to the side of the stable where he slept when the rooms were full, he stopped by the only solidly built thing on his property, a wooden food trough, a manger, no longer than the length of his arm. He bent over, his back creaking as he reached to remove the last remnants of the over-ripened corn and stale oats that the ox and ass had for dinner. A slight smile crossed his face as he remembered when he and his wife, when working together to run the inn, would snuggly wrap their infant boys in a blanket and lay them in the manager to nap.

CHAPTER 16

The Third Letter from the Corinthians

Dear Joseph the Carpenter,

*W*here on earth are you? Disaster struck today as a pack of famished wolves or ravenous desert foxes, or maybe carnivorous camels, marched through the hole in the enclosure in the middle of the night and killed the youngest foal, eating it clean to the bone and leaving its blood, bones, and entrails scattered about the place. We had high hopes for this foal. Beautiful auburn hair and a long mane that flowed like barley in the wind. And its legs, even at its tender young age, are, or I should say, were, powerful. As powerful as I'd ever seen. Joseph, I'm telling you, you would have marveled at this young colt. Hooves the size of my head. The most powerful hind end I've ever seen in a foal. Truly a promising specimen who would have surely fetched a handsome price. I don't care to dwell on it, but its guts were strewn all over the yard. Bits of liver here, long sections of intestines there, its stomach splayed and sprayed all over the place. Truly a horrific sight. Junia picked up the remains and examined them carefully, sniffing them and such. She *is a curious one! Anyway, he was a foal of great promise, now gone. Little Junia, after she was through fondling bits of the dead foal's organs, said it was "a foal that ran afoul." Clever girl. Odd indeed, but clever. We don't know where you are, so I'm sending these letters out in all directions, hoping they find their way into your caring and capable hands. Where art thou? Why hast thou forsaken us? If you get this letter, please return immediately and complete the job you so ably started.*

Yours fondly,
Aaron Corinthian

CHAPTER 17

A Slight Change of Plans

DECEMBER 24, 1 DAY BC

Four massive Arabian stallions, each branded with a stylized CA, stood perfectly still in the candlelit garden of Paragus; each horse was freshly groomed and exquisitely adorned with plush black saddle blankets trimmed with golden silk tassels. The reins were finely braided strands of leather, their utility surpassed only by their beauty. On each horse, five goatskins draped over the front of each saddle, four containing Paragus's best wine and the fifth containing water. Servants packed an assortment of nuts, dried fruit, and thinly sliced strips of dried and salted lamb for the overnight journey.

Behind each saddle sat a small silver box holding a gift for the Son of God. Melchior's contained frankincense. Balthazar's contained myrrh, which he also planned to use to soothe his chafed groin on the long night's ride. Caspar's contained the gold-painted talus bones from some long-ago dead goat that he intended to pass off as gold ingots. Paragus's contained twenty-four rare gold coins from the Babylonian Empire—an inconsequential sum compared to Paragus's wealth, but their value was enough to buy a kingdom.

Packed into an additional silver box behind Paragus's saddle, identical to the box that held the Babylonian coins, were a dozen of Zacharia's tightly rolled, perfectly crafted cannabis joints. For long journeys with his master, Zacharia had invented and then perfected the art of joint making. He would first dry the cannabis buds, then tightly roll them with leaves from grapevines that grew in the garden. Zacharia would then dip the fully rolled joints in water, gently squeeze them with his palm, and then hang them to dry in the desert air for exactly fourteen days. While traveling, the durable joints were much easier to carry and smoke compared to the long bronze pipes that Paragus used in his palace.

A light northerly breeze cooled the evening air. Stars filled the clear Judean sky, and a waning gibbous moon was bright enough to illuminate their nocturnal journey to Bethlehem. Cleaned and clothed, the Wise Men were barely recognizable from their earlier selves. Balthazar, drinking slowly from a wineskin and thinking about the best way to protect his tender groin for the long ride, nervously ran his fingers along the padded saddle blankets. He wore orange pants and a hip-length tunic, each with a pattern of bluish-green peacock feathers. Caspar, dressed in green silks and linen, walked in tight circles around his horse, tugging at the reins, cursing at having to leave on the last night of Saturnalia. He flung his green cape over his shoulders as he felt the chill from the evening breeze. Melchior stood alone, a short distance from the others, by one of the small streams that ran through the garden. Looking upward into the starry night, hands reverently folded and raised to his lips, he silently prayed and thanked God for the opportunity to meet His Son.

"Where the fuck is Paragus?" Caspar shouted.

"Haven't seen him," Balthazar replied. "Melchior, have you seen Paragus?"

Melchior shook his head and resumed his prayers.

"Zacharia, go find your master," Caspar said.

Zacharia ran back into the palace and reappeared moments later with Paragus, whose arm was wrapped around the waist of a stunningly beautiful woman who wore only a sheer undergarment, a thin sadin that betrayed the results of the chilled evening air. Like the other Wise Men, Paragus dressed in his finest clothes, a deep cerulean cape and pants adorned with clusters of small six-pointed stars made of precisely cut topaz. A yellow silk gown accentuated his great belly.

"My friends," Paragus announced, squeezing the half-clothed woman around the waist, "there is a slight change of plans. I am afraid I will not join you on the journey to Bethlehem. Lilith has just arrived from Sephoris, and it wouldn't be right for her to travel all this way only to spend the night alone. It would be the mark of a terrible host, and I have no intention of being a terrible host, so, as I'm sure you will understand, I must stay here. It is my duty, just as it is your duty to travel to Bethlehem."

"Paragus," Melchior said, "you disappoint me."

"But, Paragus," said the messenger, who had a deep gash above his right eye from his earlier collision with the bronze bowl, "Jerome and Elisheba are expecting you. If you don't come, they will punish me. Preparations are being made for each of you as well as the Wise Man from Judea. They plan to lavish you with an opulent feast, fine wines, in the finest home in Bethlehem."

"Is the feast more lavish than this?" Paragus asked.

"No, but—"

"Is the wine finer?"

The messenger shook his head.

"Is the home more luxurious, my friend?"

"Well, no, but . . . " The Messenger struggled to respond.

"But what?"

"Paragus, you are the Wise Man of Perea," Melchior said, coming to the messenger's aid. "Perea is the neighbor of Judea, and Bethlehem is in Judea."

"I'm aware of these things. What's your point?"

"Someone must represent Perea at the birth of God's Son."

Paragus turned to Lilith, who slipped her slender hand up Paragus's shirt, rubbing the lower reaches of his belly. She kissed his shoulder. He smiled.

"Zacharia!" Paragus shouted.

"Yes, sir." Zacharia ran across the garden and stood by Paragus.

"No. There must be no *sir*," Paragus playfully scolded Zacharia.

"Saturnalia," said Zacharia and Paragus together.

"In my absence, you will go," Paragus said and placed a hand on Zacharia's head.

"I'm sorry," the messenger said, "but Elisheba and Jerome will never allow a servant to witness the birth of the Son of God. They will have both him and me removed, maybe even jailed."

"Then he shall not go as a servant. He shall go as me. He shall be Paragus, the princely Wise Man of Perea." Paragus removed his cape, pulled his pants completely down, and with the help of Lilith, wiggled his yellow gown over his jiggling belly and handed the clothes to Zacharia.

"You're old, wrinkled, fat, and bearded," Balthazar said to Paragus. "Zacharia is young, thin as a reed with skin as smooth as your tiled floor, and there is not a hair on his chin. It will never work."

"This is even more farfetched than my golden fucking knucklebones," said Caspar. "I love it!"

"Maybe," Balthazar reconsidered, "it could work."

"Oh, here we go." Melchior glanced toward the heavens.

"You've never met them," Balthazar continued, "this Elisheba and, and . . ."

"Jerome," the messenger said.

"Correct. Never met either," Paragus said as Lilith rubbed his chest slowly, sensually.

"They don't know what you look like, correct, Paragus?" Balthazar said.

"I suppose not."

"But Zacharia? As a Wise Man?" the messenger said, alternating between puffs on the pipe and gulps from a chalice. "No offense to you, Zacharia, you are a fine young man, and you grow the finest cannabis in Perea, but a Wise Man, I'm sure you are not."

"No offense taken." Zacharia took a long pull on a short joint.

"Paragus, although you've never met these people," Melchior argued, "you are well known throughout the three lands. Your reputation precedes you. Among this merry group of Wise Men, you are arguably the most well known. Surely, they would have seen images or heard descriptions of you."

"Perhaps," Paragus said, completely unmoved by Melchior's arguments but quite moved by Lilith's delicate hands, which continued their soft caress across his chest and the nether reaches of his prodigious belly.

"What's he supposed to do with those?" Caspar pointed to the clothes in Zacharia's hand. "Make a tent out of them?"

"You could fit four Zacharias into those pants," the messenger said as he puffed on Zacharia's joint. He quickly added, "With apologies to you, sir, I didn't mean to insinuate that you're fat."

"Apologies are not needed, my friend. Insults and insinuations are welcome. It's still Saturnalia. Listen, my friends, my mind is made up. There shall be no more discussion. Zacharia has been by my side when I've presided over civic ceremonies, conversed with kings, advised the highest-ranking military generals, and broken bread with the highest of High Priests. No one knows me better or could be more me than him. If anyone could pull this off, it's Zacharia."

"God will not view this with favor, Paragus. You will regret this," Melchior said.

"I doubt he will," Caspar said as he lecherously gazed at Lilith.

"He's the only truly wise man among us," Balthazar said as he repeatedly dipped his hand into the myrrh and spread it liberally over his groin.

Paragus, still standing in nothing but his undergarments, hugged his servant Zacharia and bid him and the other Wise Men good luck and a safe journey.

One by one, Melchior, Balthazar, Caspar, and Zacharia mounted their horses as Paragus stood as magnificently as a fat, naked man in the desert can, waving farewell to the caravan of horses. He urged the group to ride swiftly and safely and reminded them one last time, "For the remainder of the journey, until you all return for an extended Saturnalia celebration, you shall refer to Zacharia as you would me. He shall be known as Paragus, learned Wise Man from Perea who comes bearing a gift of gold Babylonian coins for the Son of God!"

CHAPTER 18

Exodus I

DECEMBER 24, 1 DAY BC

Vashti was sleeping soundly in her bed, cuddled next to her baby, when two small, unripened figs, one after the other, hit her squarely on the forehead. She checked on the baby to make sure a similar fate had not befallen her, and to her relief, it had not. The infant continued to sleep as Vashti rose from her bed to retrieve the figs from the floor. Each fig was wrapped in a small piece of papyrus securely fastened by a thin piece of tightly tied string. *Mary.* Vashti instinctively knew Mary was in trouble. She picked up the first fig, untied the string, unfolded the papyrus parchment, and read Mary's one-word note: "Help!"

Earlier in the evening, Rachel told Mary what a servant, having heard a hushed conversation between Jerome, Elishba, and the High Priest, told her: The three were planning to have Joseph arrested before dawn and taken to Ergastulum, a notoriously ruthless prison carved out of an abandon quarry just outside of Bethlehem. Joseph had no place in the yarn that the triumvirate wished to spin about Mary and her baby, so he needed to be removed to a place where he would never be heard from again. The High Priest assured Jerome and Elisheba that agents of the Temple would capture Joseph as he slept and drag him to the prison, where they would chain him, torture him, starve him, and leave him to wallow in his own waste until he withered away to a solitary and gruesome death.

Vashti leapt to the window, where, across the narrow passage that separated the two houses, Mary waved her hands in a crossing motion. The two did not make a sound. Vashti untied the papyrus parchment from the second fig and quickly jotted a one-word note—"How?"—rewrapped and tied the note around the fig and threw it into Mary's outstretched hands.

Judging from the position of the moon, Vashti guessed it was just before midnight. Instead of being exhausted, she felt energized, motivated by a sense of loyalty to her best friend, who needed help. From across the narrow divide, Mary and Vashti exchanged quick but reassuring glances.

Vashti watched as Mary wrote a second, longer note. Then, after Mary tied it around the same green fig, she threw it back to Vashti. As Vashti read, the smile left her face. Mary and Joseph needed to leave tonight, but her parents had placed two servants in the courtyard and instructed them to stand guard. There was no explanation for why, and to Vashti, it didn't matter. All that mattered was that her friend was in trouble, and she intended to help. It took only a moment for her to develop a plan, scratch out a note, tie the note to the fig and throw the fig back to Mary, who reeled it in with both hands. The note read, "Need time. Go to the courtyard when the moon's light first hits your bedroom window."

Vashti woke her husband and nestled her sleeping baby beside him. She rushed down the stairs into a darkened room where dried fruit, herbs, and wine were stored. She found a flint and lit two wall-mounted candles—just enough light to see but not so much that would draw the attention of anyone up at this late hour. She rummaged through the clay pots that were arranged alphabetically in the cupboard until she came to the herb she was looking for—valerian. Each night, her mother and father ground a small pinch of fresh valerian root into a powder and mixed it with a small amount of diluted wine to help them sleep. She set the valerian powder aside and rummaged again, this time through wines, vinegars, and oils until she found the second ingredient she was looking for—a large vessel containing strong, nondiluted Zeitani wine, the most potent wine her parents allowed in the house.

She worked quickly and quietly, placing four heaping scoops of the powder into the dark red wine, stirring until it was fully mixed. She then stretched the top of her form-fitting nightgown and wriggled her shoulders until the gown tore slightly and fell to expose her shoulders and a hint of cleavage, which was ample before she was pregnant and even more ample after the baby's birth. She blew out the candles, grabbed two cups from the shelf, tiptoed through the front entry, and crept out into the street and under the arched entry of Jerome and Elisheba's courtyard. In the moonlight, she could clearly see the fig tree in the middle of the courtyard and two drowsy servants sitting at the bottom of the marbled stairs. While she didn't immediately see him, Vashti heard Joseph snoring rhythmically next to the stable that held his donkey in the far corner of the courtyard.

As instructed by her friend, the moment the moon's light hit her window, Mary tiptoed slowly, quietly, across the large room where she and Joseph had met defeat at the hands of the triumvirate earlier that day. On the balcony, she peered into the courtyard as Vashti poured wine into two large cups that the grateful servant-guards greedily accepted. Vashti whispered into the men's ears. They each grinned a lecherous kind of grin, their gaze fixed on the low neckline of her gown. Vashti lifted the wine pitcher, pressed it against her lips, and pretended to take several gulps. She nodded to the guards, encouraging them to do the same. They happily did.

The smaller of the guards drunkenly put his hand on Vashti's bare shoulder, which triggered a swift slap to his face. Vashti wasn't sure whether it was the wine, the valerian, the slap to the cheek, or the combination of all three, but the servant crumpled, his forehead smacking against the blunt edge of a marble step. He was out cold but still smiling. Joseph continued to snore from his corner of the courtyard.

Leading with her bare shoulder, Vashti moved closer to the second guard, the only obstacle in the way of Mary's and Joseph's escape. Vashti winked seductively, pursed her lips, kissing the air just inches from the guard's lips. He moved his head awkwardly toward her as if to either kiss her lips or nibble on her neck. Vashti put her smooth, warm fingers seductively under his chin, then raised the pitcher of wine and emptied it into his mouth. He wiped his lips with his bare arm and, in slow motion, folded onto Vashti's lap and fell into a deep sleep. With care, she put the second servant-guard's head next to the first.

Mary tiptoed down the darkened stairs, with each step feeling as though the baby was sinking lower in her belly. Sudden bolts of sharp pain punctuated the chronic dull ache in her lower abdomen as she reached the courtyard.

Vashti embraced Mary, kissing her forehead. "Are you all right?"

"We will be after we leave this place," Mary whispered, clutching her belly. "I can't thank you enough, Vash. You've come to my rescue. Again."

"I need to get back," Vashti whispered. "One day, you'll need to explain all this to me." Vashti put her hands on Mary's midsection. "You and the baby be safe, be well."

Like a silent spectre, Vashti glided across the courtyard, through the arched entry, and back into the street that connected the two houses. Mary crossed the courtyard, stopping for a moment to pluck a handful of unripened figs from the tree and tuck them into the pocket of her nightgown. The figs were a symbol of Vashti's friendship and a reminder for Mary to look for opportunities to give back to others as Vash had given to her. With a pocketful of figs, she reached the corner of the courtyard, next to the stable, where Joseph lay sleeping.

Unable to bend down, Mary planted her left foot on the ground, held on to a fence post, and used her right foot to tap Joseph on the shoulder. "Wake up," she whispered. No reaction. "Joseph." Mary forcefully dug her foot into Joseph's shoulder. "Wake up."

Joseph shot up, disoriented, as if he was ready to fight. He glanced at Mary and then around the empty courtyard, which was bathed in the light of a bright gibbous moon.

"Are you all right?" Joseph shouted.

"Shhh." Mary placed her hand on Joseph's lips, feeling the coarse, damp hair of his moustache and beard. "We can't stay here."

"You want to leave? Now?" Joseph whispered, his hands cupping Mary's face.

"We must." Mary was resolute. "We made a mistake in coming here. My mother and father and the High Priest feed off one another. They plan to jail you, and what they plan to do with our baby, I'm not certain, but it will only get worse when the five Wise Men arrive. We can't stay."

"Okay, okay," Joseph said, still hazy, still trying to focus his mind after waking from a sound sleep.

"It's my fault. I wish I'd never left Nazareth. I don't know what I was thinking. I wasn't thinking, I—"

"Enough." Joseph kissed Mary's forehead. "We both agreed to this. Let's leave now, while we can see by the moon's light."

Joseph opened the gate to the small stable in the courtyard where his donkey was tied. He threw the blanket that had been his bed onto the donkey's back and struggled to lift Mary atop. As Joseph led the donkey out of the courtyard, the clip-clop of hooves echoed against the courtyard walls. The noise seemed as though it caught the attention of the marble statues of Moses, Isaiah, and Micah, who observed through their hollow eyes, with great disdain, Mary and Joseph move past the entry and into the winding pathways of Bethlehem.

Moonlight glowed on the ochre-colored cobbled lanes, providing just enough light to guide their exodus from Bethlehem. The donkey's uneven steps jolted and jostled Mary. Her pain increased with his every step, and the sharp cramps that radiated from her lower belly were coming more frequently. Mary bit her lip and squeezed Joseph's hand tighter as Joseph led them down winding path after winding path.

"I don't know where we are." Joseph stopped and surveyed the shops that surrounded them. As a boy, he knew the village of Bethlehem well, but he hadn't been in these streets for more than thirty years. In the moonlit night, he lost his way. "This isn't how we came in."

"I can't sit up here any longer." Mary winced. "There is pain with every step of the donkey. Help me down, please."

"You're in no condition to walk."

"It can't be worse than sitting up here," Mary said as Joseph helped her dismount. "It must feel better to walk. We need to keep moving."

Mary reached out and held Joseph's hand. She found comfort in its strength and in the way it enveloped her own. With his other hand, Joseph tugged at the reins of the donkey, and they continued their journey farther into the jumbled pathways of Bethlehem. An intense pain, a cramp deep within her body, forced Mary to stop.

They stood frozen in front of a tavern where six drunk shepherds, wearing tall, red-pointed Saturnalia hats, were draped around women of the night for support. Empty wineskins and broken plates littered the ground under their feet. Busy attending to their wine and women, the shepherds didn't notice the travelers who had stumbled upon them.

"Excuse me," Joseph said, and then he repeated with a shout, "Excuse me!"

A gangly shepherd, the tallest of the party, turned toward the travelers. His pointed hat tumbled from his head onto the ground. "Happy Saturnalia!" he slurred.

Mary and Joseph exchanged glances.

"Saturnalia? It didn't even occur to me," Joseph said to Mary.

Mary closed her eyes and rubbed the underside of her belly.

"My wife is in a great deal of pain. We're trying to find our way out of Bethlehem. Can you direct us to the northern gate?"

"The northern gate—do any of you know where the northern gate is?" the tall shepherd asked his mates.

"It's likely," another shepherd responded as he, with a full cup of wine, pointed upward to the sky, "that it's in the north." The wine splashed out of the cup onto his head and ran down his face.

"Yes," said another. "If you find the southern gate, just go north from there. It's that simple." The shepherds and their scantily clad companions turned their backs to the travelers and continued with their intoxicated merrymaking.

A dilapidated inn, which looked as if it had been built during the time of Moses and not maintained since, sat in a state of decay next to the tavern. Mary and Joseph walked past the three ramshackle rooms and stopped in front of the adjoining stable. An ox and ass lay asleep, and two sheep stood, perfectly still, in their pen. In front of the sheep was a manger, and lying next to the manger, a waiflike figure was curled up on a bed of straw. Mary closed her eyes, grimaced, her breathing marked by sharp inhales and long, extended exhales.

"Joseph, we need to continue to move." Sweat covered Mary's forehead and dripped down her neck, soaking the top of her gown. She tried to smile, but the pain would not allow it.

Joseph wrapped his left arm around Mary to support her. Although determined to leave Bethlehem and her parents behind, before Mary could take another step, water rushed from between her legs, splashing the parched ground, sending muddy speckles onto her feet and ankles. Mary and Joseph locked eyes, each in a state of panic and neither noticing the slender, slightly hunched figure walking slowly from the shadows of the stable toward the moonlit street where they stood frozen with fear.

CHAPTER 19

The Birth

DAY 1, AD

The Keeper and Joseph supported Mary as they walked toward the stable. Mary wrapped one arm around Joseph's shoulder and the other around the Keeper's. Joseph glanced at the Keeper, wondering how a frail old man could support the weight of his Mary and worried that he might have to care for the old man as well as Mary before the night was through. They moved into the stable, past the well, and headed for the nearby three-room inn.

"There," the Keeper said as he pointed to the room closest to them. "I'll move the shepherds out and your wife in."

"Stop," Mary said breathlessly as the water and blood continued to trickle from between her legs. They stood by the pile of blankets the Keeper had been sleeping on beside the manger. "I can't walk. Not another step. Please. Set me down. Here. Abigaia is ready."

Joseph and the Keeper carefully lowered Mary onto the thin layer of blankets. Joseph sat behind her, supporting her back, rubbing her shoulders. He removed his worn linen vest and stuffed all the loose straw within his reach into it, fashioning a pillow for Mary's head. The Keeper walked to the well, filled two small pails with fresh water, and placed one by each of Mary's bare legs. Through cataract-ridden eyes, the Keeper could see the fear in Joseph's eyes and the pain in Mary's. The Keeper had helped his wife give birth to their two beautiful boys. That was more than seventy years ago, but the memory of each birth—the pushing, the breathing, the blood, the pain-induced screaming—was vividly etched in his mind. He looked Mary in the eye, smiled ever so slightly, and nodded a slow, confident nod, letting Mary know everything was going to be all right.

The three exchanged no words. They instead worked in a surreal silence, their actions orchestrated, each somehow knowing what they needed to do. Then it came time to push. Joseph cradled Mary's head, brushing her sweat-soaked hair from her face with one hand and holding Mary's hand in the other. Mary pushed and rested, and pushed and rested, according to the calm, confident instructions from the Keeper. It was minutes, or perhaps hours—the three had lost all track of time—before the baby's head crowned and the Keeper's instructions to push became louder and more urgent. Then, in the moments just before the sun rose on the warm windless morning of the twenty-fifth of December, as the four Wise Men were on the last leg of their journey to Bethlehem, as Jude Aya Weissman woke in the Nakhleh slum and carefully wrapped his gift for the Son of God, as Jerome and Elisheba lay sleepily in their bed dreaming pleasant dreams of grandeur, as Vashti provided morning nourishment for her baby, and as the High Priest performed his morning prayers, Mary gave birth to a beautiful baby boy.

The baby cried, Mary and Joseph wept, and the Keeper gently washed the blood from the baby with fresh well water before placing the child on Mary's chest.

"A boy!" Mary was as surprised as she was pleased.

The baby let out a shrill, guttural wail.

"And he wants the world to know he has arrived," Joseph said.

Before Mary and Joseph could thank him, the Keeper fell soundly asleep, his head resting at the foot of the manger.

"He's beautiful." Mary cradled the babe in her arms. "Look." Mary pointed just below the baby's left ear at the red birthmark.

"Another Sea of Galilee," Joseph said, shaking his head. "He carries on the family birthmark. The only blemish on our beautiful boy."

"It's not a blemish. It gives him character." Mary kissed Joseph's cheek. "Just like his father."

As Mary and Joseph marveled at their newborn son, the six shepherds, just coming in from a night of bibulous debauchery, looked with drunken curiosity at the strange sight of a newborn baby and its parents resting on straw next to a manger among the animals in a run-down stable. But the sight did not hold their attention for long as they drank and burped and laughed and farted before stumbling back to their rooms at the inn and passing out on the straw floor.

CHAPTER 20

The Fourth Letter from the Corinthians

Dear Joseph the Carpenter,

We, the entire Corinthian clan, the whole lot of us, are losing patience. We implore you to return. We insist. We are at the point where we are very, very unlikely to provide a strong referral or reference on your behalf. What started as a protective enclosure has turned into a deathtrap and escape hatch for our precious Arabians. As you might have guessed, dear Joseph, we lost another of our horses. This one just walked away in the middle of the night. We may need to tie them up instead of letting them roam freely around the unfinished corral. Perhaps this will prevent them from wandering off. Caleb thinks we should tie thick braids of twine to each of their muzzles and tie the other end to one of your fence posts. He thinks that will do the trick until you return to finish the job. Do you think that would work? Junia keeps asking me about the blind carpenter, and I'm still unsure how to respond. She is becoming unbearable. Or perhaps she's always been unbearable, and I'm just beginning to notice. It's hard to say. In either case, my patience with little Junia is wearing *as thin as the boards from which you've constructed this shabby corral. I must insist that you return to protect what remains of our fine horses as our wealth dwindles with each wayward or slaughtered horse, even if it means leaving the buxom young woman. I'm beginning to think, my faithful friend and trusted carpenter, that you have forgotten us entirely.*

Yours fondly,
Aaron Corinthian

CHAPTER 21

A Good Morning Spoiled

DAY 1, AD

As the early morning sun rose over the low-slung rooftops of Bethlehem, Elisheba woke in a fine mood with great anticipation and high expectations for the day. She was certain it would be a glorious morning. Crossing the great room, where just the day before she had sent the messengers on their mission, she paused to enjoy the sweet vanilla-honey scents of the fresh desert roses that decorated every table in the room. She hadn't even noticed them before, but this morning their orange and pink colors were vibrant and their scent filled the air. She summoned a servant and asked, in a most uncharacteristically pleasant manner, to please bring her a cup of hot Ceylon tea and thanked the servant as he delivered it with a respectful bow. *Please* and *thank you*. It was the first time in more than ten years of service that the servant had ever heard Madam Elisheba utter those words.

Elisheba closed her eyes, raised the tea to her lips, and, before taking a sip, inhaled its wonderful steamy scent. After taking one more look around the great room, she felt pleased that everything was in place for the five Wise Men; the furniture perfectly positioned, fresh flowers in ornamental vases, the miniature palms newly trimmed, new candles in place of the old, and the wood floor freshly polished. Truly a wonderful start to a glorious day.

Elisheba walked out onto the balcony, closed her eyes, lifted her head, and basked in the warmth of the morning sun. She sipped her tea, glanced down into the courtyard where Joseph had been sleeping, and saw only crumpled blankets, just as she had expected. She smiled, knowing the agents of the Temple had successfully executed their plan to abduct Joseph and lock him away in the rat-infested, disease-ridden dungeons of Ergastulum, from which he would never be seen or heard from again.

Elisheba looked down toward the stable, where she noticed that Joseph's donkey was also gone. She then traced the faint indentations of the donkey's hooves out from the stable, into the courtyard, and through the arched entryway. Alongside the hoofprints were the footprints of a barefoot man. There was no sign of a struggle in the courtyard or by the blankets where Joseph had slept. Elisheba lowered the tea from her lips, and her eyes darted from the stable to the marble staircase, where she saw the two servants, who had been instructed to stand guard diligently throughout the night, sound asleep. They were sprawled across the bottom steps, with broad smiles across their pathetic faces.

Throwing her teacup to the ground, Elisheba dashed back across the great room, now oblivious to the sights and smells of the fresh desert roses. She ran down the long corridor, opened the door to Mary's bedroom, and found a fully made bed and two green figs on the floor. But there was no sign of Mary.

Elisheba raced back to the balcony and repeatedly pulled on a thick string that ran to a large bell that sent every servant on the premises, except for the two sleeping soundly on the steps, scurrying to meet the madam in the great room. Awakened by the balcony bell, Jerome stumbled into the room. Elisheba, with the precision and demeanor of a military general, sent five of the servants with instructions to scour the neighborhoods of Bethlehem to find Mary and Joseph and bring them back to the house. And, if Mary and Joseph refused to return, she further instructed the servants to let the wayward pair know she would force them to come back in the most unpleasant way. She ordered a sixth servant to fetch the High Priest.

"This is just like her," Elisheba said, shaking her head as she paced across the great room, "always thinking of herself, never about us and certainly never about God."

"We need to find her before the Wise Men arrive," Jerome said and then blew steam from a cup of hot tea a young servant had delivered.

"It will tarnish our reputation among Temple Elders and the High Priest," Elisheba said.

"Our reputation at the Temple is one thing, but no virgin mother, and no Son of God, means no gifts and no opportunity to extend my commercial empire."

Husband and wife sat across from one another at the large table and exchanged a stream of vicious insults, each blaming the other for everything from raising an independent, strong-willed daughter to allowing her and the peasant carpenter to escape from under their noses. As they hurled insults, the servant sent to search in the neighborhood immediately surrounding Elisheba and Jerome's house, climbed the ladder and, breathing heavily, reported that he had seen no signs of the fugitives.

"Then why on earth are you back here in the comfort of this house?" Elisheba pointed at the balcony ladder. "Get back into the streets, and don't stop looking until you find them."

The High Priest trudged up the stairs, weighed down by layer upon layer of his priestly garb. The first layer was a pearl-white, thick linen tunic, covered by a light-blue vest adorned with fine jewels and gems and topped with a silken blue robe with gold embroidery. He arrived in the great room, removed the white mitre from his head, and wiped away the sweat trickling from his chin. A servant brought him a cup of hot tea.

"Is Mary ready?" the High Priest asked. "I assume by your urgent note that she will soon deliver. Where is she?"

"We don't know," said Jerome. "Both Joseph and Mary escaped. They must have been gone long before we woke."

"Who's gone?" Rachel walked into the great room, rubbing the sleep out of her eyes.

"Your sister and that carpenter," Elisheba said.

"You had no part in this?" Jerome asked.

"No, but if I had the opportunity—"

"Oh, this is not good. Not good at all." The High Priest set his teacup back on the table and hailed a servant. "I'll need something much stronger."

Elisheba nodded to the servant, who brought a large chalice of wine to the priest.

"Make sure this cup never goes empty," the High Priest commanded the servant.

"Where is the jailer from Ergastulum? He was supposed to remove Joseph last night," Elisheba said as she moved closer to the High Priest so Rachel could not hear; but Rachel followed closely behind.

"Last night?" The High Priest drank from his filled cup. "I thought it was tonight. I instructed him to take Joseph tonight. It was supposed to be last night?"

"So, it is true," Rachel said and grabbed her mother's arm. Elisheba forcefully pulled away. "I told Mary last night that I'd heard about a plan, but I didn't think even you would stoop so low."

"Watch yourself, Rachel, you're hanging by the thinnest of threads." Jerome walked with small, quick steps toward her. "You cross us again, and we'll have the jailer haul you off to Ergastulum."

"I'm sure the guards there are more pleasant than the two of you."

Another servant, having scaled the ladder, arrived on the balcony breathless from his sprint through the lanes of Bethlehem. He too reported that he had seen no signs of the missing pair and their mangy donkey, and he too was ordered to leave the comfort of the home and return to the streets of Bethlehem.

"I have word from a reliable source," the High Priest said and sipped his wine between each word, "that four Wise Men have been seen traveling by horse from the east, in a caravan from Perea. I expect they will arrive late this morning."

"Traveling in a caravan? On horseback?" said Jerome.

"Yes, on horseback."

"I thought Wise Men typically rode camels," Jerome said.

"That's the impression I had as well," said the Hight Priest.

"Yes, I'm certain of it," Jerome said. "Every Wise Man I know struts around on a camel. I've never seen a Wise Man on a horse. It doesn't seem right."

"A camel to a Wise Man is like the sand to the desert," commented the High Priest.

"What does that mean? You're not making any sense." Jerome shook his head.

"Stop. It doesn't matter if they were riding camels or horses or flying carpets. What matters is that there are only four. We sent five invitations. Any sign of the fifth?" asked Elisheba.

The High Priest shook his head and took a long drink from the chalice with his eyes closed, shutting out all other senses so his tongue could fully rejoice in the fruity finish of the Malawi wine.

Elisheba heard shouting in the distance. The voice came from the streets below and grew clearer as the voice drew nearer, finally reaching their courtyard. A servant scaled the ladder and stood before the triumvirate, trying to catch his breath.

"Sir, Madam, your Holiness," the servant bent over, placing his shaking hands on his knees, wheezing, "I've found them. They're still in Bethlehem."

"Excellent," the High Priest said.

"Where, exactly?" asked Elisheba.

"In a stable at an inn."

"There are dozens of inns, idiot. Which one?" Jerome got up out of his seat and slipped into his walking sandals.

"Be nice." Rachel elbowed her father.

"The inn by the tavern. The one run by the old man, the Keeper."

"Disgusting." Elisheba wrinkled her nose.

"The inn or the Keeper?" asked the High Priest, who rarely ventured out into Bethlehem, instead preferring to stay in the comfort of the Temple and in the homes of the wealthy.

"The Keeper, but it applies to the inn as well."

"We need to get Mary back here," Jerome said. "Now."

"But they don't want to be here. You can't force them back," Rachel said.

"Jerome is right," said Elisheba, ignoring Rachel. "We need to get them back before the Wise Men arrive and before she has the baby amongst the filth and squalor of that decrepit inn."

"Excuse me, Madam," said the servant who had brought the news of the fugitives' whereabouts. "I'm sorry. I mean no disrespect, but that won't be possible."

"You impertinent boy, how dare you suggest to Madam what is, and is not, possible," Jerome stood next to the servant, his dainty fist raised in the air.

"What do you mean?" Elisheba drew closer to the servant, putting her hand over Jerome's fist.

"What isn't possible?" Rachel asked.

"That Mary could have the baby here. In your home."

"You disgusting urchin, do you know whom you are addressing?" The High Priest now raised his fist.

"Why is that?" Elisheba stood nose to nose with the servant.

"Because, Madam, your highness, I saw," the servant said and folded his hands together as if praying for mercy or protecting himself from a fist to the face, "in the stable, resting in the straw, I saw the carpenter from Nazareth and Mary and heard the sound of a baby crying in a manger."

"Mary has already given birth?" Jerome signaled to the servant to replace his tea with wine.

"That's wonderful!" Rachel said.

"That's decidedly not wonderful," Jerome shot back.

"The baby is in a food trough meant for livestock?" added the High Priest.

"We need to fix this now." Elisheba slipped into her sandals. "You," Elisheba addressed the largest servant in the house and pointed to Rachel, "make sure she stays right here."

With Rachel shouting, trying to wriggle away from the servant, Elisheba and Jerome moved quickly down the stairs, through the courtyard, and into the lanes of Bethlehem. The High Priest followed shortly after but not before he gulped down what remained of his wine and refilled his chalice to the brim for the short slog to the inn.

CHAPTER 22

The Triumvirate and the Fugitives

DAY 1, AD

Elisheba and Jerome jostled their way through the crowded Bethlehem lanes, shoving, elbowing, and bashing anyone who dared cross their path. As they turned a corner and passed a tavern suitable only for peasants and prostitutes, the pungent aroma from the inn filled their nostrils before they could see the inn itself. An unusually warm winter's morning baked the ox and sheep shit, producing a visible steam that released the foul odor.

Mary was sitting on a cushion of straw, her gown pulled down below her breast, a thin shawl covering her and the head of the feeding baby. Joseph lined the manger with fresh straw and a clean blanket the Keeper had brought from the inn. The sheep were still asleep in their pen, and across the stable the ox let loose a torrent of urine, adding a pungent sourness to the steaming piles of shit that dotted the ground. With a fresh pail of cool well water for Mary and Joseph, the Keeper moved across the stable toward the manger. Unnoticed by Mary or Joseph or the Keeper, Elisheba and Jerome arrived, stunned and horrified by what they saw and smelled.

This is not what Elisheba had visualized. Not at all. Things were decidedly not going as planned. And, for Elisheba, rarely did things not go as planned. What was to be an event that catapulted Elisheba to her rightful place amongst the great religious leaders like Abraham and Moses and Isaiah, what was to enshrine her name into the Holy Scriptures, and what was to propel Jerome's commercial empire to the farthest corners of the earth had turned into a nightmare. Instead of welcoming the Son of God and the rich Wise Men into their home, where they would have total control of the event, they found themselves in this sty. This unholy filth. Their virgin daughter chosen by God, clothed in rags, lying in straw. The Son of God, Himself, resting in a food trough tended by an impoverished Nazarene carpenter and a decrepit old deaf man in an equally old and decrepit stable amongst the filth and squalor of equally old and decrepit animals. No, things certainly were not going as planned.

"Mary!" Elisheba rushed across the stable. "We need to get you and the Son of God home. Now."

Mary looked up from the baby at her breast to see her mother dashing toward her, her father and the High Priest not far behind, following Elisheba like little ducklings behind their mother. Jerome covered his nose to reduce the smell of the stench. Joseph moved from the manger and stood beside Mary, putting his hands on her shoulder in a gesture of support and protection. He didn't like to use his size and physical strength to intimidate others, but on this occasion, he made an exception.

"Good morning Mother, Father." Mary removed the baby from her breast and raised her gown over her shoulder. The long night of labor had sapped her strength, leaving her exhausted, but the sight of the unholy triumvirate descending upon them like vultures, disturbing their tranquil morning, gave her the energy to fight back. "I'm not going anywhere. Neither are Joseph nor our son."

"So, you indeed had a boy!" the High Priest said, bathed in sweat, with red wine spilled on the front of his gown. "Blessed are you amongst women."

"A boy. Just as prophesied," Elisheba said self-righteously. "We need to get you and the baby home. This is no place for a child."

"Not just a child," the High Priest said, "but the Son of God. It is certainly no place for the Son of God to spend his first moments on this earth."

"More to the point, I can't imagine what the Wise Men would think," Jerome said. "I wouldn't want a dog to be born in this filth. And I don't even like dogs."

"Stop it. All of you. Stop with the nonsense about the Son of God. This is our baby," Mary said and rested her hand upon Joseph's hand.

"You can't stay here, Mary. What in God's name will people think?" Jerome said.

"What will they think? About me? Or about you? I don't care. It doesn't matter. We are not going anywhere. We will rest here. The Keeper has treated us with far more kindness and care than you have shown us."

"Mary, you have given birth to our Savior, the Son of God," said the High Priest. "He should not remain in this stable. You would dishonor and displease him."

"My hearing is poor," the Keeper said, "but did he say this baby is the Son of God?"

"Yes." The triumvirate spoke in unison, their voices loud enough for the Keeper to hear.

"No," Mary said. She turned to the Keeper and held his hand. "No, it's not true. This is the son of Joseph. My mother and father and the High Priest are badly mistaken."

"Mary, you have fulfilled the prophecies of the most respected, reverent, and hallowed Holy Men." The High Priest spoke as if he were addressing a crowd. "Your son is surely the Son of God, our Savior."

"Our Savior?" asked the Keeper.

Again, the triumvirate responded with a chorus of *Yes*.

The Keeper looked down at the sleeping infant. "He's beautiful, but he doesn't look like he could save much to me."

"You must return to your parents' home to fulfill your destiny and the destiny of this child," the High Priest persisted.

"The only destiny you care to fulfill is your own," Mary said.

"We're not moving," Joseph added.

"Give us a moment," Elisheba said and guided Jerome and the High Priest to the far side of the stable.

"This is more excitement than we've had in years," the Keeper said to Mary.

"It's nothing, really, I promise." Mary patted the Keeper's hand.

The High Priest, Jerome, and Elisheba huddled where the ox stood lazily swinging his tail to ward off a persistent family of flies intent on making a home on its back. Two sheep, with flattened, urine-encrusted fleece caked with dust and pieces of straw, lay asleep in the stable next to the ox. Nestled into the warmth of the wool of the sleeping sheep, and observing with great interest the morning's proceedings, was a one-eyed, dusty, rust-colored cat with only half a right ear and ribs sticking out like fence posts. The cat loved a good bit of chaos, and he watched with delight as the triumvirate hastily huddled together. What appeared to be a smile spread across the cat's face as he lazily licked his left paw.

The High Priest, Jerome, and Elisheba each covered their mouths and noses with their sleeves as the pungent smell of shit and urine permeated the air.

"She has your stubbornness," Jerome said to Elisheba.

"What?" said the Priest. "It is hard to hear when you talk into your sleeve."

"I said she has Elisheba's stubbornness," repeated Jerome loud enough for anyone in the stable to hear.

"And this stable has your stench," Elisheba shot back at Jerome.

"That, I heard clearly," said the High Priest.

"What is that splattered on the front of your robe?" Jerome asked the High Priest. "Is that wine from my house? Did you bother to get any in your mouth, or did you just bathe in it?"

"An unfortunate waste of fine wine, indeed. I was chasing the two of you, and the wine leapt from the chalice and onto my robe as I hastened to arrive at this," the High Priest said and looked around at the surroundings, "this, this, whatever this is."

"We can't physically force her back to the house," said Elisheba, "could we?"

"With the help of our strongest servants, why not?" Jerome combed the limp strands of hair from one side of his head to the other and then back again.

"Make yourself useful, Jerome, and send for them," Elisheba said.

"Wait!" The High Priest took an extended drink from his chalice to bolster his courage. "That would cause a scene. It will upset Mary, which will upset Joseph. He is a brute of a man. People could get hurt."

"I could get hurt," Jerome said.

"That wouldn't take too much," Elisheba said and fanned her hand in front of her nose to dissipate the stench.

"It wouldn't look good if the Wise Men arrived to see that the virgin mother and the Son of God were being held hostage by the grandparents and a High Priest," the High Priest reasoned. "That would not go over well. We would lose their favor."

"And their gifts," Jerome added.

"I need to hear a better idea, and I need to hear it now," Elisheba spoke through clenched teeth.

There was a moment of silence, finally broken by the High Priest. "We might be able to use this situation to our advantage."

"How is that possible?" Elisheba asked.

"Think about certain periods of the lives of the greatest prophets—Moses, Isaiah, Micah. At some point, each was poor, living in squalor often for long periods of time." The High Priest paused, taking another gulp of wine as he formulated his plan. "Think of the Son of God, born of humble beginnings, in the humble village of

Bethlehem, among the common villagers, and among animals that God Himself created. It's like Moses wandering in the desert. It lends a sort of down-to-earth quality to the story, a certain dramatic flair—an unexpected twist."

"But the Wise Men," Jerome said. "The invitations. We've created an expectation. The grand promise of the Son of God."

"Perhaps the Wise Men will more clearly see the magnificence of the child against the squalor of his surroundings and their outpouring of gifts will be even greater."

"I'm not convinced," Jerome said.

"Do you have a better idea?" Elisheba asked Jerome accusingly. She didn't wait for his answer. "I didn't think so. The High Priest is right. This must be God's plan. It's the only explanation, and we must follow it."

Elisheba instructed the servant who had accompanied them to return home and await the Wise Men, then guide them to the stable. The servant set out running.

"And bring my scribe," Elisheba shouted to him as he dashed away.

"Excellent idea," the High Priest said to Elisheba and Jerome. "The spoken word will vary, but we need to control the written narrative."

CHAPTER 23

The Five Wise Men Arrive in Bethlehem

DAY I, AD

A hazy plume of cannabis smoke signaled the arrival of the Wise Men at the home of Jerome and Elisheba. Having continued the Saturnalia celebration on their overnight journey to Bethlehem, they arrived with empty wineskins and full bladders. They entered under the archway into the courtyard, dismounted from their horses, and emptied their bladders against the walls of the courtyard, not noticing the blank stares from the statues of the prophets. Zacharia, who was still in his servant's rags rather than Paragus's robes, inhaled the final bit of a joint. Melchior gave thanks to God for their safe journey, while Caspar cursed the fact that they were in Bethlehem rather than Perea. Balthazar complained to anyone who would listen that the overnight journey further chafed his already raw groin and that he had used most of the remaining myrrh to soothe his pain.

Elisheba's servant appeared from the balcony, descended the ladder, and warmly welcomed the group as they stood in the courtyard. "My masters have sent me to welcome you, distinguished guests. So welcome to Bethlehem and to the home of Elisheba, Jerome, and their grandson, the Son of God. But you'll have to forgive me." The servant surveyed the group of Wise Men. "I was told that four of you were riding from the east together. I see only three Wise Men and one servant."

"No, boy, there are four of us." Caspar pointed at Zacharia. "Paragus enjoys riding in his underwear."

"Paragus," Balthazar said to Zacharia, who didn't respond, "Par-a-gus!" Balthazar said a little louder, hitting Zacharia on the shoulder. "Paragus! Perhaps it's time to put your robe on."

"Oh, yeah." Zacharia giggled the giggle of one who is sublimely stoned. He unpacked the robes and dressed. The yellow tunic hung past his knees, and when he pulled Paragus's pants up, they slid immediately back down to the ground.

Rachel stood silently on the balcony, watching the gathering of Wise Men. Her gaze fixed on Paragus, who was much younger and much fitter than the other Wise Men. He looked quite pleasing in his underwear.

Melchior shook his head with a look of disgust. "Perhaps a sash would help."

"I'll bring him one belonging to my father," Rachel called from the balcony.

A moment later, she stood in front of Zacharia with one of her father's finest silk sashes, a braid of red and yellow and dark blue silk with gold tufts at each end. "Hold your pants up, Paragus," Rachel said as she knelt in front of him and stretched the sash, wrapping it around his waist.

As she pulled Zacharia closer with the sash, he felt her warm breath against his exposed stomach. He couldn't take his eyes off Rachel, enthralled by her emerald eyes, her long black hair brushed over her shoulder exposing her neck, and her olive skin radiating a warmth that went to his core. His heart skipped and then beat a step faster.

"I'll tie the sash like I've seen my father tie it a hundred times before." Rachel's hands moved skillfully until she had tied a decorative knot, which now hung from Zacharia's slender hips. She stepped back to admire her fine work. "Very distinguished, suitable for a distinguished Wise Man."

"Excuse me, good sirs." A peasant in threadbare clothes appeared at the arched entry and bowed his head as he addressed the Wise Men. "I have instructions to come to this home to witness the birth of the Son of God."

The Wise Men looked at each other with furrowed brows and wrinkled foreheads.

"Are you sure?" asked Balthazar.

"That's what I'm told it says in this invitation." The peasant handed the scroll to Elisheba's servant.

"I don't read," the servant said as he handed the scroll to Caspar.

"This fits right in with this fucking day," Caspar said. "I'm instructed to read a scroll by a servant I don't know, to a peasant I've just met, in a house I've never visited, in a village I don't want to fucking be in."

"That's Saturnalia, Caspar!" Zacharia said.

"Which reminds me we should be in Perea right now," Caspar said as he glanced at the scroll. "Yes, it's the same as the invitation we all received. Identical."

"Greetings, my friend." Melchior welcomed the peasant with a warm embrace. "So, you must be the Judean Wise Man."

"No, no. Very far from that. I'm Jude Aya Weissman, the collector of the shitpots for the city of Bethlehem. I'm no Wise Man."

"I'm afraid there has been an error," Elisheba's servant said. "This invitation was strictly intended for another. My masters will not welcome you."

"Nonsense," Balthazar said. "He's with us. If he's not going, we're not going."

Melchior and Caspar looked at one another and nodded in agreement.

"Where are the virgin mother and the Son of God, our Savior?" Melchior asked.

"My masters have instructed me to take you to them. Please get back on your horses."

"Oh, for fuck's sake, we just got here!" Caspar said.

"Back on the horses?" Balthazar cupped his hands around his groin and applied another layer of the myrrh ointment.

"For only a short distance," the servant reassured the travelers. "Please, gentle Wise Men, please get back on your horses and I shall lead you there. Master Jerome and Madam Elisheba are eager to be graced with your presence."

"Before we go, my good man," Balthazar said and held his wineskin upside down, "our wineskins are empty, and it has been a long journey. Perhaps you could fetch some of the best wine in your master's house and refill our skins."

"I'm sorry, I can't . . . " the servant said.

"Of course," Rachel nodded to the servant as she gathered the wineskins until she couldn't see over the mound that had piled up in her arms.

"Let me help you," Zacharia said, instinctively acting as a servant.

"Paragus," Balthazar said, "perhaps you should leave that to a servant."

"It's Saturnalia, Balthazar. Servant and Wise Man. Wise Man and servant. We are one and the same."

"Literally," Caspar said under his breath.

Zacharia took the wineskins from Rachel and she, with her hand wrapped around his waist, led him to a small, dimly lit room on the ground floor at the back of the house. It was filled with row upon row of wine vessels.

Rachel pointed to the back row. "That's my parents' best wine. They reserve it for special occasions, and I think the birth of my sister's baby is just such an occasion."

"Your sister's baby is fortunate to have such a thoughtful and beautiful aunt."

"You flatter me, Paragus. You are too kind."

One by one, they filled the wineskins, with Zacharia pouring from the vessel as Rachel held the skins. They returned to the courtyard with fifteen filled wineskins, enough for each of the five Wise Men to have three. When Jude Aya declined, Balthazar and Caspar fought over his ration, with Balthazar, as Caspar's elder, claiming two and Caspar one.

"Please," Elisheba's servant urged, "they are awaiting your presence."

Melchior, Balthazar, Caspar, and Zacharia tucked the wineskins into the folds of their robes and remounted their horses.

"Rachel, please do me the honor of riding with me." Zacharia extended his hand and with surprising strength and in a single, smooth motion, lifted her lithe body onto the saddle, setting her down gently behind himself. The small caravan left the courtyard, led by Elisheba's servant and her scribe on foot and Jude Aya trailing in the back. Rachel, with her legs wrapped around Zacharia's waist and her hands around his chest, hoped the ride to the inn would never end.

CHAPTER 24

The Presentation of the Gifts

DAY 1, AD

Marked by their ever-present plume of cannabis smoke and accompanied by deep, guttural, moist burps caused by guzzling wine while riding atop a galloping horse, Caspar, Balthazar, and Zacharia arrived at the stable in various states of insobriety. Rachel, after receiving a detailed tutorial from Zacharia on how to effectively inhale a cannabis joint, arrived stoned. Melchior and Jude Aya, each having sensed the importance of the occasion and each eagerly awaiting an audience with the Son of God, arrived reverently sober.

The babe lay in the manger, and Mary, after a long night of labor, had finally fallen into a deep, dream-filled sleep. She dreamed of the night in the garden in Nazareth; she dreamed of telling her infant son stories as she cradled him in her arms; she dreamed of Joseph teaching their son the craft of carpentry; and she dreamed of sitting on soft grass under the shade of a cypress tree with Vashti and her baby, Mary, telling stories, playing games, and laughing, always laughing.

Joseph sat on the straw-covered ground next to the manger, his attention consumed by the sleeping mother and child. Their son had Mary's beauty and her radiance; the only blemish, thought Joseph, was the birthmark that was identical to his. But even this, on their son, was beautiful. Without taking his eyes from the baby, Joseph leaned over and kissed Mary.

The Keeper was in front of the ramshackle rooms next to the stable, bent over a small fire, heating water for tea. The triumvirate remained huddled in the far corner of the stable; Elisheba confidently laying out the next set of tactics, identifying risks and detailing mitigations while Jerome pretended to listen and the High Priest stood inattentively, thinking only how to refill his empty wine chalice.

The horses whinnied and neighed as they stood to allow their distinguished passengers to dismount. "Mary!" Rachel cried out as she tried to descend gracefully from the saddle but fell flat on her face. Bouncing up with pieces of straw stuck in her hair and on her gown, she dusted herself off with a giggle and ran toward Mary, who woke up to her sister's welcome voice.

"She's beautiful," Rachel said. She leaned over the manger and kissed the baby's forehead.

"It's a boy, Rachel. And yes, he is beautiful."

"I am so happy for you both." Rachel embraced Mary and then Joseph and then added in a giggly whisper, "And I'm completely stoned, but don't tell anyone."

The triumvirate made their way to greet the Wise Men. The two sides, the triumvirate on one and the Wise Men on the other, met with equal, but unsaid, disappointment in what they saw. Among the five Wise Men, the triumvirate found Melchior to be the only one who matched their expectations. He dressed in the finest fabrics, carried himself regally as a Wise Man would, and in his hand was a silver box, which they imagined contained a gift of riches for God's Son. They were less sure about Balthazar and Caspar, who, while dressed in fine clothes and also holding ornate gift boxes, carried themselves more like drunk commoners, unsavory people you might find at a disreputable tavern or a house of ill repute.

They didn't know what to make of Paragus, who swayed from side to side, completely enveloped in his poorly fitting princely clothes. He just stared at them with a slight and silly grin pasted on his face for no discernible reason. And finally, they looked at Jude Aya in complete disbelief. Surely this was not the Wise Man from Judea that they had expected. Perhaps it was his servant. Together, the triumvirate approached their five guests with concealed disappointment.

Melchior, and even Caspar and Balthazar in their altered states, found the foul stench of urine and shit, the dust and filth, the presence of an ox and sheep, and the sight of a baby lying in a food trough thoroughly disappointing and somewhat alarming. Jude Aya didn't mind any of this. The scene was more pleasant, and the smells and filth were no worse than what he experienced on the job or in his home. Zacharia was just happy to have given Rachel a ride on his horse; the soft warmth of her legs and arms still lingered on his body.

But both sides, distinguished guests and distinguished hosts, put disappointments and misgivings aside and greeted one another with warmth and grace before making their way to pay their respects to God's Son.

Zacharia walked unsteadily in front of the group, tipping from left to right, his shoulders moving to the rhythm of music that only he could hear.

"Paragus, if I may ask," Elisheba said and tapped Zacharia on the shoulder, "are you drunk?"

"No. Of course not, your highness," Zacharia replied, his eyes little more than slits, his speech slowed by the cannabis, a grin pasted on his face. "High, yes. Completely. But not drunk."

As they walked toward the manger, Joseph put his hand on Balthazar's back. "The horses you rode in, are those Corinthians?"

"No, they're Arabians," Balthazar responded.

"I meant the breeder. I saw the *CA* branded on their hinds."

"Indeed, they're Corinthians. Paragus spent a small fortune on them," Zacharia said, shaking his head.

"You mean *you* spent a small fortune on them?" Elisheba asked.

"That's what he meant." Balthazar put his hand on the back of Zacharia's neck and squeezed tightly. "Sometimes, Paragus refers to himself in the third person. Isn't that right, Paragus?"

"Ow! Yes. Paragus does . . . I do."

"Last night, just outside of Jericho," Caspar said as the group approached the manger, "we saw an entire herd of horses with the *CA* brand running fast and wild, heading south toward Masada, a long way away from the Corinthian compound in Nazareth."

"No one was riding with them?" Joseph asked.

"Not a soul in sight. Only a mass of hooves, hinds, and horses."

"I see," Joseph said, crouching on a cushion next to Mary.

Mary, Joseph, Rachel, and the Keeper sat on the right side of the manger on straw-filled mats the Keeper had removed from the shepherds' rooms in the inn. On the left side of the manger, sitting on a roughly hewn bench that Joseph had assembled out of scraps of wood from the Keeper's stable, were the triumvirate, Elisheba's scribe, and the five Wise Men. The two sides sat across from one another with the manger in the middle, as if they were opposing teams ready to engage in some sport that had not yet been invented and whose rules were yet to be determined.

Everyone settled in uneasily under the sagging roof of the run-down stable. With his head still foggy from the sleepless night, Joseph's attention turned to the Judean Wise Man; there was something about his look, his demeanor, or perhaps his smell that was vaguely familiar. But Joseph couldn't place him, and his attention returned to Mary and their child.

Mary, though deeply concerned by the gathering of guests, whispered to Joseph that she did not have the physical or emotional strength to fight her parents or her parents' unwelcome guests. The days of hard travel and the prolonged painful labor had drained her of energy. She needed to focus the remnants of that energy in caring for their baby.

Before a word was spoken, Caspar, Balthazar, and Zacharia pulled wineskins from the folds of their robes and started drinking. "We hope you don't mind," Balthazar said and wiped his mouth with his sleeve as he saw the concerned looks coming from the triumvirate.

"No, of course not," said Elisheba, whose esteem for the Wise Men continued to decline by the minute. "Please, go ahead."

"If you don't mind, I would love to try your wine," Jerome said and held a large chalice that he had pulled out of the folds of his robe.

"And, if it's no trouble," the High Priest said and raised his empty chalice.

Zacharia filled the men's chalices to the brim.

Jerome took a sip, then raised his chalice and nodded in approval. "This is quite good. Truly excellent. It compares favorably to the finest and most expensive wine I keep in my cellar."

"There's good reason for that," Balthazar said.

"What is that, my fine man?"

"It's your wine."

"My wine?"

"Yes, your daughter was kind enough to let us borrow a bit to fill our wineskins."

Jerome stood up, looking menacingly at Rachel as if he wanted to slap her. Elisheba grabbed him by his tunic and slammed him back into his seat. "Stay focused on what's important," she whispered to him.

Melchior apologetically stepped in. "We have traveled through the night, a long distance across the Judean Desert to reach you. My fellow travelers are feeling parched. They simply need to be refreshed. We are grateful for your wine and to witness this moment."

"To our distinguished guests," the High Priest said and stood, making a sweeping gesture with his hand, "we have the honor and privilege to welcome you to this humble—"

"Exceedingly humble," Caspar said.

"This humble," the High Priest continued, "but entirely prophetic setting to witness the birth, or more accurately, witness the moments just after the birth, of our Savior, the Son of God, born of the Virgin Mary, who is daughter of Jerome and Elisheba, fulfilling the prophecies that were written centuries ago by Isaiah and—"

"Enough!" Jerome said to the High Priest. He then smiled at the Wise Men. "Perhaps we could begin with the giving of gifts."

"If you wish," agreed the High Priest. "But before we begin," he said and held out his empty chalice to the Wise Men, "may I trouble you for a bit more wine?"

Zacharia rose to fill the cup, winking at Rachel as he poured. Rachel blushed, a wide smile crossing her face.

"Excuse me, I don't mean to insinuate, Paragus," Elisheba said in a polite but pointed tone, "but did you just wink at my daughter?"

"No, Madam. A speck of dust or dirt made my eye twitch. I would never be so brazen as to wink at your daughter. But she is certainly lovely."

"Impertinent bastard," Elisheba whispered to the High Priest.

"We were just discussing the presentation of the gifts," Jerome reminded the guests.

"Yes, the gifts," confirmed the High Priest.

"Of course. The gifts." Melchior rose from the bench, walked to the foot of the manger, and stood at the center of the opposing groups. "If I may begin."

"No, please, no gifts. This can't go any further," Mary said, barely able to lift her head. "I know you have traveled a long distance at the invitation of my mother and father, but they misled you—"

"What Mary is trying to say," Jerome said, his loud voice rising over Mary's, "is that we apologize for the misleading directions to our home."

"We had always planned for the birth of our Savior, the Son of God, to be among the people of the village," the High Priest explained. "In these humble surroundings, so the birth symbolizes the prophetic—"

"Yes," Jerome interrupted the High Priest, "thank you for that context, but let's get back to the gifts, shall we?" Jerome turned to the Wise Men. "As you can see, Mary, the virgin mother, my daughter, is exhausted and much too distracted by the baby to look after these gifts, so, please, each of you should bring them to me as the custodian for the gifts and I shall look after them until Mary is able."

Joseph leaned over to Mary and whispered, "We'll never see these gifts, will we?"

"Never. And that's fine with me."

Joseph nodded in agreement.

Melchior, with reverence to God and a keen sense of history, began ceremoniously, "I am Melchior of—"

"Excuse me," Elisheba's scribe said, "what is the name again?"

"Melchior."

"Could you spell that for me?"

"M-E-L-C-H-I-O-R, Melchior. And to begin again, I am—"

"Sorry, I don't mean to interrupt," the scribe interrupted, "but is that your first or last name?"

"Ignore him." Jerome slapped the scribe across his leg and turned to Melchior. "Please, continue."

"I am known as Melchior, Wise Man of Persia, a land that stretches from the Mediterranean to the west and the Gulf to the east. A land of milk and honey. A land that is rich and fertile. A land with vast deserts in which water flows in a thousand different green and fertile oasis, a land—"

"You mean *oases*," slurred Balthazar, playfully hoping to disrupt the grandeur of his friend's presentation. "A single patch of verdant land in the middle of the desert is called an oasis, but—"

"But," Caspar said, catching on to Balthazar's game, "if Persia has thousands of these patches of verdant lands amidst its vast deserts—"

"Which I sincerely doubt," Balthazar added.

"Then the word must be plural, which, as Balthazar correctly pointed out, is *oases*," Caspar finished.

"And how is the plural form spelled?" the scribe asked, much to Caspar's and Balthazar's delight.

"Shut up," Jerome said and knocked the quill out of the scribe's hand. "One more question from you and I'll have one of our servants, one of the larger ones, throw you into the steaming pile of ox dung."

"As I was saying," Melchior said, regaining the floor and shooting a stern look at his two friends, "the water flows, it is a land for which God has blessed with—"

"Yes, thank you, Melchior," Jerome said and waved his right hand in slow circles, "we are all certain Persia is a lovely place. Thank you for your kind introduction to its charms, but if you could just get to the gift."

"Never mind my husband, Melchior," Elisheba said. "Please continue. Take as long as you'd like."

Melchior held the ornamented silver container and opened the lid slowly. "The gift for the Son of God is the finest frankincense extracted from the rarest trees of the genus Boswellia that grow in a thick forest in southern Persia. This frankincense is used for medicine and can heal skin ailments. It can also be ground and liquified to produce the finest perfumes on the Persian peninsula. I hope it is worthy of the Son of God. Its value is undeterminable."

"Excellent. Excellent," Jerome said and clapped his soft hands, giddy with greed. "You said its value was undeterminable, but everything must have a value, of course. If you had to give it a guess, just a rough estimate, nothing precise, what do you think it would be worth?"

"A thousand camels, two hundred cubits of the finest oriental silk, one hundred ingots of copper."

"How nice!" Jerome nodded to the High Priest. "But just so there is no confusion, is that a thousand camels *and* two hundred cubits of oriental silk *and* one hundred ingots of copper, or is it *or*?"

With a growing concern about the intense focus on the value of the gift, and a growing dislike for Jerome, Melchior laid the silver container of frankincense at the feet of Jerome and Elisheba. "It's *and*." Melchior bowed his head to Mary, Joseph, and the child. Mary and Joseph returned the gesture under the watchful eye of Elisheba and Jerome.

"Wonderful!" replied Jerome. "*And* is always so much better than *or*."

"We're off to a splendid start," the High Priest agreed.

As Melchior sat, Caspar staggered from Joseph's makeshift bench to the foot of the manger, the place where Melchior had presented his gift. He held the silver box that he had taken from Paragus's palace.

"I think I'm going to like this one," Jerome whispered to the High Priest upon seeing the gift box.

"I am Caspar of India," Caspar began, burping just as he enunciated the "I" in India, "a land of a thousand spices: cinnamon, cardamom, and cloves. A land of mysterious, ancient temples. A land where gemstones fall like figs from trees. A land in which cows roam freely—"

"Sorry to interrupt," the High Priest said. "I believe everything you are saying, even the part about the gemstones; but what do you mean when you say cows roam freely?"

"I mean cows in India run freely, without constraints or care."

"You mean before they're slaughtered?" the High Priest asked.

Elisheba leaned over to the scribe, instructing him to not write this down.

"No, we don't kill cows in India."

"Then what do you do with them?" the High Priest asked.

"We honor them. They're sacred."

"But surely you eat their meat. It's delicious. Much more so than mutton, fowl, or fish."

"No, we don't kill them."

"With all due respect, that makes no sense. Who decided that?"

"It was decided long ago, hundreds of years, maybe thousands of years before my time. I think it was a decree from Krishna. No, maybe it was Ganesha."

"And who is Ganesha?" the High Priest asked.

"A talking elephant. Well, not really a talking elephant, but a boy with an elephant head. You know, big ears, long trunk, wrinkly skin, and such."

"A talking what? I'll be damned. I thought Moses magically turning his staff into a serpent and Jonah living in the belly of a whale were clever, but this Ganesha fellow tops them both. Well done." The High Priest smiled, slapping his knee and shaking his head.

"Please, please, gentlemen," Jerome said, eager to turn the conversation away from sacred cows and talking elephants and back to the gifts. "Let's remember that we are here for the Son of God. There will be plenty of time for this type of chitchat later. Please resume the presentation of the gifts."

Caspar quickly opened and closed the silver box from his position at the foot of the manger, a distance that ensured the gathered crowd could only get a small glimpse of its golden content.

"A gift of gold ingots." Caspar handed the box to Jerome. "I'm sure you are aware of the value of gold. Keep this hidden. Don't open it until you're in a safe and secure place. There are vicious thieves in Bethlehem who would chop off your arms for that gold."

Balthazar, having drained two wineskins, fell into a pleasant sleep on Jude Aya's shoulder.

"My sight is as bad as my hearing, but from a distance, those looked like golden knucklebone pieces rather than gold ingots," the Keeper said. "Not very useful for a baby."

"I can assure you, whoever you are, old man," Caspar said to the Keeper, "those are the fucking finest goddamn gold ingots in all of India, extracted from a single gold vein in the hardest rocks in the highest peaks of the tallest mountains in all of India. A vein of gold so remote and so treacherous that no less than a hundred men died so I could bring this gift to the Son of God."

"Caspar, enough. Calm yourself," Melchior said. "You do yourself no favors with that language in the ears of God."

"Well worth it," Jerome said, "for the Son of God, of course. What are the lives of one hundred men compared to the glory of God?"

"Praise God," the High Priest added. "Caspar, you are truly a great and wise man. Your gift of gold is worthy of the Son of God and foretells of the gilded life you shall enjoy in the heavens one day. You have surely found favor with God."

"I'm sure," Joseph whispered to Mary, "the baby will find many uses for this as well."

"I heard that, carpenter. Watch your tongue," Elisheba said. "When you offend our guests, you offend me."

"Please," Jerome said, "someone wake Balthazar. It's his turn to present a gift to the Son of God."

Jude Aya shook Balthazar from his sleep and he stumbled from the bench, staggering to the spot where Melchior and Caspar had presented their gifts; but he faced the wrong direction, looking out into the stable at the ox and sheep instead of the assembled crowd. Melchior coughed and cleared his throat to help reorient his struggling friend. Balthazar, holding the silver box in both hands, turned one hundred eighty degrees to face his audience.

"I am Balth—"

"Yes, we all know who you are by now. Can we speed this up? This is going a bit long," the High Priest said, squirting wine on his robe as he tried to refill his cup.

"Balthazar," Mary said, "you do not need to present your gift. Please take whatever gift you've kindly brought and give it to the poor and those in need."

Jerome rose from his seat and raised his glass. "Spoken like God's humble servant. My dear Mary, it is clear why God has chosen you to be the virgin mother of his only Son. Always giving. Glory be to you. But Balthazar has been waiting long enough. We should let him continue."

Balthazar swaying, with one eye fully closed, and a strand of drool running down his chin, began, "I am Thalthzarab of Barabia." He paused, smiling. "One moment . . . I am Zalthabar of Arbabia . . . no, that's not it . . . I am Blalthazal, Blaltheral . . . closer . . . Balthazar, yes, I am Balthazar." He stopped, pleased he could finally pronounce his own name.

"And he is from Arabia," Melchior added.

Balthazar thanked Melchior and bowed before shifting his attention back to the others.

"I won't take the time to tell you about Arabia, but it's a wonderful place. Beeee-u-teef-ful." Balthazar teetered from side to side. "I'll just gift right to the get . . . I mean get right to the gift. A box of mrrrrrrh."

"I'm sorry, what?" Jerome asked.

"Mrrrrrrrrrryrrh, my lord."

"Murrmelord? Marmalade? I don't know what he's saying." Jerome turned to Melchior.

"Myrrh," Melchior said. "He is trying to say myrrh." Seeing the continued confusion in Jerome's expression, Melchior continued, "Myrrh. An oil used to anoint kings, priests, warriors, and holy men. The Son of God surely deserves to be anointed with the finest myrrh in the world."

"But is it valuable?" Jerome asked.

"Melchior, Balthazar," Elisheba said, "unlike my ignorant husband, I am familiar with myrrh. In fact, I'm the only woman in Bethlehem who the High Priest has anointed with myrrh. I'm aware of its value and agree that this is a worthy gift for the Son of God."

At this, Balthazar fumbled with the box, releasing its clasp, opening for all to see and inhale the essence of the ointment. He passed it slowly and unsteadily under the noses of those gathered. Each guest had the same reaction: pursed lips, wrinkled brow, and a hand politely and discreetly raised to the nose.

"My sense of smell is as bad as my sight, which is as bad as my hearing, but, at the risk of being crude, that smells like week-old ball sack sweat. Like groin rot," the Keeper said to no one in particular.

Elisheba grabbed the box from the drunken Wise Man's hands. She closed the lid and placed the box at Jerome's feet. "It is indeed a lovely gift, Balthazar, but we'll anoint the child later. No need to anoint him today."

"Melchior, Caspar, Balthazar, your gifts are magnificent. Melchior's and Caspar's more so than yours, Balthazar, but the Son of God will reward you for your generosity," Jerome said, then extended his hand toward Zacharia. "Paragus, please come forward and present your gift."

Zacharia stepped forward; his oversized pants draped in folds, flopping on the ground as he staggered to the foot of the manger, where the others had presented gifts. The red and yellow sash that Rachel borrowed from her father's wardrobe strained under the weight of the sagging material. Zacharia cleared his throat and lifted the gift box to chest level.

"Paragus," Jerome said, "your sense of style in accessories is impeccable. I have a sash just like that. I reserve it for only special occasions."

"There is a reason it looks familiar," Zacharia said and tugged on the sash.

"And why is that?"

"Because this is your sash. Rachel was good enough to lend it to me. Very generous of you, sir."

"First my finest wine, now my sash?" Jerome glared at Rachel, his tone rising with each word. "Is there anything else you removed from my house without my permission?"

Wanting to protect Rachel from her father's wrath, Zacharia untied the sash, his pants slipping to his ankles. He lifted each of his knees to fully step out of Paragus's baggy pants, leaving only a small white undergarment tightly wrapped around his groin, which left nothing to the imagination. Those gathered were aghast, except for Rachel, who smiled a simple smile, raised her eyebrows, and slowly nodded. Unfazed, Zacharia walked in his loincloth to Jerome, returned the sash, and walked back to the foot of the manger to begin his presentation of the Babylonian coins.

"I am Paragus of Perea."

"Are you quite sure?" Elisheba asked. "I was told Paragus was among the oldest of the Wise Men. You look rather youthful."

"Thank you, your highness. I have indeed aged well. You know, I get plenty of sleep, stay out of the sun, apply aloe on my face at night. I make a point of these things. Sometimes I put cucumber slices under my eyes, sometimes I don't. Keeps me young. You should try it, your highness," Zacharia said and turned to Rachel and winked.

Rachel returned the wink.

"Stop that, you two," Elisheba said and glared at Rachel and Zacharia. "This is no place for that type of behavior—in front of the Son of God. Disgraceful." Elisheba pressed on, "And I was told Paragus had grown quite fat in his old age. You're as skinny as a sapling."

"Diet, I suppose," responded Zacharia. "And exercise. I eat only fish and dates. Not always at the same time or in that order, and certainly there are other foods. I don't live on fish and dates alone; I eat pistachios and other things. A healthy diet makes a difference. And for exercise, every day I—"

"Enough," Jerome said, sending a sharp look to Elisheba. "Please, Paragus, continue with your gift; your diet, weight, and age are none of our concern."

Zacharia, rattled by Elisheba's questions and more aware of the fact that he was standing in his underwear among strangers, had completely forgotten the words he had heard Paragus repeat a thousand times before and that he rehearsed on the journey to Bethlehem. His mind was fuzzy, clouded by the cannabis and wine, so he improvised. "As I was saying," he began slowly, stalling for time, "I am Paragus of Perea. A land. Perea is indeed a land. A land . . . a land . . . filled with heart. And plenty of hope. A land where the wind comes sweeping down the plain. A land in which the waving wheat smells oh, so sweet—"

"There is not a speck of wheat in Perea," Elisheba said. "The climate is far too dry for wheat to grow."

"And I don't think there are plains in Perea," the High Priest said.

"He speaks in tongues," Balthazar said, trying to help Zacharia.

"Who is this man?" Elisheba leaned across the High Priest and whispered to Jerome.

"It's a good question, but not as important as what's in the silver box," Jerome replied.

"May I present to you," Zacharia said and placed both hands on the box, "gold coins from the ancient Babylonian Empire."

Jerome had heard rumors of rare gold Babylonian coins. Their worth was unimaginable. The prestige they would bring, unmeasurable. In the split second before Zacharia opened the box, Jerome imagined himself as a king, sitting on a gilded throne, ruling over a far-reaching kingdom.

Zacharia turned the box away from himself, toward the guests, and slowly opened it, displaying to all several tightly rolled joints. The silver box filled with priceless Babylonian gold coins remained mistakenly fastened to the saddle of the horse.

"These are the gold coins you speak of, Paragus?" Jerome said accusingly.

"What is this?" Elisheba asked, now convinced that this man, hardly a man, more like a boy, was not Paragus.

Zacharia turned the box so that he could see its contents for himself, now realizing his error. "This is a different kind of gold," Zacharia said, unsure of how to proceed, wishing he was back in the palace of Paragus sitting on a thick silk pillow on the floor, puffing away at a pipe, "the strongest herbs cultivated in the hills dotting the Perean countryside."

"This? For a baby? The Son of God?" The High Priest was incredulous.

"Enough! Remove this man and the foul things he brings!" Elisheba commanded two servants from the Temple as she pointed at Zacharia.

Melchior, Caspar, and Balthazar exchanged nervous glances.

The servants moved quickly, each grabbing one of Zacharia's arms.

"Wait!" Joseph rose, walking toward Zacharia. "It would be rude, and terrible manners, to not accept Paragus's gift. I shall take one as a gesture of goodwill."

"And Joseph, I also don't wish to be rude," Mary said, winking at Rachel. "I will take one or two, if it pleases Paragus."

As the two men removed Zacharia, Joseph pulled three joints from the box and thanked him.

"Strike this man and this incident from the record," Elisheba instructed the scribe. "There shall be no mention of Paragus, or whoever that boy was."

Melchior excused himself from the gathering and followed Zacharia as he was being led to his horse by the two brutish servants. When the servants left to return to their position behind the High Priest in the stable, Melchior stayed with Zacharia and the two whispered to one another briefly, each nodding in agreement as they looked back over their shoulders toward the stable.

Before Zacharia mounted his horse, he reached behind the saddle and handed Melchior a neatly folded bulky cloth, the cape of Paragus. Melchior looked at Zacharia with a sly smile and nodded. "Well done. I know exactly what to do with this," Melchior said as they embraced before Zacharia climbed into the saddle.

Zacharia waved to those who remained huddled around the manger as his horse walked out of the stable and onto the dusty roads of Bethlehem.

Melchior walked back to the head of the manger, where Mary and Joseph sat and ceremoniously bowed before them and the child before presenting them with the carefully folded cape. He leaned in and whispered to Mary to keep the cape folded until the others left, when she, Joseph, and the baby were alone.

"What did he say to Mary?" Jerome asked Elisheba and the High Priest.

"No idea," Elisheba said.

"Excuse me, Melchior," Jerome said. "We didn't hear what you said to our daughter."

"Nothing, really. Just an old Persian blessing."

"There is one more gift to be given," Jerome said and looked warily at Jude Aya. "Shall we get on with it?"

Jude Aya rose, nodding at Joseph and Mary and deeply bowing to the child who lay sleeping in the manger. Unlike the four Wise Men before him, he dressed in ragged clothes with the stains of sweat, dirt, food, oil, and shit. His hair was long and tangled, and his beard looked like it was trimmed using two rounded rocks.

"Come here," demanded Elisheba. "You don't look like a Wise Man. Our servants dress with more dignity. I sent invitations to the Wise Men of India, Arabia, Persia, Perea, and Judea. Are you telling me you're the Wise Man from Judea?"

"No, Madam."

"An imposter then!" The High Priest pointed a crooked finger at Jude Aya.

"No, High Priest, I'm not an imposter."

"Not a Wise Man from Judea and not an imposter," Jerome said. "Enough of your riddles. Tell us who you are and how you got that invitation, and move away from me. You stink like a filled shitpot."

"Ah, Jude Aya! Of course!" Joseph walked to the foot of the manger and embraced him. "I'm Joseph. Do you remember me? Yesterday, exchanging the shitpots. I was in the courtyard. We cleared them together."

Jude Aya recognized Joseph and returned his embrace.

"You know this man?" Jerome asked Joseph.

"Somehow, this doesn't surprise me," Elisheba said and looked at Jude Aya and Joseph with contempt.

"A shit slinger and a carpenter. Perfect," the High Priest said.

"Again, I will ask." Elisheba's inquisition continued. "Who are you, and why are you here?"

"Jude Aya is my given name. Weissman is my family name. I come from just around the corner, the Nakhleh slum." Jude Aya pointed toward his hovel. "I received this." He handed Jerome the invitation, and Jerome handed it to Elisheba. "I'm afraid I don't belong here. I'm not worthy to be in the presence of the Son of God."

"Find the messenger who delivered this and jail him," Elisheba said to the High Priest. "As for you," she said and turned her wrath toward Jude Aya, "you must go. You are filthy and not fit to present gifts to the beasts in this barnyard let alone the Son of God!"

Jude Aya turned, shoulders hunched, to walk away.

"No, Jude Aya, you are welcome to stay." Mary pointed to the empty straw mat next to Joseph and the Keeper. "Please, sit by us."

"But isn't that where Rachel was sitting?" asked Jude Aya.

"Where is Rachel?" Elisheba stood and quickly surveyed the stable.

"Has anyone seen Rachel?" asked Jerome, more annoyed than concerned.

"I haven't seen her since Paragus—" the High Priest was saying.

"Put that out of your mind. She would never have the resolve to do what you were about to suggest. She, unlike her younger sister, respects her parents' words," Jerome said. "Let's get back to the gifts."

"Thank you, Mary," Jude Aya said and settled in the small pile of hay beside Joseph. "You and Joseph have shown me much kindness. And, if I may, I have a humble gift for your lovely child. It isn't as grand or valuable as those presented by the Wise Men, but I would be pleased if you accepted it." He handed Mary a bundle of linens he had neatly folded and tied with string.

"Stop! Mary, don't touch that!" Elisheba shouted. "You don't know where that has been or what's wrapped inside."

"Undoubtedly lice or mice," said the High Priest.

"Or some peasant plague," Jerome added.

"Stop, all of you," Mary said with what little strength she had. "Joseph and I will gladly receive this gift."

Nodding to Jude Aya, Mary took the bundle and untied the string, which held thick, neatly folded linens. "Thank you, Jude Aya. It's perfect," she said.

"What in God's name is it?" asked Jerome.

"Swaddling clothes." Jude Aya bowed his head to Mary.

"What the fuck are swaddling clothes?" Caspar turned to Jude Aya.

"They're used to wrap the child in, to keep him warm, and . . . " Jude Aya became uncomfortable. "You need many of them as babies are prone to, well, soil their clothes."

"Soil their clothes?" cried Elisheba, the volume raising with each word. "This is the Son of God, for God's sake! Do you think the Son of God has any need to soil his clothes?"

"I haven't really considered it, but I assumed that because he's a baby—"

"Blasphemous poison from the mouth of an ignorant peasant. Are you implying that God shits too?" accused the High Priest.

"No. Well, I don't know," Jude Aya said, growing more uncomfortable. "I mean, I suppose it could be possible."

"You *suppose* it could be possible?" the High Priest mocked Jude Aya.

"Theoretically," Balthazar said, tired of the High Priest's arrogance, "it could be true."

"It could explain where the Sadducees came from," Caspar said.

"No more of this talk." Elisheba pointed at Jude Aya. "You blaspheme God and the Son of God by suggesting that He would soil clothes. Sacrilege."

"Mother, unless you shit your gown," Mary said as she picked up the baby and gently swung his bottom close to Elisheba's nose, "judging by the smell from the manger, we'll have a need for swaddling clothes. And lots of them."

CHAPTER 25

The Fifth Letter from the Corinthians

Dear Joseph the Carpenter,

We are ruined. They are gone. All of them. We tied them to the fence, but apparently the Arabians are more powerful than the pitiful fence you built. I don't mean to be harsh, but in hindsight, the stable and fence you built were less sturdy than you promised and far from what we expected. We tied the mighty beasts to the fence posts, but one reared and bucked in defiance, and the others, watching closely, all began to rear and buck and kick and stomp and convulse. Their strength and weight brought down the entire fence like a pile of kindling sticks. The Arabians, and with them, our wealth, have scattered to the wind. We have reached the end of our rope. We don't know what to do. Seven generations of the Corinthian family have raised the finest Arabian horses in all of Galilee, and now that is all gone. And little Junia isn't as concerned about the horses as she is with what happened to the blind carpenter. I could scream! We are very disappointed in you, Joseph. I am not one to hold a grudge nor am I one to overreact to life's little challenges, *but I must conclude this letter with two firm messages. First, wherever you have wandered, and whomever you are with, if you see a pack of Arabian horses with a CA branded on their hinds, please return them to us with haste. Second, you're fired.*

Yours fondly,
Aaron Corinthian

CHAPTER 26

Baby Names and Divine Designations

DAY 1, AD

After the morning's presentation of the gifts, the various factions split to regroup and replenish. The High Priest and Jerome took refuge in the tavern next door, where they drank with the shepherds who were staying at the inn. Joseph stayed close to the manger while Mary fed the baby alongside him. There, they planned how and when to escape her parents in Bethlehem to return to the peace of Nazareth. Mary's desire to leave Bethlehem, and all its chaos, outweighed her concern over her frail condition. Elisheba stood outside the stable instructing the scribe what to write, often ripping the scroll and the quill from the cowering scribe's hand and writing the narrative herself.

The Keeper, with the little money he had, lumbered to the market stalls and bought cheese, dates, grapes, almonds, olives, and dried herbs for his guests. When he returned, he boiled a large vat of water over an open flame in the courtyard's corner and made herbal tea. Jude Aya, never one to sit still, cleaned the stalls and removed the urine-soaked hay, replacing it with a fresh bale.

Balthazar, Caspar, and Melchior joined the Keeper in the courtyard, finding refuge under the olive tree's intermittent shade, which shifted with the breeze. They rolled out their silk blankets, fluffed their feather pillows, and spent the early afternoon under the tree, taking turns puffing away at one of Zacharia's joints. They were each transfixed by the motion of the slender silver olive leaves waving against the azure sky. Theirs was a heavy, hazy silence, broken only by Balthazar's repeated refrain of "Who are these people?" and Caspar's question "What the fuck are we doing here?"

One by one, group by group, as the late afternoon sun threw long shadows across Bethlehem, the guests returned, each taking the same place they had earlier in the day.

"May I ask the child's name?" Melchior placed his hand on the baby's forehead.

"Of course," Mary said, "but we've not named him yet. We'd planned on a girl. Abigaia was to be her name."

"A lovely name," Melchior replied. "It means *my father's joy*. Well chosen, a perfect name for your next."

"But for a boy we're considering Joseph, after the fath—"

"Impossible," Elisheba interrupted. "Your son, God's Son, shall be named *Immanuel*. It's in Isaiah's prophecy." Elisheba grabbed the papyrus scroll from the unsteady hand of the High Priest and read, *"'Behold, a virgin shall conceive, and bear a son, and shall call his name Immanuel.'* There can be no discussion. Immanuel it must be."

"No, it mustn't." Mary fixed her eyes on her mother's eyes, and neither relented.

"Here we go again," Balthazar whispered to Caspar.

"I've got two silver shekels that Mary wins this one," Caspar said.

"It's a bet." Balthazar dug two shekels from the folds of his robe.

"Are there any other prophecies that mention the name of the Son of God?" Caspar asked.

"No," Elisheba said, "only Isaiah. And the only name is Immanuel."

"We still prefer Joseph," said Joseph. "The name has served me well."

"Mary, Mary," the High Priest burped out the last Mary. "You can't name the Son of God *Joseph*. It's absurd. Think about it. It will be shortened to Joe. It may well suit the traveling carpenter, but it is no name for God's Son. Can you imagine? *Joe, Lamb of God.* Immanuel is the name intended for God's Son. Your mother's right. God relayed it to Isaiah himself."

"Hold it," Caspar said, his eyes barely more than slits, his speech slowed by the cannabis. "Did you say *Lamb of God?* What the fuck does that even mean, *Lamb of God?*"

"It is important that the Son of God have titles," the High Priest said. "And, of course, you need titles that are fit for the Son of God." The High Priest lifted a long piece of papyrus from a pocket deep within the many folds of his wine-spattered robe. "So, I've written a list of potential titles, and the *Lamb of God* is one."

"A lamb seems like an odd thing to call the Son of God," Caspar said.

"On this, I agree with Caspar," Balthazar said, re-entering the fray sensing the potential for mischief. "Wouldn't you want the animal to be something that people fear and revere? Something more like a tiger, cheetah, or—"

"A hippo-fucking-potumus," Caspar said. "You should consider a hippo."

"I do love how their little ears wiggle on top of their big round heads," the High Priest said and gestured on top of his head with each of his forefingers, which earned him a sharp look and a hard jab from Elisheba.

"I love how their ears wiggle too," said Caspar. "Fucking adorable."

"I've never seen a hippo," Jude Aya said.

"Once," Balthazar began, "as a child, I was on the banks of the Euphrates with my father. Across the river was a group of three, maybe four men bathing, splashing, and cooling off from the afternoon sun—"

"Where are you going with this, Balthazar?" Elisheba was growing impatient with the Wise Men.

"I'm getting there. These interruptions slow me down, but I'm getting there. Now, where was I?"

"The banks of the Euphrates with your father," Melchior said, not sure what Balthazar was trying to say but eager to find out.

"Thank you, my friend. So, the men were bathing, splashing about, enjoying each other's company, and engrossed in their conversation. They didn't see a hippopotamus a short distance away, fully submerged in the water except for its eyes and those little ears—"

"Were they wiggling?" Caspar asked.

"Was what wiggling?"

"The ears of the fucking hippopotamus."

"Caspar," scolded Melchior, "refrain from swearing. We're with Mary and her child. There is no need for that kind of language."

"And please finish the story quickly," Elisheba said. "I still don't see how this is at all relevant."

"Yes, the hippo's ears were wiggling. In fact, they were wiggling just before it charged out of the water, with speed I could have never imagined, and trampled over the bathing men one by one. But that's not the worst part. It crushed their bodies. Thoroughly. Completely flattening their skulls, their blood flowing into the river. Buzzards made a feast of them."

"Now that's a powerful animal. Certainly worthy as a title for the Son of God," said Caspar. "A lamb couldn't do that!"

"You may have a point," said the High Priest, "but I don't think that a skull-crushing hippopotamus is the animal we want to associate with the Son of God."

"Quiet! Stop this. The discussion of animals is not important. What is important is the name of the Son of God, and his name, as prophesied, shall be Immanuel," Elisheba said as her green eyes intensely fixed on Mary. "Mary, my daughter, this is not my choice. It is not your choice. It is God's choice."

"Immanuel is a fine name, Mother. It's just not his," Mary said, nodding to the sleeping baby.

Uncomfortable with the tension between mother and daughter, Jude Aya spoke. "May I offer an alternative?"

"So, now we're getting advice from the shit slinger," Jerome said to Elisheba and the High Priest. "Let's ignore the great prophets. Let's ignore the High Priest. Let's ignore the grandparents and listen to an ignorant shit slinger."

"Please, Jude Aya, ignore my father. He knows not what he says. Go on."

"I think the High Priest has a point about the name Joseph. It will be shortened to Joe, a suitable name for the honorable carpenter but maybe not fitting for the Son of God."

The High Priest and Elisheba nodded in approval, surprised by the insightful wisdom of the shit slinger.

"But," Jude Aya continued, "Immanuel may not be right either."

"Blasphemer!" Elisheba pointed her finger at Jude Aya.

"You betray the Word of God as spoken through the prophets," the High Priest said.

"I have a friend named Immanuel," Caspar said. "Not really a friend, just a guy I kind of know. More of an acquaintance. He's actually kind of a dick. Nobody really likes him. Everyone calls him Manny."

"This was going to be my point, Caspar. Thank you," Jude Aya said. "Use caution with any name that can be shortened. People are lazy. They take shortcuts. Joseph becomes Joe. Immanuel becomes Manny."

"This is wrong, Mary. We must fulfill the prophecy," Elisheba pleaded.

"What do you suggest, Jude Aya?" Mary asked.

"May I suggest," Jude Aya took a deep breath, "Jesus?"

The Keeper, who had difficulty following the discussion from the beginning, asked, "Did you say Cheeses?"

"Yes, Jesus."

"Cheeses," repeated the Keeper, looking into the eyes of Mary and Joseph. "This is none of my business. I am but a humble keeper of a humble inn. I am here only to serve and care for you. The minds of these Wise Men are sharper, much more learned than mine, but I don't understand why you would want to name any child after a foul-smelling chunk of coagulated milk."

"I, I'm not sure I understand your point." Mary placed her hand on the Keeper's knee. "*Jesus* is what Jude Aya suggested. I don't understand the reference to milk."

"All cheeses are, more or less, coagulated milk."

"Wait," Joseph said and turned to the Keeper, finally understanding the confusion. "The name is Jesus, with a *J*." Joseph repeated, this time pointing to his lips as he pronounced the name slowly for the Keeper to hear, "Jesus with a *J*."

"Forgive me," the Keeper said and shook his head. He leaned in closer to the child. "That is indeed a fine name. It's the one my mother gave me over one hundred years ago."

"Your name is Jesus?" Mary asked.

"It is, but it's been so long since anyone called my name that I had almost forgotten."

"Then it's settled," Mary said. "Our baby shall be named Jesus."

Joseph nodded in support.

"I thought he was saying *cheeses* too," Balthazar said to Mary and Joseph. "You'll need to enunciate more clearly, or people will think God sent a piece of goat cheese to cleanse the world of its sins."

"No, Mary, this can't be. This discussion isn't over." Elisheba glared at Mary.

"The discussion *is* over, Mother. His name is Jesus."

Sensing the naming battle was lost and eager to move on to titles, the High Priest took the opening. "Now, we shall discuss the titles I have composed to bestow upon the divine child born of God."

"That's nonsense," Mary said. "He is beautiful and precious, but he is not a divine child."

"It is not nonsense. It must be done. All kings must have titles," insisted the High Priest.

"It's only fitting," Melchior agreed.

"We won't take part in this madness. You can talk all you want, but Joseph and I will not be here to listen." Mary tried unsuccessfully to get up from her seat on the straw floor, but she was too weak. Joseph stood, placed his arms under each of Mary's arms, and lifted her. Once he was sure Mary was steady, he knelt to take the sleeping baby from the manger.

"Stop, carpenter, the child is sleeping. I'm the child's grandmother. You take your walk; the child will be safe here. You two go on."

Mary nodded to Joseph. Her mother was many things that Mary found disagreeable, but she knew her mother would care for the child, particularly a child she believed to be the Son of God. With Joseph and the Keeper by her side and Jude Aya following closely behind, Mary gingerly left the stable and entered the courtyard, where Joseph lowered Mary onto a bench while the Keeper and Jude Aya fetched tea.

Melchior joined the High Priest and Elisheba at the foot of the manger. "The world has been waiting for this," Melchior said, gazing at Jesus. "The Son of God. Our Savior."

The High Priest and Elisheba nodded in agreement. Balthazar and Caspar staggered over to the small group gathered around the manger. Jerome lay in the fetal position on the bench, soundly sleeping, resting his head on a stack of empty wineskins he had fashioned into a pillow.

"That mark," Caspar said and pointed to the small patch of red under the baby's ear, "looks exactly like a miniature version of the one Joseph the carpenter has."

Elisheba and the High Priest looked at one another; the High Priest moved directly between Caspar and the manger, blocking the Wise Man's view.

"God Himself," said the High Priest, gesturing to the heavens, "plays tricks. Tests us. Even with his own Son, our Savior. I don't know what you were implying, but make no mistake, this child is the Son of God. Mary is indeed a virgin, and the carpenter is merely, well, a carpenter who has a donkey and a reason to be in Bethlehem."

"There is no doubt," said Melchior. "I believe. We believe."

"When will he do something?" Balthazar asked. "Something godlike?"

"He was just born, Balthazar," Melchior chided his stoned friend. "We can't ask too much of a little baby now, can we?"

"It's not written in the prophecy," the High Priest explained. "The prophecies of Isaiah and Micah foretold only of his birth."

"But why does he just lie there?" Balthazar poked gently at Jesus's left foot. "Shouldn't he do something as God would want?"

"Like what exactly?" asked Elisheba.

"I don't know. Are there miracles to perform, any seas to part?" Balthazar asked.

"He is not a circus performer," the High Priest said.

"He is the Son of God, and only God knows," Elisheba said, her utter disappointment in the Wise Men, except for Melchior, now complete. "God has his plans. This is not for us to consider."

"But, my friends, what is ours to consider," said the High Priest in an eager and cheerful tone, "are the titles fit for the Son of God. I'll share a few." He again referenced his long sheet of papyrus. "I have divided the titles into two types—those that elicit respect through power and fear and those that evoke goodness, peace, and gentleness."

"But let's not start with the *Lamb of God*. I think we all agree that it is a terrible place to start," Caspar said.

"Fine," the High Priest said. "Then, to evoke how essential the Son of God is to our daily lives here on Earth, I have the *Bread of Life*."

"Fuck off. Really? Equally terrible, actually worse, than the *Lamb of God*," Caspar said.

"I have a sister who can't digest bread," added Balthazar. "When she eats it, she bloats up, feels terrible, has gas that smells worse than a camel's ass. I agree with Caspar, the *Bread of Life* is out. What else?"

"If you don't like my suggestions, let's turn to Isaiah. He spoke of multiple titles for the Son of God," the High Priest continued undeterred. "He said, '*unto us a child is born, unto us a son is given . . . and his name shall be called Wonderful, Counsellor, The mighty*

God, The everlasting Father, The Prince of Peace.'"

"Again, terrible," Caspar said. "Ganesha, the talking elephant boy, could make up better titles. I'm not at all impressed by this Isaiah fellow."

"*Prince of Peace* is my favorite," said the High Priest.

"I like it," Melchior said and nodded enthusiastically. "Very suitable for the Son of God. An exquisite title."

"It's okay," Elisheba said.

"Are you saying Prints or Prince?" asked Balthazar.

"I'm not clear what you're asking," replied the High Priest. "I don't hear any difference between the two."

"Exactly my point. *Prince* as a king, queen and prince or *prints* as a scrivener, scribe?"

"*Prince*, as king, queen, and prince, of course. A silly question."

"And *peace* as in the opposite of war or *peas* like the little green round vegetable?"

"Great Wise Man," the High Priest cautioned, "you are perilously close to blaspheming the Son of God on his first day on Earth. Be careful where you tread, my good man."

"So, which is it?"

"Peace, as in the opposite of war."

"Better. That could work. *Prince of Peace* is certainly better than *Prints of Peas.*"

Jude Aya, wanting to give Mary and Joseph time alone, walked in from the courtyard and sidled up to the informal title committee by the manger.

"May I join?"

Melchior, Caspar, and Balthazar answered affirmatively at the same time Elisheba and the High Priest answered negatively. Jude Aya stayed.

"What is it you're trying to decide?"

"Titles to bestow upon the Son of God," said Melchior.

"Why?"

"To emphasize that, you know, he is the Son of God," the High Priest said, second-guessing himself as he spoke.

"Yours is not to ask questions, shit slinger. You are only here because of my daughter's stubborn insistence," Elisheba said, still smoldering over the baby's name.

Jerome awakened from his wine-induced slumber and staggered to join the others at the foot of the manger. "Any titles that strike fear or respect and exude power are best. It's better to be feared and respected than it is to be loved."

"I have a few of those, yes. Would you like to hear them?" the High Priest asked Jerome and Elisheba.

"Please," said Elisheba.

"The Almighty, The Almighty Warrior, King Almighty."

"I'm not sure I see that in this mild, sleeping baby. Those don't fit," Melchior said. "I rather like the *Prince of Peace*."

"It's a good start. What else do you have?" Jerome asked, searching for a filled wineskin but finding only empty ones scattered in the straw.

"This next set is inspired by Moses smiting the Egyptians. They exude both power and fear. *The Prince of Smite, The Smiter of Evil, Smite Lord, The Almighty Smiter*."

"Much better," Jerome endorsed enthusiastically.

"What about the *Smitten Lord*?" asked Balthazar.

"Smitten?" asked the High Priest.

"Yes. Smitten."

"Doesn't that mean *to be in love*?" Elisheba said.

"I thought smite means *to strike down mightily* like a great warrior," said Caspar.

"That is indeed what smite means," confirmed the High Priest.

"Then why wouldn't smitten mean roughly the same thing?" Balthazar asked.

The group thought silently for a moment.

"I'm not sure," the High Priest said.

"It's a good question," Caspar agreed.

"But because it doesn't mean the same thing," Elisheba said definitively, "we can consider smite, but we should strike smitten."

"I'll go back to the *Lamb of God*," said Jude Aya. "That has a certain appeal. I think mothers would like that."

"But fathers would prefer something with *smite, warrior,* or *almighty* in the title," Jerome said.

"Perhaps instead of trying to choose a title, we eliminate the worst choices," Balthazar said.

"Or we could each vote for our favorite, and the title that collects the most votes wins," Caspar suggested.

"This isn't a democracy," Elisheba said. "Not everyone gets a vote, and not all votes are equal."

"That sounds like some democracies," Balthazar said.

"There is no reason we should settle on just one title," the High Priest reminded the assembled committee. "We should adorn him with as many titles as we see fit."

"Did you consider *Christ*?" asked Jude Aya.

"Consider it for what, shit slinger?" Jerome asked.

"As a title for the Son of God, for Baby Jesus."

"Ridiculous. It's not on my list." The High Priest waved the piece of papyrus in front of Jude Aya's face. "What does it even mean?"

"It's derived from the Greek word meaning *the anointed one.*"

"How does an impoverished, putrid shit slinger know anything of the Greek language?" Jerome asked.

"It won't do. The Greeks are a decadent and faithless people. An empire that has fallen and remains deeply in ruin. I don't like it," Elisheba said and paced with her arms crossed and her head down.

"Ever since the Greeks banished Draco and his enlightened laws," Jerome said, "they've descended into a weak and worthless society. They are the past, not the future. There is no reason to look to Greece for inspiration."

"*Christ,*" Melchior tested the sound to his ear and to his tongue. "It's not bad, though."

"It's the best of a bad lot," agreed Caspar.

"*Christ,*" Melchior repeated. "I rather like it."

"It's awful," Elisheba argued. "How would it be used as a title?"

"You could say the *Christ Child* or *Jesus Christ*," said Jude Aya.

"*Jesus Christ?*" cried Elisheba. "That's no title for the Son of God. *Jesus Christ?* That hardly rolls off the tongue."

"Uninspiring," added Jerome. "*Jesus Christ?* It strikes neither fear nor respect. It won't do."

"*Jesus Christ,*" the High Priest said the name and title slowly, listening to himself as he spoke. "*Jesus Christ.* I have to say, I'm warming to it. It could work nicely. *Jesus Christ.* Yes, it has a ring to it, and its meaning, *the anointed one,* is perfect."

"*Jesus Christ,*" Elisheba said, testing the sound of the title one more time. "It doesn't sound like a title; it sounds more like a last name. People will think *Christ* is his last name."

"They'll think he's from the *Christ* family," Jerome agreed.

"*Jesus Christ.* It's confusing," Elisheba said. "It won't do, and that's final."

"But—" Jude Aya began.

"Silence." Elisheba's patience with the peasant had worn out. She moved in front of him, her nose nearly touching his. "You have opposed me every step of the way. It's not enough that you've named my grandson, now you're bestowing titles upon him. You, a slinger of shit. I have had enough of you. Your influence over Mary and the carpenter is unwelcome. You leave immediately, or I will press charges and have you jailed."

"On what grounds?" Jude Aya asked.

"Grounds?" Jerome stepped in. "You think there needs to be grounds when a person of my stature demands that a person of your stature be thrown into a prison? You may know a few fancy Greek words, shit slinger, but you are woefully ignorant about how things work in Bethlehem."

Elisheba continued, spraying Jude Aya's face with spittle. "Go. Now. And, like I did with Paragus, I will ensure that you are stricken from the records, your presence erased. Be gone from my sight, from this pathetic stable, and return to the poverty-stricken, filthy hovel from which you oozed."

Jude Aya bowed reverently to Baby Jesus, who still lay sleeping in the manger. Walking with his chin up, he strode through the same stable gate from which Zacharia had also departed.

Jerome gently grabbed Elisheba's shoulder and led her away to a corner of the stable where he argued that leaving the story to only three Wise Men instead of five would diminish the grandeur, the magnificence of the birth. He advocated for including each of the five, but in the end, as it was in most cases, Elisheba's point of view prevailed.

As the crowd departed from the stable, scattering in all directions, Mary and Joseph returned to the manger. Jesus lay sleeping in peace. Out of the watchful eye of Mary's parents, Joseph and Mary returned to finalizing the details of their escape from Bethlehem. As they packed their ragged belongings, Mary lifted Paragus's heavy, carefully folded cape, which Melchior had presented earlier in the day. In the solitude and stillness of this moment, Mary found, deep in the cape's folds, a silver box containing the gold Babylonian coins.

CHAPTER 27

Pa Rum Pa Pum Pum

DAY 2, AD

The first of them came in the early morning, while the moon was still bright and the sun had not yet made its way to the eastern horizon. They were an elderly couple who had heard the news of the virgin birth of the Son of God from a neighbor, who had heard from their cousin, who had heard from two women excitedly talking in Bethlehem's market square. Next was a family of eight, all of whom frequented the Temple in which the High Priest gave his regular sermons. They had heard from a Temple servant, a reliable and trustworthy teen, who the High Priest used as a local messenger to spread news. They were followed by a devout local silk merchant, a smattering of curious shepherds, skeptical civic leaders who wanted to understand what the gossip was about, and bored villagers looking for something, anything, to add interest to their otherwise pedestrian days.

Bethlehem was a small village, and word of a mysterious virgin birth of a child who was said to be the Son of God spread wide and fast and with varying degrees of detail. By the time the morning sun rose over the low-lying honey-colored clay and mud homes of Bethlehem, two hundred people had quietly gathered within the rickety fence of the Keeper's stable to glance at the infant and his virgin mother.

The Keeper, who had anticipated and attended to every need of Joseph, Mary, and Jesus, sat on an uneven stool in the courtyard, preparing unleavened flatbread over the embers of the previous night's fire and boiling tea water over a separate flame he lit just before dawn. Melchior, Caspar, and Balthazar were waking from a night of sound sleep on their cushioned pillows, having slept in the same clothes they had arrived in the day before—the rich, clean elegance of their garments now looking crumpled, disheveled, and dusty.

Joseph, who had enjoyed a deep sleep, woke to find Mary seated on a blanket on top of a pile of straw, with Jesus quietly slurping breakfast from Mary's breast. Joseph stretched his arms and yawned and for the first time realized that hundreds of people and a smattering of animals, including an ox, camels, sheep, and a dusty, rust-colored cat with matted fur and ribs that stuck out like fence posts, had gathered in the stable.

"What is this? Who are these people?" Joseph kissed the top of Mary's head so as not to disturb Jesus.

"I don't know. They began to arrive some time ago and continue to trickle in. They're just sitting there," Mary said, "not saying a word, just staring at me and Jesus. I don't like it."

"You've had little sleep?"

"Very little, but I'm okay. Jesus is hungry, fussing all morning. He has your appetite." Mary stretched out her hand for Joseph to hold.

Joseph again surveyed the crowd, which continued to grow. "I don't like the looks of this. Your mother and father's doing?"

Mary shrugged. "Maybe. We need to get out of Bethlehem. Between yesterday's circus and how this day is starting, we can't stay."

The Keeper made his way from the courtyard to Mary and Joseph, carrying the flatbread, two tarnished copper kettles, and a tray of clay cups. The Wise Men followed closely behind. After them came the unholy triumvirate of Elisheba, Jerome, and the High Priest. They had spent a late-night drinking wine and scheming how to orchestrate the events of the coming day.

"We've eaten. We won't need any of that tasteless tea," Jerome said with an upturned nose, "or that dry, tasteless wafer you call bread. God, I hope it's for the animals. It looks horrible."

"Piss and vinegar, even this early in the morning," Mary said.

"Watch your tongue, my daughter."

"I was just going to say the same to you, my father."

"Elisheba, Jerome, look. Just as I told you," the High Priest said excitedly, pointing to the gathered crowd, "they have arrived!"

"This is your doing?" Joseph said, sitting close to Mary, his protective instincts heightened whenever the triumvirate was nearby.

"This is God's doing, carpenter. When will you understand? It's God's will. I simply foretold that crowds would gather."

The triumvirate and the Wise Men took their place on the same long bench they had sat on the day before. Continuing to feed Jesus, Mary sat with Joseph and the Keeper on the opposite side on loose piles of straw covered with the inn's ragged and worn blankets.

Elisheba walked to the end of the manger closest to the open part of the stable, the same spot where the Wise Men had presented their gifts. Instead of facing Mary and Joseph, she turned and slowly scanned the crowd. A smile came across her face, the morning sun making her green eyes sparkle. She took three long strides toward the crowd.

"Behold!" she shouted, raising her outstretched arms toward the heavens, drawing the attention of the people away from Mary and Joseph and their baby.

Mary, still weakened from the travel and her long labor, rose slowly from her seat. Still holding Jesus, she walked with short, slow, wary steps to Elisheba and pulled her mother's arm down from its raised position. "Mother, stop. What are you doing?" Mary whispered.

The crowd was silent and still. They had been waiting for this moment.

Elisheba took Mary's hand and raised it over her head toward the heavens. "Behold, people of Bethlehem, for this is Mary, a virgin, who has given birth to the Son of God. Rejoice, for he is born to be your Savior and our King, and we shall call him Immanuel."

"Jesus!" Mary shouted to the crowd, jerking her hand out of her mother's tight grip. "His name is Jesus. And he is not—"

The High Priest grabbed Mary's shoulders, ushering her to her straw-filled blanket by the manger. Joseph wrapped Mary and Jesus in his protective arms.

"And he is not what?" yelled one who was among the crowd.

"Yeah, what isn't he?" another joined in.

"And he is not," Jerome, standing next to Elisheba, shouted back, "and he is not . . . he is not . . . at all opposed to accepting gifts on behalf of God."

"What kind of gifts?" the question came from the back of the crowd.

"All kinds," Jerome shouted. "Gifts that are suitable for the Son of God Himself. But also, perhaps, suitable for his family as well, including grandparents—particularly the grandparents."

"What's an example?" asked yet another member of the crowd, whose numbers continued to grow.

"Well," shouted the High Priest, who had joined Elisheba and Jerome in front of the gathering, never wanting to miss an opportunity to speak. With a sweeping gesture of his right hand, using the sleeve of his blue robe to accentuate his words, he pointed to the three Wise Men, who were quietly healing their hangovers with freshly brewed tea. "These three Wise Men—Caspar of India, Melchior of Persia, and Balthazar of, of, um . . . "

"Arabia," Balthazar said, just loud enough for the High Priest to hear.

"Dumb fuck," Caspar whispered.

"Me or him?" Balthazar asked but didn't really care.

"Him."

"Yes, Balthazar of Arabia," the High Priest said and returned his attention to the crowd. "These three Wise Men brought gifts of gold, frankincense, and myrrh."

"What's myrrh?" The question came anonymously from the crowd.

"Why doesn't anyone know anything about myrrh?" Balthazar complained to Melchior and Caspar.

"Because it's a shit gift," Caspar replied, the steam from his tea warming his face.

"Does he need swaddling clothes?" shouted another from the crowd.

"No, emphatically no. No swaddling clothes," Jerome answered.

"What about a nice hat?" another shouted.

"What would a baby do with a hat?" Elisheba shouted back condescendingly.

"What would a baby do with myrrh?" an equally condescending member of the crowd shouted in return.

"I've forgotten how unsavory peasants can be," the High Priest whispered. Jerome and Elisheba nodded in agreement.

"What about a toothbrush?" The questions came from seemingly everyone who had gathered.

"A toothbrush?" Jerome was losing his patience. "He is one-day old, you idiot; babies are not born with teeth."

"He's the Son of God, isn't he?"

"Yes, he's the Son of God," the High Priest said, lending the weight of his authority to the answer.

"God has a full head of hair. I'm sure of it," someone in the crowd said. "And likely teeth. Why wouldn't His Son?"

"Because he's just a day old. A baby," Jerome said.

"What's his name?" The questions continued to pour in.

"This is Jerome." The High Priest put his hand on Jerome's shoulder.

"No, you imbecile. What's the baby's name?" The crowd grew bolder, slightly hostile.

"Jesus, the Son of God," Jerome answered.

"The Christ Child," the High Priest added, eager to test the title that the committee had settled on. "Jesus Christ."

"Is Christ his last name?"

"I told you that was a bad title," Elisheba said, elbowing the High Priest.

"It's not his last name," the High Priest said, now exasperated. "It's his title. It's Greek."

"Is the baby Greek?"

"No, of course not. He was born here, in Bethlehem."

"Then why does he have a Greek last name?"

"For God's sake. It's not his last name. It's his title," the High Priest shouted back, then turned toward a servant and signaled for wine. Jerome commanded the servant to make it two.

"Why did you stick him in a food trough?"

"Yeah, why did you put him there? Isn't that for animals?"

"The Son of God should have a proper bed."

The crowd was becoming angry.

"What kind of grandparents are you?"

As the crowd continued to bombard the triumvirate with questions, Jude Aya entered the stable and wound his way through the masses, being careful not to step on the toes of those who had gathered. Four scruffy, forlorn youths followed him, each carrying a musical instrument and dressed in rags like Jude Aya. The drummer, first in line behind Jude Aya, pounded out an uneven marching beat on the small drum that hung around her neck. Their entrance silenced the din of the crowd, except for a young man who was sound asleep, snoring with such ferocity that the quieted horde could hear his guttural inhaling and exhaling in between each erratic drumbeat.

"Jude Aya!" Mary cried out, cradling Jesus in her arms. "You're a welcome sight. Who have you brought with you?"

"Mary and Joseph," Jude Aya spoke with pride, "these are young minstrels from my neighborhood. I thought their music might brighten your day."

"Did they come bearing gifts better than swaddling clothes?" Jerome asked, disgusted by the four peasant children who trailed Jude

Aya. Elisheba and the High Priest stood crossarmed with unwelcoming scowls. Next to them sat the Wise Men, who continued to nurse their hangovers drinking hot tea and rubbing their pounding temples, attempting to ease the pain that grew with every beat of the drum.

"They have no money for gifts, sir. These children come from poor families, like my own."

"Their music shall be their gift!" Mary said. "And we shall treasure it more than any material gift."

Jerome rolled his eyes.

"Please," Mary addressed the four young minstrels, "do us the great honor of playing for us."

The crowd, which now swelled to more than three hundred, made room for the minstrels to play. Mary, with Jesus fussing quietly in her arms, sat with Joseph. The triumvirate sat on the long bench where they spent much of yesterday, looking completely disinterested in anything having to do with Jude Aya.

"Have you ever seen a more pathetic sight? These urchins," Elisheba said with an upturned lip and dismissive wave of her bejeweled hand.

"I want to get their names in case they try to steal something," Jerome added.

"Please play," encouraged Mary.

"But," Jerome said and stood, only slightly taller than the oldest minstrel, "first introduce yourselves, urchins."

The youngest and slightest of the group, a barefoot boy with dirt-stained, ragged red shorts and a worn-out fleece vest, stepped forward. His unkempt hair covered his left eye.

"I'm Ezekiel Drumher, sir."

"And do you have brothers or sisters, boy?" Jerome barked.

"Yes, sir."

"Don't be shy, boy. What are their names?" Jerome continued, a prosecutor cross-examining the accused.

"Abraham is my brother, and Sarah is my sister, sir."

"Older or younger?"

"Sarah is the oldest. In the middle is Abraham, and I am the youngest."

"I see," Jerome said, peering from over his wine cup with his small sunken eyes, "so you are the little Drumher boy?"

"That's right, sir."

"And what instrument do you play, my son?" Melchior asked in a kind, fatherly voice, wanting to break the tension from Jerome's inquisition.

"I don't play an instrument, sir. I sing."

"But then," the Keeper asked with keen interest, "why do you call yourself the little drummer boy?"

"The Keeper has a point," Caspar said, holding his head between his hands. "If you're the little drummer boy who sings, then who plays the drums?"

"The eldest Singer girl," replied Ezekiel.

"Are you fooling with us, boy?" Jerome said menacingly.

"No, sir," said the leader of the minstrels, a girl of eleven or twelve. "I am Alma Singer, the eldest girl in the Singer family. I am the Singer who plays the drums." Alma stepped forward and gave a quick drumroll, which only intensified the pain in Caspar's head.

"This is nonsense." Jerome was in no mood for games. "A group of minstrels where the drummer sings and the singer plays the drums? Is this some sort of trick, shit slinger?"

Melchior, again trying to create a less antagonistic environment, turned to the minstrels. "The little Drumher boy, Drumher being the family name, is the singer. The eldest Singer girl, Singer being the family name, is the drummer. Do I have that right?"

"Yes, sir," replied Alma and Ezekiel.

"Lyre!" exclaimed Caspar, pointing in the general direction of the minstrels.

Melchior turned to Caspar. "Quiet! That was uncalled for. You should be ashamed. There is no reason to believe the Singer girl . . ."

"Who plays the drums," added Balthazar.

" . . . is a liar. Apologize. Immediately," Melchior insisted.

"I'm referring to the instrument. It's a lyre," Caspar explained.

"What a bizarre thing to say. Are you still drunk?" Balthazar asked. "Instruments are inanimate objects. They have not life nor thoughts. They are not capable of either telling the truth or clever enough to invent lies."

"It's the name of the stringed instrument, you idiot," Caspar said to Balthazar. "Even you should know that." Caspar returned his head to his hands and closed his eyes as the constant low nasally sound of the distant snoring grated on each of the raw nerves in his head.

"Ah, I see, my friend," said Balthazar to Caspar, "you're not as much of an ass as I thought."

The last of the minstrels stepped forward, raising her hands in the air, twisting her wrists in precise concentric circles. "And these are cymbals," she said.

"The last two days have been filled with signs and symbols; but what exactly are you referring to, my dear?" Balthazar asked.

The young girl stretched her arms to show Balthazar the cymbals that adorned her fingertips. "These are cymbals."

"Again, my dear," Balthazar said patiently, "I don't mean to be difficult, but symbolic of exactly what?"

"Symbolic of what a fucking imbecile you are." Caspar elbowed Balthazar in the ribs. "What the child is holding in her hands are called cymbals."

"Oh, I see. Never mind."

"Please," Mary said, encouraging the minstrels as she was trying to settle Baby Jesus, who grew fussier in anticipation of his next meal. "Please play for us."

"I hope the playing is more rhythmic and less grating than the grotesque snoring of the derelict young man," Jerome said to Elisheba and the High Priest.

The young minstrels played with great determination but with little skill. It was a tune, or something that resembled a tune; a cacophony of sounds, as if the gurgling burp of a sickened cow married the protracted fart of a flatulent camel. The noise aggravated the triumvirate, intensified Caspar's headache, but delighted Mary and Joseph and seemingly even captured the attention of Baby Jesus. As the minstrels finished their first uneven piece, someone in the crowd remarked that the motion of the oxen's tail and the hooves of the lamb's legs kept time with each uneven beat of the drum. Nestled in the hay, the rust-colored cat courteously clapped his two front paws together, pleased by the unpleasing ruckus. It was a magical scene for the crowd of commoners who had gathered, and they enthusiastically applauded while the isolated snoring from the young man in the corner continued.

"Will someone please wake that man up?" Elisheba commanded the crowd as the clapping subsided.

In the far corner of the stable, her back supported by a fence post, the slumbering man's wife shook him vigorously. Still, the sleeping and snoring continued. "I'm sorry," the wife addressed the crowd, who had stopped paying attention to the minstrels and were now focused on the snoring man. "He's in a dead sleep."

"Who is dead?" asked the Keeper.

"I couldn't quite hear the wretch," Elisheba said.

"I think she said someone's dead," the High Priest said.

Hearing that someone had died, Mary, who had been feeding Jesus, shot instinctively out of her seat with concern. She took Jesus from her breast, cradled him in her arms, weaved her way through the crowd, and rushed to the aid of the wife of the dead man, who, as Mary found when she arrived, was still very much alive but soundly asleep.

The wife looked up at Mary apologetically. "I'm sorry. He sleeps as if he were dead. I can't wake him."

Jesus, angered by being stripped away from his morning meal, filled his lungs with air, closed his eyes, and his face reddened.

The wife turned back to her sleeping husband and shook him again. "Lazarus, wake up!"

But still he slept.

Baby Jesus, fed up with not being fed, produced an ear-piercing wail from the bottom of his lungs, so loud that it reverberated across the stable. So loud it woke Lazarus out of his deep, dead sleep.

"It's a miracle!" the wife marveled. "The clapping of the crowd couldn't wake him, the music from the minstrels couldn't wake him, but Jesus has raised Lazarus from a dead sleep!"

Word spread from one corner of the crowd to another and back again. What started as low murmurs of Jesus raising Lazarus out of a dead sleep evolved into loud proclamations that Jesus had raised Lazarus from the dead. The crowd shouted joyful praise to God for this miracle; a sure sign that yesterday's uncertain rumors of the birth of God's Son were today's certain truth of His existence, as proven by this miracle.

"Grab your quill, quickly," Elisheba ordered the scribe. "Write this down. Get every detail. This must be recorded and retold."

"About the minstrels?" asked the scribe.

"No, you incompetent imbecile. About Jesus raising the dead," the High Priest said.

"Are you certain that's what happened?" the scribe asked. "I thought—"

"I don't pay you to think. I pay you to write what I tell you to write," Elisheba said and waved dismissively at the scribe.

"Balthazar," the High Priest said and turned his attention to the Wise Men, "yesterday you were looking for a miracle? Well, now you have one."

CHAPTER 28

The Shepherds' Story

DAY 3, AD

"So, you want us to say that an angel appeared to us. Is that right?" asked the shepherd who, along with five other herders, was nursing a hangover from their prolonged Saturnalia celebration. The pounding in their heads made it difficult to focus on what the High Priest was saying.

Jerome and the High Priest, plotting how to spread the news of the birth of the Son of God, enlisted the help of the shepherds, whom they had met at the tavern just two days earlier. The High Priest believed that the more people who knew about the virgin birth of the Son of God, the more fame, influence, and power he would attain. Perhaps his power would even outstrip the power and influence of his priestly archrival in Jerusalem. Jerome believed that the more people who knew about the birth of the Son of God by the Virgin Mary, the larger the pool of gifts and opportunities to extend his trading empire. The shepherds were a pathetic and impoverished lot, but their numbers were great, and when combined, their gifts could be of material value.

The six shepherds had gathered in the courtyard of the inn, their knapsacks packed, reluctantly ready to leave the heathen excesses of Saturnalia and return to their flocks in the western hills of Judea. From the tavern, they had viewed the events of the previous days with an interest that ebbed and flowed but mainly ebbed in favor of the flow of wine and women.

Jerome and the High Priest could not distinguish one shepherd from the next; ill-mannered, uneducated men with scraggly beards, wearing plain, poorly stitched together simlahs and sheepskin cloaks badly soiled with dirt, grass, food, and wine. They wore sandals exposing their grimy feet covered with cuts and bunions and toenails that looked like the inside of a withered fig that had fallen from a tree and lay rotting on the ground. Their faces were dull, wrinkled, and weathered. The beastly group of men were far below the type of people Jerome and the High Priest cared to interact with, but to advance each of their causes, they were willing to make sacrifices. The shepherds listened with varying degrees of attention.

"That's right," the High Priest said. "We're asking you to say an angel appeared to you."

"And you're saying the angel compelled us to come to Bethlehem to see a baby who is supposed to be our Savior?"

"Correct."

"But we came to Bethlehem to celebrate Saturnalia."

"To get drunk and fuck," said another.

"And you are to be congratulated. It looks as though you've accomplished those two tasks expertly," Jerome said as he lifted a bag of coins from the pocket in his robe.

"But what if we paid you to tell a different story?" the High Priest said. "A story of wonder. Of miracles. A story that will earn you a place in history. A story about an angel and a newborn, the Son of God, our Savior, your Savior."

"Surely you and your families could use the contents of this bag to buy new clothing, better food, finer wine than what you're accustomed to," Jerome said as he dangled the coin purse in front of the group.

A shepherd grabbed the purse and tossed it to another shepherd, apparently the only one who could count without using fingers or toes. "How much is there for the six of us?"

"Plenty," said the accountant shepherd. "More than our flocks could bring in a year, maybe two."

"You've got our attention," said the first shepherd. "Tell us, who exactly is the baby saving?"

"Well, everyone, I suppose. All of mankind, of course." Jerome was quickly getting out of his depth.

"From what?"

"Well, many things. Lots of things. Things that are bad," Jerome said defensively. "I think it is more than obvious."

"Name one," said another of the shepherds.

"This is more of a question for him," Jerome said as he pointed at the High Priest.

"You shepherds ask too many questions." The High Priest did not like to be challenged by anyone, let alone by a shepherd of low station. "He will save us from wars, famine, drought, and disease. These will all go away with the birth of the child. The list of the evils that the Son of God will save us from is long, and I don't have the time to enumerate them all. Not to you."

"Does the angel have a name?" a third shepherd asked Jerome.

"Is that important?" Jerome was becoming impatient.

"I don't know, but in case we're asked," replied the third shepherd.

Jerome turned to the High Priest again. "Do angels have names?"

"Some do, others do not. Let's keep this simple for these simple men. Let's say *no*. It is simply a nameless angel that appeared."

"How should we react?

"What do you mean?" the High Priest replied.

"To the angel. How should we react? I mean, we're out in the field, looking after our sheep, perhaps chasing a stray one here, nudging a lazy one there, and suddenly, we see this angel coming from the sky. We've never seen an angel before. Should we be happy? Excited? Or frightened and concerned?"

"For the purposes of this encounter," said the High Priest, who had not considered these details, "you would have been frightened at first, intimidated by the angel. But quickly, the angel would reassure you that there was nothing to fear, that he brings only good tidings of great joy. This eases your mind. Makes you feel better about the angel."

"Does the angel speak?"

"No, it pantomimes, you boob," Jerome replied, regretting the idea of engaging with the shepherds. "Of course, the angel speaks. That's how it communicates with you."

"What about wings? Does this angel have wings?"

"Of course, it has wings. It's the defining physical feature of an angel." The High Priest, like Jerome, was tired of the questions.

"And remind me again," said the first shepherd, "what exactly does the angel communicate?"

The High Priest took a deep breath. "This is the last inane question I will answer. The angel comes down from Heaven while you are tending your flock. I don't know exactly what you do out there in the grasslands tending your flock, but that's what you were doing when the angel appeared. Then the angel, who indeed has wings, and who indeed can talk, tells you that in the town of Bethlehem a baby was born, and the baby is the Son of God, who will be our Savior. You got that?"

"I think so. We all have that?" one shepherd said to the rest as they all nodded in unison.

"And that's the baby we're talking about?" said another shepherd, pointing across the courtyard to the manger, where Jesus lay sleeping.

"Yes," Jerome answered curtly.

"Should we mention anything about the manger or the rags used as swaddling clothes?"

"I hadn't considered. But yes, I think your impoverished shepherd friends will enjoy those details. Include the bit about the manger and swaddling clothes," Jerome said, then walked away from the group.

"Now, go forth and spread the good news," the High Priest said, ushering the shepherds out of the Keeper's courtyard and back to their flocks of sheep and the flocks of people who populated the far-flung fields from which they came.

CHAPTER 29

The Granting of Miracles

DAY 3, AD

In the waning heat of the evening sun, the Wise Men returned to the inn after visiting Bethlehem's market square. There they had filled their goatskins with local wine and their leather food sacks with dates, figs, and sage-encrusted flatbread for their journey back to Perea. The inn was pleasantly quiet, with the shepherds having returned to their flocks and the large crowd that had arrived the day before dispersed at Mary's polite but firm urging. Only Mary, Joseph, Jesus, and the ox and donkey remained in the stable; the Keeper dutifully attended to the needs of all.

Once Melchior, Balthazar, and Caspar had finished their preparations, they gathered in one of the small, confined rooms at the inn at the request of Jerome and the High Priest. The five men, plus Elisheba's scribe, sat shoulder to shoulder, knee to knee, cramped and uncomfortable on uneven stools. This was to be Jerome and the High Priest's final effort to secure the loyalty of the Wise Men and to ensure that they, upon returning to their respective kingdoms, would convey the truth, as dictated by the triumvirate, to all the citizens in their lands. Knowing that a simple gift of money, like the bribe paid to the shepherds, would not be interesting to the wealthy Wise Men who enjoyed every luxury of life, the High Priest and Jerome had to present an alternative that the Wise Men would find irresistible.

"Before you leave, we have gathered you here to thank you," the High Priest began in a formal tone, "for making the journey to witness the miraculous birth of the Son of God, from the virgin, whose name is Mary and who is the daughter of Jerome and Elisheba."

"Could we do this somewhere more comfortable?" Caspar said.

"This stool is already making my balls ache, and I'm going to be riding that damned horse through the night again," Balthazar said, then folded his cape and placed it on the hard, uneven surface of the stool for padding.

"Never mind them," Melchior said. "It's our duty as Wise Men to come when we are called, particularly when it is to serve God." Melchior's faith in the prophecy and his belief in the baby being the Son of God had diminished due to the events of the last two days. He had grown to dislike and mistrust Jerome, Elisheba, and the High Priest. He had developed a great fondness and paternal caring for Mary. And he had a deep respect for her carpenter companion. The triumvirate's words and actions created doubt in Melchior's mind about the truth of the events he had witnessed and that had inspired his hope as he left Perea just days before.

However, Melchior was a pragmatist. While he had doubts, he intended to err on the side of demonstrating devotion to God and now to God's Son. If he was wrong in his devotion, then it would cost him nothing more than a small amount of time and a fraction of the frankincense he possessed. But, he reasoned, if this was truly the Son of God, then he would gain great favor when passing from his earthly life to his heavenly life. So, he continued to play the role of devout servant to a God he deeply believed in and the Son of God who he wasn't quite sure about.

"We have recorded your presence here at the birth of our Savior as well as your magnificent gifts that were truly fit for the King of Kings, the Christ Child," the High Priest said. He stood and bowed to each of the Wise Men in the cramped room. "We shall ensure that your deeds and generosity are known to all, and we shall also ensure your names are indelibly stamped and inextricably tied to the birth of Jesus Christ in story, in image, and in song."

Melchior bowed his head in return. Balthazar and Caspar fidgeted on their stools.

"I won't ask about Paragus, but where's Jude Aya?" Balthazar asked. "Why isn't he here with us?"

"Not that we could fit one more person into this shithole of a room," said Caspar.

"He's no prince, no Wise Man," Jerome said. "He has no wealth. He brought swaddling clothes, for God's sake. That is hardly gold or frankincense. It's hardly even myrrh."

"What do you mean, *even* myrrh?" asked Balthazar.

"Nothing. I meant nothing. It is a fine gift." Jerome tried to recover. "It's just that—"

"Just that what?"

"I mean, next to gold, I think—"

"I'm tired of people dismissing my myrrh." Balthazar leaned forward, his nose just inches away from Jerome. "Just make sure it gets equal treatment as the gold and frankincense in these stories you intend to tell and songs you intend to sing about us."

"I assure you it will," Jerome said, placating the Wise Man for whom he had one more request. "Besides gathering you here to thank you, we ask one more favor of each of you, and in return, the Son of God will grant you a miracle, which he will perform on your behalf in the fullness of time."

"Please. Ask anything." Melchior bowed his head slightly. "What would you like for the three of us to do for the two of you?"

"Not for us," the High Priest corrected, "for the Christ Child."

"Of course, for the Christ Child," Balthazar said, exchanging smirks with Caspar.

"We would like you to spread the good news that you have witnessed to all the citizens in your kingdoms," the High Priest said, maintaining his formal air. "The birth of Jesus Christ, the Son of God, our Savior, to the Virgin Mary, in the little town of Bethlehem, just as the great prophets Isaiah and Micah foretold."

"This shall be done," said Melchior, speaking for the three.

"And," Jerome said, putting his hands on his heart, "we think it is appropriate, only fitting, that grandparents also become an integral part of the story—Elisheba, of course, the grandmother, and me, Jerome, the grandfather. I'm sure you can imagine how important grandparents are to the rearing of any child, let alone the Son of God."

"No, I really can't," replied Balthazar.

"If that is your wish," said Melchior, the devout pragmatist, "then it shall be done."

"No, it shall not," Balthazar said.

"You mentioned something about a miracle?" Caspar fidgeted in his seat, eager to get on with the miracles so they could leave the cramped room.

"Yes, the miracles." The High Priest nodded toward the scribe. "He will record them faithfully, and we shall, in turn, convey them to Jesus at a time when He and God, His Father, are ready. Please, Melchior, go first."

"If I may." Melchior cleared his throat and folded his hands as if he was praying. "I have thought about this question before, so I am well prepared and humbled by the opportunity. I make my request with the understanding that the Son of God is omnipresent, omniscient, and omnipotent. The miracle I ask is for peace on Earth. For centuries, kingdoms have risen and kingdoms have fallen on the might of the sword and with the blood of innocents. Wars have taken the lives of men, women, and children across the lands of Assyria, Babylon, Egypt, and Israel. Armies have destroyed armies; brothers have killed brothers. The ground is stained red with the blood of good and innocent people. I ask that Jesus, the Christ Child, the Prince of Peace, grant the miracle of peace, so that all people, all children of God, no matter where they live, what they believe, what they look like, or how wealthy they are, live in peace and happiness. This is the miracle I desire."

"Wonderful, Melchior," the High Priest said, turning to the scribe. "And so it is recorded, and so it shall come to pass." The High Priest turned to Caspar. "Please, wise and honorable man, what would you ask of the Son of God?"

"Melchior is always a tough fucking act to follow. The miracle that is on the top of my mind is a little more modest than world peace."

"Please continue."

"I have a cousin. He lives in Cana." Caspar rubbed his hands together as if attempting to warm them. "He's not actually a cousin, but a very good friend—the type of guy you would consider a cousin. Really, almost a brother to me. His name is Simon, and he is a very dear man. But he is also very poor. The same level of poverty as Jude Aya or the Keeper; pathetically, painfully fucking poor. Wretched."

"Excuse me," the High Priest said, placing his hand on the scribe's papyrus scroll. "No need to capture all the fucks and fucking. Just capture the essence of what the Wise Man is saying."

"So, he can barely provide for himself and his family. Simon just had a son. And he loves beer."

"Sorry," the scribe said. "I want to make sure I'm getting the essence correct. Did you say Simon's son loves beer?"

"His son was just born. That's ridiculous. He wouldn't be drinking beer, now would he? It's Simon who loves beer."

"I don't see where you're going with this, Caspar. You have the opportunity for a miracle from our Savior," Melchior said. "Why are you going on about your cousin Simon, who is not your cousin, and his son and his love of beer?"

"I'm getting there, if you would all just stop interrupting me."

Caspar folded his arms across his chest. "Simon is thinking ahead. Way fucking ahead. He is thinking fifteen to twenty years into the future. He's thinking of the marriage of his son in Cana. This is typical of Simon. I told you what a nice guy he is, very thoughtful. Already worried that he will not be able to throw a proper wedding feast for his son. He's so poor that he fears no respectable woman would want to marry his son if there is not a proper wedding feast."

"But you are as rich as the day is long," Balthazar said. "Why don't you just pay for the wedding feast?"

"I promised to pay for the food, and we shall have the grandest banquet of roasted lamb and desert hen, the freshest pomegranates, the sweetest oranges, and the juiciest grapes from the four corners of earth. There will be bread with herb-infused olive oil from the best orchards in Cana. However," Caspar said, then paused, "my generosity has its fucking limits. I told him, I told Simon, I said, 'Simon, I'll buy your son a feast that any bride would gush over, but you need to provide the beverages.'"

"Where are you going with this?" Melchior asked.

"Not clear to me either," the High Priest said.

"Same," said Jerome.

"Be patient. I'm almost there. So, there is a well on Simon's property. It's the only valuable thing he possesses. Similar to the Keeper's well, the water is fresh and cold. While Melchior was thinking about world peace, I was thinking that Jesus, when he is ready, could perform the miracle of turning the water in the well into beer for the wedding feast in Cana. Just for that one special day."

"That's the miracle you're asking for?" Melchior was incredulous.

"That's it?" Balthazar shook his head in disapproval. "You need to think bigger."

"Exactly," Melchior agreed.

"Why ask for beer when you could ask for wine?" Balthazar slapped Caspar on the shoulder. "If you really want your cousin's son to impress his bride and their family, then don't settle for beer. Beer is for barbarians, for peasants. But wine! Ah, wine is from the gods. Have Jesus turn the water into wine, and that bride will not only happily marry your cousin's son, but she will gladly drop her gown to the ground for his pleasure. That, my friend, will be a miracle worth remembering!"

Melchior, head in hands, lips pursed, eyes closed, shook his head disapprovingly.

"He makes a good point," Jerome said.

"I hadn't thought about it in that way," Caspar said, nodding in agreement. "That's a fine idea. So, the miracle I ask for is that Jesus turns water into wine at the wedding feast of my cousin Simon's son in Cana."

"And so it is recorded, and so it shall come to pass," the High Priest said as he watched the scribe record the requested miracle onto the papyrus scroll.

Melchior tapped the High Priest on the knee. "Can you ask Jesus to do that *after* the miracle of world peace? I don't mean to be judgmental, but world peace seems a bit more important."

"I'll make that request," the High Priest said with surprising modesty, "but ultimately it will be up to Jesus to determine how he wants to sequence these miracles as I am merely the messenger in these matters."

"Since world peace is covered and I don't have any poor relatives or poor friends whom I call relatives, I've been mulling over a few ideas," Balthazar said.

"And?" the High Priest said.

"Imagine the miracle of a colossal camel capable of crossing the Judean Desert or scaling the Hebron Mountains in just ten steps. With such a beast, we could return to Paragus's Saturnalia celebration in the blink of an eye. No more long camel or horse rides."

"I didn't think it was possible, but that's even more shallow than Caspar's water to wine miracle," Melchior said.

"It may not be at the same level as world peace or water into wine, but it was just one idea. I have others." Balthazar paused, waving his arms slowly for dramatic effect. "What about the creation of a sword, that, when in my possession, and only in my possession, could wipe out entire armies with just one swing? Literally the ability to slaughter an opposing army with just one swing. Whoosh and gone."

"Very dark," replied Caspar.

"And in direct conflict with world peace," Melchior said.

"What would happen if we requested two miracles that were diametrically opposed to one another?" Balthazar asked.

"It is a fine question, but one I don't have the answer to." The High Priest leaned forward. "I suppose only Jesus knows, and he is, at this moment, fast asleep or drinking from his mother's breast. Perhaps you should choose another."

"Why not make it for something good? Something beneficial, like feeding the poor or healing the sick," Melchior suggested.

"That could work. You're on to something there." Balthazar stroked his beard and closed his eyes. "Since I was a child, I've always had this fear, this repulsion, of leprosy."

"Disgusting fucking disease." Caspar shook his head.

"Terrible," Jerome agreed.

"When I was a child, maybe five, no more than six—" Balthazar said.

"Is this going to be another story like the hippo?" Jerome asked.

"Of course not. Well, maybe a little. Yes, indeed. Very similar, actually. Anyway, my father and I were in the market square of Damascus. We had gone to the market, as we did every Monday, to buy cinnamon, sage, and turmeric for my mother. I used to love these outings. The sights, smells, and sounds of the market—I loved it. But, one day, there was a leper sitting cross-legged on the pathway just across from the market. A beggar. He fidgeted and fussed on his blanket and couldn't get comfortable. Then, with a heavy sigh, he bent down to scratch his left foot. The itch must have been intense because he scratched—and scratched and scratched again until finally one of his toes fell off."

"Which toe?" asked Caspar

"How should I know? It doesn't matter. That's not even the worst part. The leper, upon seeing his detached toe lying on his blanket, went from disbelief to despair and then to outright anger. So angry was he that he picked up his toe with his right hand and threw it. It sailed in a perfect arc across the street, where it landed on top of a neatly arranged pile of sundried, oil-cured olives."

"Terrible," Jerome said.

"But that's not the worst part. Neither the olive merchant nor his customer noticed the leper's scabby toe amongst the ripened olives, and his customer, without looking, reached into the pile." Balthazar was now acting out the part of the customer. "He picked up the toe thinking it was just another olive, plopped it into his mouth as he would any other olive, and swallowed the toe with one bite."

"This is worse than the monkey picking at your vomit," Caspar said.

"And that's not even the worst part."

"Of course not," Melchior said with growing disgust.

"The leper had thrown his toe with such force," Balthazar said, acting out the throwing motion with his right hand, "that his finger, I believe his middle finger, but could have just as easily been his index finger, separated from his hand. It went flying like a small twig being hurled by a young boy, landing on the ground next to a pile of fish entrails under the fishmonger's stand. Well, the poor leper's severed finger attracted the attention of two street dogs, who raced to the finger and began fighting over it, each one taking an end and tugging against the other. The dogs rolled under the fishmonger's shabby wooden table, knocking it over with scores of musht, kinneret, and sardines spilling out into the street. Emerging from the melee was the larger, more muscular mutt with the leper's mangled finger hanging from his mouth as if he were smoking one of Zacharia's joints."

"Stop! Enough, Balthazar," Melchior said. "This is surely not a true story."

"But it is, Melchior."

"Then get to your miracle," Melchior said.

"Ever since that day, the image of the leper's toe and the man who chomped it down has haunted me. And I can no longer look at any dog without conjuring up the image of the leper's finger dangling from its mouth. This brings me to my miracle. When Jesus encounters a leper, I'd like him to heal the leper of this dreadful disease."

"And so," the High Priest clarified, "you'd like Jesus to cure leprosy?"

"Oh, no, no. That seems like too much to ask. Too much of an imposition. But if he could just cure any leper that he arbitrarily meets when he is out and about, that is the miracle I seek."

"You're sure now?" the High Priest said. "You are asking Jesus not to cure leprosy but just cure a single leper or two that he may happen upon."

"Exactly. Yes."

"And so it is recorded, and so it shall come to pass." The High Priest nodded to the scribe.

"To confirm," the scribe said, wanting to ensure he recorded the wishes of the Wise Men correctly, "we have the miracle of world peace, the miracle of turning water into wine at a wedding, and the miracle of curing a random leper or two. Further, to be clear, you are not asking for enormous camels or lethal swords. Do I have that right?"

"Yes," the three Wise Men answered in unison.

"But what if Simon's son never marries?" Caspar asked.

"That's a good point. And what if Jesus never encounters a leper?" Balthazar added.

"Those are risks you'll need to accept," counseled the High Priest. "The only request that is certain is the ability for Jesus to deliver world peace. There are no contingencies, no variables in that request. That's entirely within God's purview."

"Good. Done. Now, gentle and honorable Wise Men, go back amongst the people in your kingdoms," Jerome said, "and spread the word of the birth of the Son of God, the Child Jesus, born of the Virgin Mary and under the caring, watchful eye of Mary's loving parents, Jerome and Elisheba."

And with that, Melchior, Balthazar, and Caspar left the crowded room and crossed the courtyard into the ramshackle stable to mount their horses to begin their overnight journey. They were heading to Paragus's palace to extend the Saturnalia festival interrupted by the birth of the baby who, as they left, lay sleeping in the manger.

CHAPTER 30

The Sixth Letter from the Corinthians

Dear Joseph the Carpenter,

*T*he Corinthian family has retained me as their legal counsel to seek damages for the shoddy work you performed and for the work you promised, but utterly failed, to do. My client believes you misrepresented your capabilities and that you delivered a sloppy, slapdash excuse of a fence when you promised the sturdiest of stables. It is wholly due to your negligence that the herd of majestic Arabian horses, which was the sole source of income and considerable wealth for generations of the Corinthian family, was either eaten by ravenous beasts, transfigured into a radiant light on Mount Tabor, or run off into the extensive wilds of Nazareth. Further, it has come to my attention from reliable colleagues that you have escaped to Bethlehem with your betrothed, who, as it turns out, although still a virgin, gave birth to the Son of God. (As an aside, my hat is off to her for the virgin birth. Amazing! Well done! Really well done! Please give her and the Son of God my sincerest congratulations! I understand the excitement a newborn brings as we just welcomed our little bundle of joy, Judas, into our family!)

Now, back to the matter at hand. My colleague reported that a parade of Wise Men visited you and your virgin wife and provided valuable gifts. Reportedly among these were boxes of gold, frankincense, and myrrh. It is the full expectation of the entire Corinthian clan that you, based upon this recent windfall of wealth, pay an amount that equals the value of the twenty-one (21) Arabian stallions that were lost. Plus, the Corinthians are rightfully and lawfully requesting payment for punitive damages for the extreme degree of emotional stress you have caused the entire Corinthian family, particularly Junia, a once promising young girl who now only sits in the corner repeatedly mumbling something about a blind carpenter who picked up his hammer and saw. We expect this to be paid in full by the twenty-fifth of January. We are uncertain of the exact year as there is already talk in both legal and religious circles of renumbering the years on the account of the birth of the Son of God. There are those who believe this year should be the year zero, and there are others who believe it should be the year one, and there is even a small, but vocal, minority asserting we should just continue with the same old numbering scheme because it worked just fine before. I personally don't care which numbering system is used. They each have their merits. I just hope they choose soon so it won't further delay the purchase of desk calendars as I like to hand those out to the office staff. In any case, the Corinthians expect to be paid in full by the twenty-fifth of January, regardless of the numeric value of this particular year.

Simon Iscariot,
Senior, Esq. Attorney

CHAPTER 31

Exodus II

DAY 4, AD

E arly morning on the fourth day after his birth, and after having slept through most of the first three days, Baby Jesus was just now becoming vaguely aware of his changed circumstances, and he was not pleased. Not one bit. He had been quite content in the warmth and silence and solitude of his mother's womb. There, he'd had everything he needed; nourishment flowed at a steady, perfect pace, no noise disturbed his sleep, no foul stench pierced his nostrils. Jesus felt the womb was like a small slice of Heaven.

That all changed when he was, without prior consultation or consent, violently forced down a dark, narrow canal only to be shot out of an indescribable orifice along with thick goo and blood and something that looked like a flattened eggplant seasoned with paprika. To make matters worse after that trauma, a persistent, irritating bright light replaced the calm darkness of the womb. Nourishment was no longer predictable or proactively provided; instead, he had to wail for his food. And the smells of this strange new world, a combination of oxen shit, sheep piss, and multiple types of human body odor, were a grave disappointment when compared to the unadulterated purity of the womb.

Although his eyesight was still fuzzy, Jesus didn't like the looks of the creatures who inhabited this strange new world. They were giants, much larger than himself and powerful, capable of lifting him in all directions, up and down and side to side. Jesus found the nests of hair on their heads grotesque compared to his own clean, smooth baldness. A subset of these creatures was made even more hideous, with gnarled nests of hair growing wildly on their chins. Jesus wanted nothing to do with this strange, monstrous new world, but he didn't know if any path would allow him to return to the warm, familiar comfort of the womb. Determined to let those around him know of his displeasure, he inhaled deeply and let out a piercing stream of wails that no one, not Mary, nor Joseph, nor the Keeper, could stop.

On a narrow lane, not far from the stable, Vashti could hear the baby's cries. Earlier that morning, she had learned from her parents that Mary and Joseph had not made it out of Bethlehem the night she had helped them escape; instead, they found refuge in the stable of the old inn. Upon hearing they were still in Bethlehem, Vashti immediately left to find them. She cradled baby Mary on her shoulder, winding her way through the crooked lanes of Bethlehem until she heard the cries of the newborn.

As she journeyed through Bethlehem, baby Mary's eyes were wide open as she marveled at everything she saw—the pale blue morning sky, the ruddy red buildings, the brownish dirt of the narrow lanes, the flapping of white linen laundry strung on thin strings in front of homes, and the brilliant yellow of her mother's scarf on which her head rested. The world was a wonder to Mary Magdalene.

"Mary, Joseph!" Vashti shouted across the stable, her pace quickening. "I just heard the news. I came as quickly as I could." With her baby resting on her shoulder, Vashti hugged her friend Mary and kissed the wailing Baby Jesus on his reddened forehead. "He's beautiful!"

"I can't calm him," Mary said, her eyes full of tears, her lips quivering. "I tried to feed him, to cuddle him, rock him back and forth, but nothing works."

Vashti sat next to Joseph and Mary, lowering baby Mary from her shoulder and turning her so she was face-to-face with the wailing Jesus. At that moment, the wailing stopped. The two babies, Jesus on his mother's lap and Mary Magdalene on her mother's lap, looked at each other with wide-eyed wonder. Vashti thought she saw Jesus smile. Mary thought she heard baby Mary coo.

Jesus was impressed by what he saw—a creature pleasing to his eye, not a giant like the others, no gnarled nest of hair on top of the head or the tip of the chin. A pleasant doughy figure, just like himself. He felt a certain kinship.

"Did you see that? Did you hear that?" Mary turned to her friend. "I couldn't calm Jesus, but baby Mary did. It's just like you and me when we were young."

"Jesus?" asked Vashti.

"We named him after the Keeper. He has been so kind to us."

"He's beautiful. And Joseph, I see your mark on the child." Vashti kissed two of her fingers and placed them softly on the baby's birthmark. "You both should be so proud."

Baby Mary reached out and touched Baby Jesus's toe, which caused him to make a googling sort of noise that babies make when they are delightfully satisfied. It was at this moment that Jesus thought this curious new world might not be so monstrous. That wonderful things and beautiful creatures like the one before him might abound and that he might, over time, come to enjoy this new world even more than he enjoyed the womb.

"We need to leave now." Mary took Vashti by the arm, putting her tears and tiredness aside as she spoke to her old friend. "My mother and father have turned the birth of our beautiful child into a sideshow."

"I've heard as much. My mother explained bits and pieces. None of it makes sense. People are saying Jesus is the Son of God. That it was a virgin birth. That you've fulfilled a six-hundred-year-old prophecy. I heard this from my mother, and it's what I heard on the streets this morning."

"Exactly why we need to leave. They have twisted and turned our child's birth to suit their desires and in ways that won't be good for Jesus."

"Is any of it true?"

"Of course not. This is my mother and father spinning a tale to gain glory and fortune for themselves. Before these stories grow any further, we're leaving for Nazareth."

"We can't let distance separate us again." Vashti wrapped her arm around her friend and kissed her forehead.

"Or separate our Jesus from your little magical Mary. They will grow to be friends, just like the two of us."

Vashti embraced Mary, kissed Jesus on the forehead, and hugged Joseph. "These two will be friends forever."

The Keeper, with a crick in his knee that had developed over the last few days, made his way across the stable, bringing thin slabs of salted unleavened bread and a small pot of honey that he had been saving for a special occasion.

"We can't accept this," Mary said. "You've already been too kind, given us so much."

"I would be pleased if you did. You'll need strength not only for yourselves but for the babe."

Mary smiled. Cradling Jesus in one arm, she put her other around the Keeper's thin waist and hugged him. "Thank you," she said loudly so the Keeper could hear. Joseph bowed to the Keeper, hands folded in thanks.

Before climbing atop the donkey, Mary gave Vashti a last hug. Then the young family made its way out of the stable to begin the journey back to Nazareth.

CHAPTER 32

The Wise Men Reunite

DAY 4, AD

Musicians playing raucous Saturnalia music, colorfully clothed jesters juggling long red sticks with flames burning at each end, and scantily clad, sensually curved dancers greeted Melchior, Balthazar, and Caspar as they entered the garden of Paragus. Weary from their overnight ride, the Wise Men felt a sudden pulse of adrenaline fueled by the sights, sounds, and smells that greeted them. Servants rushed to the travelers with enormous platters filled with grilled lamb and piled high with whole-cooked desert fowl. Other servants carried trays overloaded with heaping mounds of fresh grapes, pomegranates, dates, and large, perfectly round oranges as well as pistachios and almonds. The abundant feast of the fine foods was a welcome sight, but the tired travelers were most delighted by the pungent cannabis smoke and the opulent array of chalices of wine ready to be emptied. As promised, Paragus had extended the Saturnalia festivities.

Just as he had when the caravan left for Bethlehem, Paragus stood shirtless in his garden, greeting the returning Wise Men with a wave of his right hand while his left explored the ample, dimpled bottom of a half-naked dancer. From a cloud of smoke billowing from two hash pipes, Zacharia and Rachel reclined, pleasantly stoned, their limbs so entangled, so intertwined, that they looked like some kind of magical two-headed octopus. So occupied with one another, neither Zacharia nor Rachel noticed the arrival of the three. The monkey, who found his nourishment in spilled wine, spilled food scraps, and the occasional vomit of Wise Men, wandered the palace floors, confident he would find all these forms of sustenance before the night was over.

"You missed a shit show, Paragus," Caspar said after dismounting from his saddle and before gulping down a chalice full of wine.

"And do you agree with Caspar's assessment, Melchior?" Paragus asked as they walked with long, eager strides into the grand room and settled comfortably into their familiar places on the cushioned sofas.

"It wasn't what I was expecting, but God works in mysterious ways. The prophecies were indeed fulfilled." Melchior sipped from his chalice. "But fulfilled in a most peculiar way."

"And you, Balthazar?" Paragus asked.

"It was shit. We slept on the ground in a stable. They served us tasteless bread and watered-down wine. A group of unskilled minstrels led by a drummer who couldn't keep a beat played an irritating concert of ingratiating tunes. That's not even the worst part." Balthazar placed a cushiony pillow under his seat on the already cushioned sofa. "I can barely sit down. I gave the last of my myrrh to the virgin's father and the baby."

"Jesus Christ," Melchior said.

"Who is that?" Paragus shooed away the half-naked dancer who had been sitting on his lap, replacing her with a full plate of lamb brought by an attentive servant.

"He is the child born of the virgin—the Son of God, who fulfills the prophecies," Melchior said.

"Jesus? Really?"

"They named him Jesus?" Rachel's voice boomed as she walked hand in hand with Zacharia into the room. Rachel sat on the sofa next to Melchior and sipped from a wine-filled chalice brought by one of the many servants who buzzed around the reunion of Wise Men. Zacharia sat on the floor, his back resting on the sofa, between Rachel's legs.

"After much debate."

"I like it. It's beautiful in its simplicity. I'm sure my mother and father hated it for that same reason."

"Your mother wanted Immanuel." Caspar said as he somehow simultaneously inhaled from the pipe and drank from his chalice.

"That sounds like her."

"My friends, what do you intend to do now?" Paragus asked.

"Eat your food, drink your wine, and smoke your cannabis," Balthazar said, already having done each of the three.

"I mean, were any requests made of you? Any expectations set?"

"Mary and Joseph—" Melchior said.

"Who?" asked Paragus.

"Mary is the virgin mother, and Joseph is, well, a carpenter, her traveling companion. I'm not sure who Joseph is exactly." Melchior turned to Caspar. "Did you catch that?"

"I'm sorry to break it to you, Melchior, but he's the father."

"Of the baby? Jesus Christ? No," said Melchior. "I think he is simply a traveling companion of Mary's."

"Yes, Melchior. A fucking traveling companion, with emphasis on the fucking."

Melchior brushed off Caspar's crass comments and raised his hand to signal for wine. "Mary asked of nothing from us. She was not interested in the gifts. She cared only for the infant. She couldn't have been kinder—the type of young woman any father and mother would adore."

"Except for our mother and father." Rachel rubbed Zacharia's shoulders.

"They were certainly less pleasant and more demanding,"

Melchior said. "They requested we spread the word of the birth of the Son of God, born of the Virgin Mary, to everyone in our kingdoms. As disagreeable as I found your parents, I intend to carry out this request."

"Not me." Balthazar placed one more pillow under his seat for added cushion. "There was something about the whole thing that seemed wrong."

Melchior turned to Rachel. "Mary is your sister. What are your thoughts?"

"With no disrespect, Melchior, I agree with Caspar and Balthazar. Mary told me as much. She wanted no part of this."

"But the prophets foretold this. It can't simply be coincidence. It must be divine destiny."

"Divine destiny?" Balthazar set his chalice down and leaned forward. "Those prophets were fallible men with faults and foibles who may, or may not, have had interactions with God. Nothing felt right about these last three days. I'm not spreading the word."

"You do so at your own peril. If this was divine and God chose us to communicate this message, not doing so will surely provoke righteous indignation from our God in Heaven."

"I'll take my chances."

"But for now, my friends," Paragus said, always the peacemaker, "we shall consume vats of the finest wine, gorge on this exquisite feast, and smoke the strongest cannabis from the most ornate pipes. Let this celebration begin this glorious morning and go long into the intemperate night as we embrace the excesses and equalities that are the very essence of Saturnalia."

CHAPTER 33

The Gifts Exposed

DAY 4, AD

The High Priest and Jerome sat at the far end of the long table in the great room, sipping their morning tea and nibbling on figs. It was the same table where, only a few days earlier, the messengers gathered to receive their instructions. The two men, who had waited patiently for this moment as they tied up loose ends with the shepherds and Wise Men over the last few days, stared greedily at the three silver boxes before them. Elisheba sat at the opposite end of the table, reading and editing the scribe's account of the events surrounding the birth of their grandson.

"Have you seen the fourth gift, the one from Paragus? He mentioned rare gold coins," Jerome said to Elisheba, who remained absorbed in the scroll.

"It's none of my concern. I have what I want right here." Elisheba continued her examination of each letter, each word, and each sentence the scribe had recorded. "This is more important and far more enduring than your obsession with material things. Your

209

concerns are fleeting, mine are eternal."

"Could Melchior have wrapped the coins in the cape that he presented to Mary?" asked the High Priest.

"He wouldn't have betrayed us. And Mary, self-righteous Mary? Never would she accept such a gift."

The High Priest returned to the three silver boxes on the table. "Which one shall we open first—the gold, the frankincense, or the myrrh?"

"Let's open the least valuable first and save the best for last. We'll start with the myrrh and end with the gold," Jerome said, opening the box of myrrh and wrinkling his nose, the same reaction he had in the stable. "I thought the fragrance would be more pleasant, less pungent."

The High Priest took the box, examined its contents carefully, reached in with his thumb and forefinger, and gathered a small, tangled bunch of black and grey curly strands of hair, holding it up for Jerome to see.

"What is it?"

"It's hard to tell." The High Priest brought the clump of hair closer to his eyes. "It kind of looks like pubic hair."

"Let me see that." Jerome grabbed the curly hair from the High Priest and held it up to his eyes, then to his nose. He inhaled deeply and gagged. "The Keeper said it smelled like balls. He was right. Goddamned Balthazar. I didn't trust that bastard from the beginning. You keep that," Jerome said, sliding the box of myrrh to the High Priest with one hand and grabbing the box of frankincense with the other, "and I'll keep this."

"Fine, just fine." The High Priest sulked. "And then I'll keep the gold."

At once, the two men greedily grabbed for the box of golden ingots like two spoiled children fighting over a favorite toy. They tugged and pulled and brawled over the box until the lid sprung open, scattering the ingots across the floor. The two men paused, exchanged glances, then dove to the floor, scrambling on their knees to gather the ingots in their covetous hands. They scratched and kicked and slapped and spat at one another and rolled around the floor, picking up the ingots at every opportunity. Jerome yanked the mitre from the High Priest's head and tossed it high into the air, hoping the High Priest would chase his hat instead of the ingots. His ploy didn't work, and in retaliation, the High Priest tugged on Jerome's hair, but the strands were so flimsy, so limp and greasy, that they slipped through his fingers and out of his grip. They wrestled and rolled on the floor until they recaptured all the ingots.

Disheveled, lightly bruised, and breathing heavily, they sat back down at the table marveling at the ingots and at the generosity of Caspar, whom they had underestimated as a foul-mouthed young fool rather than a generous giver of gifts.

"We are rich," the High Priest said, putting his mitre back on his head crookedly.

"Beyond our dreams."

The two avaricious men fawned and fondled their respective collection of ingots and dreamed of the lavish luxuries and heightened power they would enjoy as a result of their windfall.

As a servant refilled Jerome's and the High Priest's tea, he commented that the gold pieces were the finest looking set of knucklebones he had ever seen.

"Ignoramus," Jerome said, rubbing a gold piece between his thumb and forefinger. "Know your place, which is to serve and be silent. Your opinions are not welcome here. You are a simpleton who doesn't have the good sense to distinguish between gold ingots and knucklebones. You lack the intelligence to recognize that this gold is mined from a vein in the highest, most remote, and most treacherous mountains in India. One hundred men, certainly better than you, died so that they may honor us with this gift. Take away this tea and fetch us two large chalices of sweet wine. The High Priest and I will celebrate properly."

"You know," the High Priest said, closing one eye and holding an ingot closer to his open eye, "they are all shaped a bit like talus bones."

"You're too eager to believe the uneducated opinion of an ignorant house servant." Jerome laughed at the High Priest as he raised an ingot to his left eye. But, as Jerome examined the gold piece more carefully, his smirk of superiority disappeared.

"Bring me a knife," Jerome shouted at the servant as he examined one ingot after another in rapid succession. "Quickly! Now!"

Jerome yanked the knife from the servant, cutting a deep gash across the servant's palm. "Don't bleed here, boy. Clean this up. And don't drip blood on the carpet. It cost more than your life is worth."

Jerome took the knife in his right hand, an ingot in his left, and began chipping methodically until a small piece of the gold veneer fell away. Bringing the gold piece closer to his eyes and quickening his pace, he chipped off flake after flake after flake until the only thing left was the dull yellow-white talus bone of a dead goat. He grabbed another ingot and frantically scraped the veneer until the brilliant gold transformed into another dull talus bone. He grabbed a third ingot, and the result was the same.

Jerome, with veins popping from his withered neck like sickly earthworms too feeble to break the surface of a thin layer of dirt, with teeth gnashing, and with tears streaming down his cheeks, gathered the gold-painted talus bones and threw them at the bleeding servant. He shouted at the top of this shallow lungs, "May God damn that bastard Caspar."

<hr />

On the other side of Bethlehem, far from the fine home of Jerome and Elisheba, the Keeper was busy doing his daily chores. As he lay fresh straw for his ox, his thoughts turned to the previous days. He couldn't remember when there had been so many people, so much commotion, and so much life coursing through his humble inn. He hadn't felt so vital, so needed, and so useful since he cared for his sick, suffering wife over the last months of her life. Though he had known Joseph and Mary for only a short while, he already longed for Joseph's companionship, Mary's kindness, and the wonder of their newborn child.

After spreading the straw, he fetched water for the donkey and walked to the manger, where he had spent so much time over the last days and nights. He removed a few strands of old straw, picking them out one by one. He then picked up the thick wool blanket that Jesus had been wrapped in, brought it to his cheek, closed his eyes, and thought of the child. At the far end of the manger, a faint glimmer hidden under a mound of straw caught the Keeper's eyes. With the blanket tucked under his arm, he walked to the head of the manger, removed the straw, and found a dozen gold Babylonian coins. Along with the coins was a piece of papyrus wrapped around a small, unripened green fig by a worn piece of string. The Keeper untied the string and unfolded the note, which read, *"You are loved. We will forever be grateful for your kindness and care."*

A short distance from the Keeper, in his jumbled haphazard hovel in the middle of the Nakhleh slum, Jude Aya sat on the ruddy-red dirt floor he and his family called home. Surrounded by family and friends, he was recounting the strange and wonderful events he had witnessed and taken part in over the last three days. The Singer and Drumher families were among those gathered, and each parent was delighted to hear of the role their musical son and daughter had played in the goings-on. Jude Aya described the understated grace of Mary, the steadfastness of Joseph, and the tenderness of their child. He explained that many who witnessed the event insisted the child was the Son of God. He acknowledged that he felt the same, that he had been in the presence of God's Son.

Jude Aya had just begun to recount the story of Lazarus when

Sharma, his eldest daughter, brought in a neatly folded cerulean cape lined with gold threads and decorated with hundreds of stars made from small amber gemstones.

"This is identical to Paragus's cape—the young, thin Wise Man I was telling you about," Jude Aya said. "Who gave this to you, Sharma?"

"A couple. Very nice. They said they were leaving on a long journey back to Nazareth. The mother was riding atop a donkey, and her newborn was wrapped in swaddling clothes. Maybe the ones you brought as a gift, Father. They asked me to bring this to you." Sharma lay the jeweled cape at her father's feet.

Jude Aya set the cape in his lap and unwrapped its folded corners with reverence. As he lifted the last corner, a small silver box was revealed. The family and friends who had gathered around Jude Aya had never seen such a finely crafted case. Jude Aya flipped the clasp, slowly opened the hinged lid, and found a dozen sparkling gold Babylonian coins. Along with the coins was a piece of papyrus tied around a small, unripened green fig with a worn piece of string. Jude Aya untied the string and, unable to read himself, handed the note to Sharma.

"The note says," Sharma said, clearing her throat, *"You are worthy of so much more than we can give. Thank you for your friendship. Peace and love to you and your family."*

CHAPTER 34

Revelations

DAY 8, AD

The young family traveled in silence, Mary atop the donkey, cradling the swaddled baby, and Joseph holding the reins, leading the donkey along the last stretch of the Jordan River on a dark and cool Galilean night. On the fourth night of their journey back to Nazareth, the light from the waning moon was much dimmer than it had been on the night of Jesus's birth. Mary held their son tightly to her breast, softening the jarring, clomping footsteps of the old donkey. She kissed the sleeping child and smiled; she couldn't remember when she was as happy.

"Mary?"

"Yes."

"I need to tell you something that I should have told you months ago." Joseph looked Mary in the eye, his voice somber, his words reluctant to leave the safety of his mouth.

"Go on."

He put his hand on Mary's knee. Even in the dim moonlight,

Mary could see the troubled look on Joseph's face.

"What is it?"

"You know I'm older, quite a bit older, than you."

"This is not news to me."

Joseph smiled at Mary's attempt to make him feel at ease, to make a difficult discussion lighter.

"And with age comes experience. And some of these experiences I . . . I . . . am not proud of."

"I love you for who you are now, and who you are now is the culmination of past experiences. The only thing important about your past is that it made you the man I love now."

"But some of these experiences, before we met, were with other women."

"Still, you tell me nothing that matters. It changes nothing."

"But I lay with other women, Mary. Do you understand what I'm saying?" Joseph bowed his head, ashamed.

"I'm not naïve." Mary put her hand under Joseph's bearded chin and gently raised his face upward so his eyes locked with hers. "When I first met you, I assumed you had been with other women. At your age, I mean, I just assumed. Then that night, that incredible night in the garden—that night I knew for certain. Your experience showed." Mary smiled and raised her eyebrows.

"I'm sorry, Mary. I should have told you earlier."

"There was no need then, and there's no need now. You are now mine, and I am now yours. That is all that matters."

Joseph took Mary's hand, and bringing it to his lips, gently kissed her. He stayed by her side, with the same troubled look, as they ascended the barren hills of Galilee. "I have been with five other women—the last many years ago."

"I don't need an account of your past, Joseph. It doesn't change a thing."

"But I have no other children."

"I assumed that was the case, that you would have told me otherwise."

"Does this trouble you?"

"No, why should it? I don't understand what you're getting at."

Joseph stopped. He tied the reins of the donkey around the trunk of a long dead olive tree. Mary cradled Jesus on her shoulder as Joseph helped her down from the donkey. He held Mary's shoulders and could feel the warm shallow breaths of the sleeping child.

"Do you think it is strange that I've been with other women and none have a child by me?"

"No."

"But then, with you, it was different. We have a child. I was thinking . . . " Joseph stopped.

"About what?"

"About what your mother and the High Priest said about Isaiah and Micah."

"No, Joseph."

"But maybe it's not a coincidence. Maybe it's the fulfillment of prophecy."

"No, no, no." Mary shook her head. "It's a coincidence. It's not prophecy, and it's certainly not divine."

"But the circumstances—"

"I'm no virgin, you know that, and I've only been with you. Jesus is our creation."

"Yes, but—"

"But what? Jesus is a mirror image of you—your eyes, the birthmark. Stop this. You're beginning to sound like my mother."

"But what if God worked this miracle through me and Jesus *is* the Son of God?"

"Look, Joseph, even for the most devoted believer in the existence of God, there are times of doubt. While I've not seen this in my mother, I have seen this in the High Priest and I could see it in Melchior at times. And for even the most ardent nonbelievers, there are times of a belief in God, of a Supreme Being. This is natural. These aren't bad things. You don't need to apologize. But Jesus is our baby. We have created this beautiful baby. There was no divine intervention."

Joseph reached again for Mary's hand and kissed her. "You, my wife, the mother of my child, are right, as I've come to expect."

"My concern," Mary said, "is what happens from here."

"What do you mean?"

"With all that just happened. With my parents spinning the story of a virgin birth, a divine conception, the birth of the Son of God. The presence of the Wise Men."

"Buffoons."

"Yes, but influential buffoons. The type of buffoons who write history. And the crowd of people who came to see Jesus, praising God for his birth. And the High Priest. They will all tell the story as my parents wish it to be told. The scribe will write what my mother and father tell him to write. There will be some distorted record of the events of the last week. Stories are already being told. It got out of hand so quickly."

"We leave that all behind," Joseph assured Mary.

"But there are already many who eagerly and earnestly believe that Jesus is God's Son."

"Just as you calmed my concerns, let me calm yours." Joseph raised Mary and Jesus back on to the donkey and pulled on the reins firmly to continue the last leg of their journey. "Before sunrise, we'll be back in Nazareth with Jesus. We will return to our modest home and live our ordinary lives. Jesus will simply be one of the thousands of Galilean babies born each year. He will grow up just like every other boy and girl in Nazareth. Maybe one day he can be my apprentice, and eventually he'll be a much better carpenter than me. None of the things that happened over the last several days will be remembered. The story of a virgin birth, the story of a baby believed to be the Son of God, and the visit of the Wise Men will all fade away in a fortnight, to be forgotten forever."

CHAPTER 35

To Codify and Canonize

AD 108

*And there were in the same country shepherds abiding in
the field, keeping watch over their flock by night. And,
lo, the angel of the Lord came upon them, and the glory
of the Lord shone round about them: and they were sore
afraid. And the angel said unto them, Fear not: for,
behold, I bring you good tidings of great joy, which shall
be to all people. For unto you is born this day in the city
of David a Saviour, which is Christ the Lord. And this
shall be a sign unto you; Ye shall find the babe wrapped in
swaddling clothes, lying in a manger.*

THE NEW TESTAMENT, GOSPEL OF LUKE 2:8-13

Luke sat on a hard wooden chair, at a sturdy, austere desk, every
inch of which was covered by scrolls and piles of papyrus sheets
that he had bundled and secured in neat stacks with well-worn string.
A voracious reader and lifelong student, his collection contained
authoritative works from some of the most renowned and respected
scholars, philosophers, religious leaders, and scientific thinkers over
the last five hundred years. The floor-to-ceiling shelves behind Luke's

desk overflowed with scrolls and more loosely tied bundles of papyrus. The subjects ranged from treatises on the human body, to legal and political critiques, to social histories and philosophical tomes.

Fluent in Hebrew, Aramaic, Latin, and Greek, Luke was most drawn to Roman and Greek authors. Among his favorites were Dionysius, who wrote the history of Rome, and Josephus, who wrote the history of the Jewish people. Luke marveled at how these two men could piece together cohesive histories by skillfully weaving information from dozens, or perhaps hundreds, of different sources.

Luke had spent much of his long life reading, writing, and researching at this very desk while studying to be a physician. More recently, he spent his days, which turned into weeks, and weeks into months, and months into years, poring over piles of scrolls—some written by prophets who lived hundreds of years ago and others from more recent events that he had collected in his travels to Nazareth, Jerusalem, and Bethlehem. Luke, like his heroes Dionysius and Josephus, was a researcher and storyteller at heart. Amidst the piles of scrolls and papyrus sheets, he kept a large journal on his desk to record notes, observations, and questions for a book he was writing about the life of a man who lived, and tragically died, nearly a hundred years earlier. His name was Jesus.

On this particular evening, Luke was immersed in the writings of Mark the Evangelist, one of a growing number of people writing accounts of the events that had occurred during Jesus's lifetime. Not an educated man, Mark's writings were simple and unrefined but contained extensive detail. His work included stories of the miracles and radical teachings of Jesus and convincingly argued that Jesus was the Son of God. Mark had a growing reputation, particularly among the peasants and poorly educated commoners, as an expert source of information about the life and death of Jesus. The only thing missing from Mark's account was the story of Jesus's birth.

Two candles placed atop the desk provided light in an otherwise completely darkened room. The flickering candles created intermittent light and shadow, which made the inanimate scrolls strewn across Luke's desk come to life, breathing in, then breathing out. His long-trusted valet and companion, Amecheus, sat on a hard wooden chair on the edge of the candlelight. Amecheus served as an assistant to Luke when Luke practiced medicine, and he was now prepared to search, and bring to his employer, any text or scroll that Luke called for. As Luke's knowledge and wisdom grew, so did Amecheus's. And, although Amecheus was only his valet, Luke considered him his intellectual equal. He welcomed Amecheus's curiosity and valued his opinions and questions.

"It's interesting," Luke said, "that despite Mark's lack of education, his rudimentary grammar, and his questionable syntax, he writes convincingly about the final years of Jesus's life."

"He knew Jesus for a long time?" Amecheus said.

"I don't think so. But Mark was a close companion of Peter, who, in fact, knew Jesus during his short ministry. Peter was one of the twelve men who served in Jesus's inner circle, his most trusted and loyal friend who devoutly followed him and who, after Jesus's death, spread the word of his life and the meaning of his death. Mark refers to Peter and the other eleven men as the twelve apostles. I believe Peter may have been the primary source of Mark's information about Jesus."

"Why are you interested in this man called Jesus? Your medical books and instruments of healing are collecting dust. You turn away the people who seek your medical counsel."

"I am too old. I no longer have the energy to counsel those who need healing. Leave that to a younger man. I'm writing to satisfy my intellect and the curiosity of an old dear friend, Theophilus."

"The Roman governor in the southern territories?"

"Exactly."

"I didn't know you sympathized with the Romans."

"I don't. He was my friend long before he became a governor. And precisely because he's a high-ranking Roman official, he needs to be discreet about his interest in Jesus. The Roman rulers, those who rank far above him, do not tolerate anyone who diminishes their absolute power, and if Theophilus acknowledged Jesus as the Son of God, there would be trouble. It would cost him his position, maybe even his life, so he asked me to quietly gather as much information as I can about the birth, life, and death of Jesus. What do you know of Jesus?"

"Very little. I've heard a range of stories—some portraying him as a charlatan, some as an earnest but insane prophet, and others as, indeed, the Son of God."

"Which do you believe?"

"I've never stopped long enough to consider. What about you?" Amecheus returned the question.

"Mark the Evangelist firmly believes that Jesus is the Son of God."

"And you?"

"I'm coming around to that belief. There's an abundance of corroborating prophecies and testimonies. The evidence is overwhelming."

"I'm not sure it is," Amecheus said. "Your evidence is based on the words of Mark the Evangelist, whom you've never met and who may not have known Jesus well or possibly not at all. His writings are heavily influenced by a fisherman named Peter, who some called Simon Peter and others simply called Simon, who also only knew Jesus during his brief ministry, the last part of his life. Their accounts are weakly supported by various claims and stories from people who may, or may not, have known Jesus at all. This is all framed by questionable prophecies from many centuries ago."

"You may doubt the rigor of my research, but it's exactly how history is sewn together—piece by piece, stitch by stitch. It's in the same tradition as Dionysius and Josephus. They certainly weren't eyewitnesses to everything they wrote about, but they researched, collected information, and spoke to people who knew other people who were there."

"But how do you separate fact from fabrication?"

"History is, out of necessity, a bit of both," explained Luke. "Like

Josephus, I see my task as having to pull together a cohesive story based on bits of written history and oral storytelling. One third is verifiable fact, another third is highly plausible lore, and the final third is a mix of myths, legends, and tales that act as a sort of glue that holds the whole thing together. This is how history is written."

"That's how fiction is written."

"Let's get back to Mark." Luke brought the loose sheets of papyrus into the flickering candlelight. "The thing missing from Mark's writing is the birth of Jesus."

"Why does that matter?"

"Because every great historical figure needs a birth story. Think of Moses, of Alexander the Great. Think of Romulus. Each has a birth story that grabs the reader's attention immediately. A good birth story pulls you in. Now, the prophet Isaiah," Luke said, shuffling through scrolls on his desk, "and the prophet Micah both foresaw the birth of the Son of God. See," Luke said, handing Amecheus two separate scrolls, "here are their words. But they wrote them centuries before the actual birth."

"One can't foretell history."

"You can if you're a prophet.

"I'm not convinced."

"And," Luke said, shuffling methodically through the piles on his desk, "I have notes from a fellow named Melchior, who was some sort of learned man, a Wise Man, who supposedly witnessed the birth."

"What does he say?"

"His account is not detailed, but he states that the birth took place in Bethlehem."

"Which is consistent with the prophet Micah," Amecheus conceded.

"And he also confirmed that a virgin gave birth."

"Which is consistent with the prophet Isaiah."

"Exactly. I view these two facts as incontrovertible."

"Did he mention anything else?"

"Here, in this note," Luke said as he pulled a sheet of papyrus out of the pile, "there is a brief reference to two family members, Jerome and Elisheba, the child's grandparents—apparently a very unpleasant couple."

"And how do they fit in?"

"They don't. At least from what I can tell. Neither Micah nor Isaiah mentions them, so I'm setting them aside."

"That makes sense," Amecheus agreed.

"Another account comes from a companion who traveled with Melchior—someone named Caspar, another Wise Man. But his account is so filled with vulgar language and detailed descriptions of the virgin breastfeeding the baby that I've completely discounted it."

"Certainly not the type of glue we need to hold the account together," Amecheus agreed again.

"There are also rumors of a series of letters, purported to be related to a traveling carpenter who brought Mary on his donkey from Nazareth to Bethlehem. The letters were supposedly written by a once wealthy, but now derelict, family, the Corinthians. They were the carpenter's employer, and the letters purportedly corroborate the birth of Jesus. But, since I've not seen the letters myself, and there is no carpenter mentioned in the prophecies, I'm completely disregarding these letters as I have Caspar's musings."

"That's wise. So, let's consider what we know for certain," suggested Amecheus.

"That Jesus was born in Bethlehem, that is widely agreed upon."

"The City of David," Amecheus added.

"Ah, yes, good. The city of Bethlehem is so prosaic. It's the type of language Mark uses in his storytelling. We need something more lyrical, more poetic. Theophilus will appreciate that." Luke grabbed the scroll on which he was writing about the life of Jesus, dipped his quill, then scratched out the word *Bethlehem* and replaced it with the *City of David*.

"What else do we know?"

"It was a virgin birth," Luke said.

"Yes, good. What else about the birth?" Amecheus asked.

"Nothing. There is nothing else about his birth." Luke raised his head and rubbed his tired eyes, which were strained by the dim light. Looking beyond the piles of scrolls and the flickering candles, his eyes fixed on a small, rudimentary mosaic he had created years ago and that now hung on his wall. It was a simple, rough portrayal of a small sheep being carried on the shoulders of a rugged shepherd. "Of course!" Luke excitedly resumed his search through the piles on his desk. "I had forgotten, but there is an account of a group of shepherds abiding with their flocks in the fields outside of Bethlehem."

"You've mentioned them before."

"The account describes, ah, here it is," Luke said, holding up a tattered papyrus sheet, "how an angel appeared to them—nearly scaring the life out of them—and told them to go to Bethlehem—we'll call it the City of David as you suggest—to witness the birth of the Son of God. It includes small, vivid details like the child wearing swaddling clothes and that the child was born in a stable with a manger for a crib."

"The swaddling clothes seem credible, the manger less so. But it conjures an image."

"This gives us enough verifiable material," Luke said, dipping his quill into an inkwell, "to create a beautiful and factually accurate passage about the events surrounding the birth of Jesus from the shepherds' point of view. This is the last piece of the puzzle that rounds out the life story of Jesus. It fills the gap left by Mark. Now, I need to put all of this into lyrical prose that is worthy of Theophilus."

CHAPTER 36

Christmas Eve Mass

VATICAN BASILICA AD 2021

*"In the darkness, a light shines. An angel appears, the glory
of the Lord shines around the shepherds and finally the
message awaited for centuries is heard: "To you is born this
day a Savior, who is Christ the Lord."*

POPE FRANCIS, DECEMBER 24, 2021

S o began the Pope's Christmas Eve homily, and within the first
seven sentences that rolled off the Pope's moistened tongue, he
cited the Gospel of Luke twice and the prophecy of Isaiah once. The
references to Luke and Isaiah were no surprise to anyone of the fifteen
hundred parishioners dressed in their fine winter clothes or to the dour
clergymen in their silken robes who had gathered in the gilded Vatican
Basilica. Nor were the references to Luke and Isaiah a surprise to the
millions of faithful watching the Mass on Eurovision, or Facebook
Live, or Shalom World TV, or listening on Sirius XM or Vatican
Radio. The stories from Luke's Gospel in The New Testament and
the prophecies of Isaiah in The Old Testament were the comforting,
familiar sustenance of all Christmas Eve Masses around the world.
They were, after all, the foundation that proved the divine birth of
Jesus, just as they had for thousands of years.

Certainly, the Pope's predictable beginning of his homily was no
surprise to the cat who sprawled out on the cool marble slabs several

meters to the left of the Pope's Presider chair, in an alcove hidden amongst the shadows of the marble columns that framed the gilded altar of Saint Wenceslas. The attentive, rust-colored, one-eyed cat, with half his right ear missing and ribs that stuck out like fence posts, reveled in the reassuring passages from Isaiah and Luke. They, as well as Micah, felt more like old friends than distant prophets from long ago.

The cat, as he had countless Christmas Eves before, had somehow evaded the watchful eyes of the impeccably trained Swiss Guards, went unnoticed by the dozens of dull docents, and was completely undetected by the hundreds of well-hidden, highly sophisticated security cameras. As the lyrical Latin words rolled from the Pope's tongue and into the cat's one good ear, the cat licked his paw and a slight, self-satisfied smile crept across his face.

The cat had arrived in the Basilica much earlier in the day as dozens of workers swarmed around the papal altar, making final preparations for the evening Mass. The workers replaced hundreds of faded poinsettias with fresh, bright red ones. They fussed over the towering candle holders on the altar, which stood like gilded Roman centurions, making sure they were aligned to an exacting standard. They placed the Presider's chair, the Pope's gilded throne padded with delicate white silk cushions, precisely in the middle of a slightly elevated platform covered in plush red carpet that matched the red of the poinsettias. The cat enjoyed the bustling preparations for Mass almost as much as he enjoyed the Mass itself. The Vatican Basilica, a rich palace built of marble and filled with gold and priceless treasures, felt like a second home to the cat. It was among his most favorite places to seek refuge, particularly during the Advent season.

When younger, the cat's favorite hidden nook to view the Midnight Mass had been in the shadows under the armpit of the statue of Saint Andrew, which directly looked out to the papal altar under Bernini's massive bronze Baldacchino. The comfortable cranny had provided an unobstructed one hundred eighty-degree view of the proceedings. The cat reminisced of his early years when he would warmly curl up under Saint Andrew's smooth marble arm and let his imagination wander to the musty crypts beneath the Basilica floor, where it was rumored the semidecayed corporeal head of the actual saint lay safely locked away in a secure vault.

The cat's other favorite spot as a youngster had been on top of the Monument to the Stuarts, with its two magnificent fully grown winged angels sorrowfully protecting the entrance to the dead royals' tomb. But the cat stopped going there after he witnessed a highly aroused deacon fondling the angels perfectly rounded, perfectly smooth marbled bottom with one hand and causing a commotion in his trousers with his other hand. Even to this day, this Christmas Eve Mass of 2021, the cat couldn't bear to set paws anywhere near the seductive bottoms of the Stuart angels or the painting of Maria Clementina Sobieska, who, with rosy cheeks and a wanton smile, looked lustfully upon the smooth-bottomed angels—an enthusiastic voyeur who fully delighted in the awkward gyrations of the amorous deacon.

Prior to this year's celebration of Christmas Eve Mass, the cat had never set paws in the Saint Wenceslas Altar. He was pleased with the comfortable coolness of its marble, the darkness of its shadows, and its view of the papal altar. As an old cat, he was also pleased that this perch didn't require the physical strength and agility that were needed to climb under Saint Andrew's armpit or atop the Stuarts' tomb. Nestled between two pillars, the cat comfortably settled onto his roost just as the procession of priests, deacons, bishops, cardinals, and all manner of holy men entered the Basilica. And there, toward the rear of the procession, walked the Pope with a slightly slumped back, his head down, his left hand holding the Papal Staff like a walking cane, his right hand resting on his stomach in Napoleonic fashion.

As the parishioners reverently stood for the procession, they raised their outstretched arms to the heavens, producing a sea of smartphones to snap a series of quick photos and short videos they would later post on Facebook and Instagram alongside pictures of their cats and dogs doing the darndest things. The cat thought the Pope seemed to labor under the suffocating weight of the many layers of perfectly pressed, heavily starched pearl-white robes, the outermost of which was decorated with a gold and red stripe that ran the length of the garment from chin to shin.

The cat impatiently clicked his claws against the marble as the Mass began with some minor deacon chanting a veritable calendar of world events that had occurred over the last several thousand years. It was a highly abridged history lesson, the accuracy of which was somewhat dubious. But it wasn't long before the main event started as the Pope walked to a small gold and red velvet altar where a white linen with gold trim covered a mysterious statue. Like a magician dramatically raising a blanket to expose a bunny hidden in a hat, the Pope lifted the linen high in the air with both hands to reveal a lifelike statue of Baby Jesus lying in a manger.

After this, the Pope then deftly flicked his gilded thurible with his wrist, producing a billowy stream of incense smoke that enveloped Jesus. As the thin clouds rose and disappeared, the cat got his first clear look at the babe in the manger—a fair-complexioned lad with a healthy pallor, light pink cheeks, delicate eyebrows, a demure smile, and a perfectly shaped head covered with thick locks of light brown and blond hair. Although (or perhaps it would be more accurate to say "because") Baby Jesus looked more like he was born in the Nordic north rather than the Middle East, all who had gathered stood in adoration of the babe.

In what was surely a tip of the Papal cap to the Wise Men Melchior and Balthazar, the Pope lumbered up the altar steps, received a freshly filled thurible, and spread grey puffs of frankincense- and myrrh-infused incense while navigating around the massive altar. As he swung his arms back and forth, his sleeves, like that of an ancient conjurer, moved in ethereal waves that mirrored the wafting smoke. The aroma of frankincense and myrrh permeated the Basilica. The intense wisps of incense penetrated the N95 masks, which were worn by every deacon, bishop, and parishioner to protect them from Covid-19, which had killed millions over the preceding two years. While the cat nodded in appreciation of the frankincense and myrrh to emphasize the gifts of the Wise Men, he covered his nose to avoid the acrid aromas as they irritated his delicate nostrils and made him sneeze reflexively.

While the Mass continued, more readings were read, prayers prayed, and songs sung as the assembled parishioners first stood, then knelt, then sat, next stood, followed by more kneeling, which led to standing one last time before finally sitting back down—all performed in perfect unison. The cat remained still, indifferent to the aerobic movement of the crowd.

Then, at last, came the homily, the cat's second favorite part of the Mass after the Eucharist; for in the homily, the Pope may choose his own words to describe the meaning of Jesus, the meaning of Christmas, and the meaning of everything without the constraints of the ritualistic recitations of Bible passages that someone else wrote. The cat's expectations were high.

The Pope's references to Isaiah and Luke to open the homily, the cat knew, were simply stage setting. It was the Pope's version of offering a tasty teaser before serving the main meal. With his glasses balanced on the bridge of his nose and his white zucchetto firmly atop his head, the Pope nimbly moved from Isaiah and Luke and implored parishioners all around the world to ask Jesus for the "grace of littleness." He further explained what he meant by littleness: "Let us stop pining for a grandeur that is not ours to have. Let us put aside our complaints and our gloomy faces and the greed that never satisfies!"

The cat was pleased with what he heard—the Pope extolling the goodness and graces of littleness and the rejection of greed as he stood in his fine silken robes under a gilded dome ceiling directly in front of an altar filled with gold candleholders, chalices, and plates, which sat amidst the massive, marbled Basilica, which housed priceless works of art by Michelangelo, Bernini, Giotto, and Bolgi. Espousing littleness and the rejection of greed amongst these riches, the cat thought in admiration, was rhetorical genius. Pure rhetorical genius.

The Pope continued his homily by describing the dimensions of littleness, of which there were many and their surface area vast. He seemed to know them all very well. To further connect the concept of littleness to the birth of Jesus, the Pope returned to the Gospel of Luke, citing his faithful description of the devout shepherds who were called to Bethlehem by the angel of the Lord: "They found him because they lived in the fields keeping watch over their flocks by night . . . " The shepherds, the Pope then pointed out, were " . . . the most simple people, and closest to the Lord."

Poor and simple shepherds, the embodiment of littleness, thought the cat. Normally not disposed to fits of sentimentality, these words warmed the cat's heart, and tears welled in his one good eye. But before he could shed a tear, his stomach convulsed several times before he finally threw up a tiny fur ball that dropped to the marble floor with a silent splat. His warm heart, as it turned out, was instead a minor case of indigestion.

Prior to the Mass, the cat had compiled a mental list of biblical references that any diligent Pope should cover in a Midnight Mass homily. Much to his satisfaction, the cat checked each of the references off his list one by one. Isaiah, check. Luke, check. The angel and the shepherds, check, check. The manger, check. But where were the Magi? *Surely,* the cat thought, *the Pope wouldn't omit the Magi.* But then again, the cat reconsidered, this homily was about littleness, and it was difficult for the cat to imagine how the Pope, even one as rhetorically skilled as Francis, could bridge the theme of littleness to the grandeur of the Magi. But then he did it.

The Pope paused, inhaled deeply, dug into the depths of his bag of rhetorical tricks, and drew the Magi into the mix. For what is the opposite of littleness, if not bigness? And what, or more accurately, who, embodies bigness more than the Magi? He reminded all that, " . . . around Jesus everything comes together: not only do we see the poor, the shepherds, but also the learned and the rich, the Magi." The cat presumed the Pope was referring to the three most famous Magi— Melchior, Caspar, and Balthazar—but perhaps he was also referring to Paragus and Jude Aya. Or maybe the Pope was not even aware of their presence that faithful day. It was difficult to say for certain.

What was certain, the Pope pointed out as he finished his homily, was that " . . . there the shepherds and Magi are joined in a fraternity beyond all labels and classifications. May God enable us to be a worshipping, poor and fraternal Church . . . " The cat's good ear twitched with delight as the Pope used the words *poor* and *fraternal* in a single sentence to describe the Church. To describe it as poor, the cat thought from his marbled perch by the gilded altar, was a bit of a stretch, perhaps a bridge too far, but he delighted in the audacious contrast between what his ears heard and what his good eye saw.

But *fraternal*, the cat thought, would surely resonate with all who had gathered. The cat was sure it resonated with the small group of nuns who wore black, dull linen dresses and who were tucked away to the side of the altar where the Baldacchino's massive bronze pillars blocked their view of the Pope but provided an unobstructed view of the large number of deacons, cardinals, and bishops seated in the center of the Basilica. Surely the word *fraternal* resonated with these holiest of men, whose brightly colored white and gold robes, red zucchettos, and white mitres stood in stark and welcome contrast to the dullness of the nuns' wardrobe.

And *fraternal* certainly described each member of the choir consisting of young boys, tender teens, and handsome men. And while the Pope concluded the homily without a single mention of Mary, she was ever-present in a diminutive statue to the right of the papal altar and in the *Pietà*, Michelangelo's masterpiece that captures the sorrow, solemnity, and strength of Mary's expression as she holds her dead son in her arms.

After the homily, the cat watched as the Pope and his cadre of well-manicured deacons prepared the Eucharist, the meal in which the blood and body of Jesus is served in snackable tidbits so as not to raise any hints or allegations of cannibalism from ignorant and misguided atheists. It was the cat's favorite part of the Mass.

Earlier in the day, between watching the final decorations being placed on the altar and securing his spot in the Wenceslas alcove, the cat had the sublime pleasure of visiting the room, hidden amongst a labyrinth of hallways, where the Eucharist had been prepared. He arrived in the empty, unguarded chamber, hungry, not having had any breakfast in the morning nor dinner the night before. Stacks of thin wafers wrapped in clear plastic sat tantalizingly on top of an oak table, tempting the famished cat. He leapt onto the table, walked across its length, used his snaggled claws and sharp incisors to loosen the wrapping, and gorged on the tasteless wafers until his throat became so dry that he could no longer swallow.

With a parched throat and a penchant for Italian wines, the determined cat walked back across the table, where he used his paw and his forehead to tip over a tall golden chalice from which wine poured across the table until it dripped into a large puddle on the floor. The cat leapt from the table to the floor, landing with a splash in the middle of the puddle; he lapped up the wine until the tiny muscles in his small, red-stained tongue cramped from exhaustion. The deacons had chosen well this year as the blood of Jesus turned out to be a rich, full-bodied Nebbiolo with notes of black cherry and hints of tobacco and with grippy tannins and a smooth satisfying finish. With red-stained whiskers, the cat licked the last bit of wine from his fur and returned to his Wenceslas perch, where he remained in a drunken slumber until the Papal processional at the start of the Mass.

The Mass ended with "O Come, All Ye Faithful," an uplifting eighteenth century carol featuring the Vatican choir and a booming baroque organ. The cat, never a fan of organs, especially the booming type, jumped from the Wenceslas Altar and crossed the marbled nave, weaving his way through the streaming masses as they strode with renewed spirit down a long hallway that led to an exit through the Door of the Sacraments.

As the cat walked amongst the throng of believers, carefully dodging in and out of black Ferragamo boots, colorful Converse sneakers, and dull but practical orthopedics, he heard righteous whispers of thanks and praise. He heard the faithful speak of Isaiah and Micah, who, through God's divine instruction, foretold the birth of Jesus. He heard the parishioners praise Luke, who had chronicled the birth of Jesus in painstaking detail, using the highest standards of historical research available to him. The praise extended to the hallowed Wise Men, who had traveled across the desert to selflessly shower Baby Jesus with priceless gifts. The praise was also for the littleness of the devout shepherds, who had bravely left their flock to witness the sacred event at the urging of a heavenly angel.

But the parishioners reserved their most fervent praise for a baby named Jesus, born of a virgin mother and the Heavenly Father in a simple manger that sat in a run-down stable in the humble town of Bethlehem more than two thousand years ago to bring goodwill and peace to his people on Earth. *Or*, the cat thought, *was it to bring a fiery end to the world?* He could never quite remember which.

Acknowledgments

As a first-time novelist, I needed plenty of feedback along the way and would like to acknowledge and thank those who helped bring *The Misconceived Conception of a Baby Named Jesus* to life. First, a thanks to Patty Lewis Lott for having the courage to be the first reader of an early draft and who also provided fine-tuning on a much later draft of the manuscript. Her insightful suggestions and specific tweaks sharpened my focus. Also, a thanks to Roisin Heycock, the developmental editor who helped with the story elements and shaping the characters. She provided pointed feedback without bruising my ego or shaking my confidence. To Becky Bruhn, who raised brilliant questions about the central characters. Her questions helped me add dimension and depth to Mary, round out Joseph, and expand the number of appearances made by the one-eyed, rust-colored cat. Finally, a thanks to John Koehler and Joe Coccaro and the team at Koehler Books for adding me to their distinguished author portfolio and for having the courage to add this somewhat controversial novel to their library. And a thanks to Suzanne Bradshaw, who created a cover that captured, in single image, the essence of the entire 200+ page book. Their guidance and support throughout the process proved invaluable and was very much appreciated.

I would be remiss if I didn't also acknowledge the prophets Isaiah and Micah and the Gospel writer Luke. Without them, this book would not have been possible. I've tried to contact each of them directly to extend my personal thanks, but they are nowhere to be found. Regrettably, I'm beginning to suspect they may have died many, many years ago.

Made in United States
North Haven, CT
11 February 2025

65635430R00148